DUST TO DUST

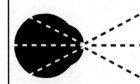

This Large Print Book carries the
Seal of Approval of N.A.V.H.

DUST TO DUST

THE PROPHECY #1

HEATHER GRAHAM

THORNDIKE PRESS
A part of Gale, Cengage Learning

GALE
CENGAGE Learning™

Detroit • New York • San Francisco • New Haven, Conn • Waterville, Maine • London

GALE
CENGAGE Learning

LIBRARY OF CONGRESS CATALOGING-IN-PUBLICATION DATA

Graham, Heather.
    Dust to dust / by Heather Graham.
        p. cm. — (The prophecy ; book 1) (Thorndike Press large print core)
    ISBN-13: 978-1-4104-1690-2 (alk. paper)
    ISBN-10: 1-4104-1690-9 (alk. paper)
    1. End of the world—Fiction. 2. Life change events—Fiction.
3. Large type books. I. Title.
PS3557.R198D87 2009
813'.54—dc22   2009010599

Published in 2009 by arrangement with Harlequin Books, S.A.

Printed in the United States of America
1 2 3 4 5 6 7 13 12 11 10 09

For Amber Smyser,
Valerie Querns, Mike LeClaire,
Cozmo Johnson, Jonathan Wenstrup,
Christine Adolf and
Jennifer Stratford —
and, very specially,
Scott and Josh Perry.
You all make L.A. a very special place!

DEAR READER,

Beginning a new mini-series called The Prophecy, *Dust to Dust* is a stand alone book and the first in a series that will eventually entail four novels, each separate, though all with a specific goal. Included in these stories are characters from past books, characters who are part of The Alliance and who will have new roles throughout the series.

So in case anyone wants to learn more about those characters, here is a list of who they are, in what book they were featured and under what name that book was published, the real me or the pseudonym me — Shannon Drake!

Best,
Heather

Beneath a Blood Red Moon, Shannon Drake, 1999 featuring Maggie Montgomery and

Sean Canady

When Darkness Falls, Shannon Drake, 2000 featuring Lucian DeVeau and Jade Mac-Gregor

Deep Midnight, Shannon Drake, 2001 featuring Jordan Riley and Ragnor Wulfsson

Realm of Shadows, Shannon Drake, 2002 featuring Tara Mason and Brent Malone

The Awakening, Shannon Drake, 2003 featuring Megan and Finn O'Casey

Dead by Dusk, Shannon Drake, 2005 featuring Stephanie Cahill and Grant Peterson

Kiss of Darkness, Heather Graham, 2006 featuring Bryan McAllister and Jessica Fraser

Blood Red, Heather Graham, 2007 featuring Lauren Crow and Mark Davidson

PROLOGUE

I Became

There wasn't anything really wrong with me from the start. I was just your average Joe. They might not have hired me for the cover of *GQ,* but I wasn't a bad-looking guy. (Sadly, in all this, my looks haven't changed. I haven't acquired a rippling six-pack or anything.) I have a nice-enough face. My features are a little too classic for some. I've been told I would make a great cavalier, that I kind of look like King Charles. Not the Second — the one who had dozens of women and probably just as many illegitimate kids. No, I look more like Charles the First — the one who favored the divine right of kings and lost his regal head. Anyway, the point of all this is that I'm no muscle-bound hunk. I'm not a rail, but I am more wiry than built-up, and I usually depend a lot more on speed and agility than the size

9

of my biceps. Kind of a lean, mean, fighting machine — fonder of argument and debate than bashing in a face.

I did — and still do, despite the changes — like life. No, that's not entirely true. I like it even more now. I've become more aware than ever of the delicacy of every single minute of human existence.

Before, I simply liked the flow of life. People, places, things — especially art. Luckily, I made a good-enough living. At the age of thirty, I'd managed to sock away enough to buy my own graphics-and-design shop. I was confident about my future, and did well enough as a son, friend and lover. I'd had a few flings, one serious, which lasted three years, several that went on for months, but . . . *she* wasn't out there. The right woman for me just never turned up.

Maybe there was a reason.

Anyway, on the night I Became, I was in Los Angeles. I was there with Zach Whalen and Emory Smith.

Zach *is* a muscle-bound hunk. Six-four, a good inch and a half over me, and a solid — and I do mean solid — two-hundred-forty pounds. Zach is of Danish descent. He'd fit right in with a Viking raiding party. And he's a good guy. Looks like he should be in a wrestling ring, which he is sometimes. But the love of his life is music. He manages a karaoke club, and in his spare time, he's a bass guitarist with the Luckless Three.

Aptly named.

They're pretty good, actually, but every time they get a gig that pays really well, one of them suddenly has an "artistic difference" with the others. Go figure. They get along just great when they're entertaining at a cousin's wedding for fun. Maybe, at heart, they're just not in it for the money.

Emory likes to draw, and he *loves* to have a few beers and sing karaoke. He's an accountant. Six-one even, square-shouldered and preppy in every way. We make a strange threesome.

The three of us are different enough that I don't think we would have ended up being friends if we'd met late in life, but we've been friends since we were kids. We were raised not just in the same neighborhood but on the same street.

Anyway, three months ago, we had gone to L.A. just to do some partying and because a group called — oddly enough — Lucky Three was playing at the Viper Room. One of the guys was an old college roommate of Emory's, so Zach had been allowed to sit in for a few numbers. We'd purposely taken motel rooms right on Sunset so that we wouldn't need a designated driver, though I'd actually been out with Zach a few times when he had pretty much needed a designated *walker*. Still, that night we were only a little inebriated when we headed back to our motel.

And then it happened.

I don't want you thinking that I started off as a coward or anything. I like to think of myself as even tempered, logical, capable of the eloquence and charm to defuse a bad situation most of the time. But when cornered, I could hold my own in a fight. I just wasn't the type you'd put up against a pair of heavyweights.

A group of thugs was in a side alley behind a restaurant-slash-bar that had apparently just closed. The first thing I heard was their victims screaming.

"Shit," Zach muttered, shaking his head, as if that could clear it of a half dozen beers.

"Son of a bitch," Emory added.

And there we were. Three guys, none of us small. But I'd be one hell of a liar if I didn't admit that it passed through each of our minds that there was a gang attack going on and that knives or guns might well be involved.

Still, what the hell?

"I've hit 911," Zach announced as we headed toward the action.

There was some reassurance in that statement. If we were going to get messed up, at least the cops would get there soon enough to clean up the damage.

As we neared the scene, I could see that the victims were an elderly couple. The man was gurgling now, because he was being strangled. The woman was sobbing as she was beaten by two men, one who looked to be of mixed race and another who was massive and white as snow. Two others were holding the man still while a third had his hands around his throat. One looked Hispanic, the second was thin but wiry and holding a huge knife, and the one doing the strangling was just plain huge.

"Shit," Zach muttered again.

And then we waded in.

Emory headed straight to the woman's aid. I followed Zach as he went after the trio attacking the man.

The guy with the knife turned at our approach, and Zach dodged quickly, but he was still caught across the abdomen. He swore and got the guy good in the jaw, but he was hurt, and I knew it.

By then I had run past him to the old man on the ground. He had powdery blue eyes that had a strange glow about them. "We're getting you out of here," I said.

"You!" he gasped, and stared into my eyes as if he had suddenly recognized a long-lost friend. "You," he repeated with sincere pleasure. Despite the situation, he smiled. "You've come."

"We're here to save you," I said, praying that was true. I didn't know how Zach was doing behind me, or how Emory was faring.

The old man gripped my hand. Hard. "It's only the beginning," he said. "Only the beginning. Thank God you are here. It was hard to hold on long enough, but . . . now you're here. Capricorn. You've come."

"Sir, it's all right. We're going to get you to a hospital."

"You are Capricorn," he said, and he spoke as if relieved, as if he'd reached the Pearly Gates and discovered they were wide open.

He was babbling, I told myself. But then he looked at me again, and I realized that there was no weakness in his eyes, just a light so strange that it was nearly as disturbing as the thugs surrounding us.

And that's when *it* happened.

I might have imagined it. But I didn't. It was real. The light in his eyes seemed to

14

stream out and touch mine. I felt as if I were being electrocuted for a moment, as if lightning had ripped between the two of us.

I stared at him with utter confusion, but then, after a moment, there didn't seem to be anything strange about the man at all. He was smiling like a tired warrior, like a Viking ready to enter the halls of Valhalla.

"Son of a bitch!" Zach roared from behind me, and I knew he'd been cut again.

I was enraged.

I had taken karate as a kid, along with the rest of Mr. Halloway's middle-schoolers, but I'd never pursued it after that. I had gone to a boxing gym and sparred a few times, and I had a good right jab, but that was it. But I was suddenly on fire. I don't remember any of my movements being voluntary; I was just a whirl of motion. In seconds I'd broken the wrist of the man with the knife. A few more seconds and his two comrades were lying unconscious on the ground. Emory was losing his struggle with the mammoth white man and his accomplice, and I sped in against the two cretins like a whirlwind. They, too, went down almost instantly.

And then, there we were. The three of us. In the dark alley. Zach gripping his sliced-up middle and staring at me. Emory, his jaw

15

swelling like a dozen bees had been at him, was staring, too. There were sirens in the night, and the noise was deafening as the first officers arrived on the scene.

Naturally, confusion ensued.

One of the cops called for an ambulance. Zach and Emory were all beat up but standing, and the five thugs, all on the ground, looked broken in various places. The old man was still on the ground, while the old woman looked as if she'd passed away. She lay staring sightlessly up at the sky. I thought at first, that the three of us were going to wind up arrested, but the old man kept talking, even as more cops arrived, even as the med techs shifted him onto a gurney. He kept insisting, "He is the savior. And now the end begins."

Something drew me to him, and I stood by his side while they prepared to hoist him on up into the ambulance. I took his hand.

"Listen, you've got to calm down," I told him. "It's going to be all right."

I saw the men standing over by his wife — at least I assumed she was his wife. I saw the way they looked at her, and knew I'd been right. She was definitely already gone.

It wasn't going to be all right.

The man I had never met before was clinging tightly to my hand. "This is just the beginning," he said. "They're out there, and they will be looking for you. The angels have spoken, and the time nears. It's not an explosion like a dying star but a gnawing away. Little things, the elements, the earth — but the earth is always changing. The earth has more time, though, if evil can be stopped. Prophecies speak of what might be, but they're never sure. The future can always be changed. And you are not alone." He paused in his babbling for a moment, and his eyes closed. For a moment I thought that he had died, too. But then his eyes opened again, that strange glow fading now. His voice, when he spoke again, was weak. "You must find the other eleven. Your two, the other earth signs, first. Strength comes from strength. And then the Oracle. She is near, and she is calling to you. I have felt the whisper in the air of the night. She is calling to you all — but you most of all, for you are Capricorn, you are the first — for the time to begin the saving of the world is now."

This was all a little too absurd, even for L.A. I was beginning to think that someone was going to jump out from behind a Dumpster and tell me that I was being punked or something.

I tried to calm the man down, though I

was pretty sure that was a vain endeavor. "I'm not a Capricorn," I said. *But I was lying. I had been born on January seventeenth. It was just that the old man's words and the feel of the night were beginning to creep me out, and I felt a need to fight back by denying everything.*

He smiled at me, and I knew *he* knew I was lying.

For a moment he looked young and full of vigor. His grip on my hand was powerful. So powerful it hurt.

"I am done. *We* are done. But for you it is just beginning, and that is how it must be, how it was written. You are earth, and it is your job to find the others. Time is slipping away. When you begin, the rest will follow. First there are four, the earth, the wind, the water and the air, and then there are three for every four. And those twelve are one. Gods and goddesses, sisters and brothers, all are one, and the most holy places of all are the battlefields. You must find your kind, and then you must find the Oracle. Evil gains entrance when our hearts fail. Men are like rats in cages, and the evil within us calls to the evil without."

Then his forceful grip simply slipped away as he was staring at me, and I realized I was staring back at a dead man.

I turned away and saw that my friends, those two guys I had known just about my entire life, were looking at me as if I'd suddenly grown horns and a tail.

Or a halo and wings. After all, we had plowed in together, but I had saved their asses.

I lifted my hands. "Adrenaline," I said with a shrug.

"Yeah," Zach said.

"Sure," Emory agreed.

But something sinister seemed to have risen in the air. Something even more frightening and malicious than the murder of the elderly couple. Or maybe it was part of the attack. The air held a lingering miasma, but it was fading, as if the wind were dispersing it. Except there was no wind.

There was still a lot going on around us. The thugs were being arrested. The paramedics had announced the deaths and now were awaiting the medical examiner. While they waited, we were questioned. Over and over again. By the end of the interrogation, we knew we'd be coming back to L.A., because the attackers were going to be tried for murder.

By the time we were finally free to go and began walking in silence back toward our motel, dawn was on the way.

When we stood in the motel courtyard and split up to go to our rooms, Zach told me good-night calmly enough, but he was looking at me again as if I had horns. Emory clapped a hand on my shoulder, but he, too, looked somber.

And why not? We had just been witnesses to a double murder.

But it was more than that, I was sure.

When the other two walked into their rooms, I stayed outside for a moment. Colors were beginning to caress the darkness with pastel shades.

Suddenly it felt as if someone touched me. It was so real that I whirled around to look, but there was no one there.

But then I heard a whisper. As sure and certain as anything.

"You *are* Capricorn. And you *will* rise to the fight."

I spun around again, looking for whoever had spoken.

"What fight?" I asked out loud. No one was there to hear me, but I still felt foolish. I was talking to myself in the shadows that came with the first tentacles of the dawn. The words I'd heard had seemed to be coming from inside my head, as if, from a great distance, a sweet voice with a subtle accent was speaking to me via some kind of ESP.

Swearing softly beneath my breath, I slipped my keycard into the lock. Screw this! No good deed goes unpunished, and this was apparently my punishment. I was going to sleep, and when I woke up, I was going to start drinking. Hell, I was in L.A. to party.

A night's sleep, or several hours at least, and the strangeness would all fade, I told myself.

But — and thank God I didn't know it at the time — that wasn't to be.

Hell no.

It started that night, when I slept — or tried to.

The dream came instantly. I was walking along what I knew was an ancient path. And I knew I had been drawn there because there was something I had to find. At first there were trees alongside the rough stone I traversed. My mind fought against being there, but my feet kept moving. Ahead of me there were what looked like telephone poles rising into the air. In moments I realized they were not telephone poles, they were crosses, each one bearing a body. Miles and miles of those who had been crucified stretched before me.

The crosses disappeared, and the earth

beneath me became hard-packed soil. The air bore a redolence that was strange and sad, like decaying moss, and I realized that I was surrounded by stacks of the dead. They were long decayed, many only bones, disarticulated skeletons, some held together by faded, gauzelike strips of shrouds, with bits of metal here and there — rings, brooches, weapons — glimmering in what seemed to be the yellow glow of lamplight coming from some place far ahead. As I paused, the head of a skeleton to my left suddenly began to turn of its own accord, as if controlled by the ghosts of muscles and tendons long gone. I stared in horror as the jaw began to work. A terrible rasping whisper hissed through the broken and toothless jaw. "The Oracle is calling."

Broken bits of finger bone began to join together, and the skeletal hand at his side was suddenly whole and pointing toward the light. "Go," the voice commanded in a tone of strange desperation.

I was torn by fear. I might have turned back then, because of that desperate need we have to survive, even in our dreams. But the wind that had come with his voice was behind me. I had no choice but to move forward. Suddenly it seemed that all the dead were awakening, urging me forward.

Heads lifted, arms pointed, and a massive call went up. "Go. The Oracle is calling. Salvation can come only from those who are called. Hurry. Hurry!"

I shouldn't have been so terrified; the skeletons were trying to help me. But they *were* terrifying, as they stared with their empty eye sockets and spoke in voices that were papery, coarse and part of the wind.

Finally I reached the place where the light began: a wall of burning sconces with a massive tomb in front of it. An ancient oil lamp sat upon that pagan sarcophagus, which had clearly seen use as an altar, and nearby, shrouded in a black hood and cloak, a presence stood. I started forward, and then I saw . . .

From another corridor in the maze of catacombs, someone else was arriving. As tall as I was, and as imaginary as I myself was in that place. He had no substance. He walked as I did, he came from my world. He, too, was headed for the light, and he stopped, startled, as he suddenly became aware of me.

He turned, and I saw that he was a bit older than I was.

As we stared at one another, the cloaked figure lifted a hand and began to speak, and I realized that it was a woman. "Come to me. Those who are not called must hasten those who are." As her hand fell, I heard a horrendous commotion and turned to look back down the corridor. The skeletons were rising, rebuilding themselves. Then . . .

Perhaps the terror woke me. That thing in a dream where we won't let ourselves fall, lest we die in real life. Whatever it was, I was awake, sitting up in my bed, sweat pouring down my chest. I was in my motel room in Los Angeles, and the multihued neon sign outside my window was blinking madly.

I threw off my covers, stood and turned on the bedside lamp. Not good enough. I needed the dirt and grit and cacophony of the city, the noises, the action, the good and the bad. I threw on some pants and stepped outside into the courtyard. And then I realized I was still smelling the hard-packed dirt and death from the catacombs of my dreams. I shook my head to dispel the cloying scent. The smell of grease from a nearby diner started to replace it, followed by a hint of night-blooming jasmine. Much better. I turned to go back in, and then I noticed my feet.

They were filthy. And not just with the normal dirt of a big city. This dirt was an odd color, a strange pasty gray.

As if . . .

As if I had walked through miles of catacombs.

Miles and miles of the dead.

1

"What on earth is that, Mel?" Maggie Canady asked, leaning over to stare at the cocktail napkin on which Melanie Regan had been doodling.

"What is what?" Melanie asked.

She hadn't paid the least attention to what she had been doing, and now she stared down at the napkin. She had flipped it over, so there was no logo to deter the free movement of her pen or mar the pictures she created.

Pictures. Real pictures. Recognizable. *Detailed.*

There were four of them, and they were so well situated on the napkin, she might have marked off the corners with a ruler.

The top left corner was very evidently a sketch of a fire, so detailed that the flames almost seemed to move. Even more hypnotic was the sketch on the opposite corner.

It was of a waterfall, forceful, filling the

air with spray as it fell to the pool below. There was something wild and even violent about it.

The bottom right corner showed a fiercely blowing wind, sweeping away the cloud cover.

She hadn't even known that the wind could actually *be* drawn. Not without showing something blowing in it. But what she had put on the paper was the wind. And like the fire and the waterfall, it seemed to have life, to be real and almost tangible.

The bottom left corner showed an earthquake, and it was amazingly realistic. It wasn't a sketch of buildings toppling or a bridge crumbling. It simply showed the ground, but the ground split asunder. Once again, it was almost as if it were happening as she looked at the napkin. Something violent and almost mobile seemed to be captured on the fragile paper.

She set the pen down.

"I didn't know you could draw like that," Maggie marveled.

Melanie clenched her hands in her lap. "Neither did I," she admitted.

Maggie looked at her as if she had just grown a third eye in the middle of her forehead. "Wow," she said.

Melanie waved a hand in the air and

forced what sounded like an easy laugh. "I don't think it's such a big deal. They say that we only use about a tenth of our mental capacity at any time. We were talking, and I guess I was distracted, so part of my subconscious mind kicked in or some such thing. Who knows? Anyway, I'm sure I couldn't do it again if I tried."

And she meant that. She couldn't usually so much as draw a stick figure.

She grabbed the beer in front of her and took a long swallow. She realized that she was barely keeping her cool, and that, too, was strange. She had learned long ago how to hide her thoughts and emotions, to play it easy in any given situation.

After all, she'd been around. Los Angeles wasn't actually home for her. She'd spent a lot of time touring Europe, hung out in New York City for a while and lived for many years in New Orleans, which was really home for her. It was where she had found a sense of herself, and where she had made so many good friends. They called themselves the Alliance — and even far apart, they remained close, always ready to help one another out. Maggie was one of those friends, and she couldn't believe she felt uneasy in front of Maggie, who knew everything there was to know about her. But she *did* feel ill at ease, and all because she could suddenly draw.

Maggie sat back, arched a brow and took a long sip of her own beer. "I would have thought, if you were magically going to become a great artist, you — being you — would have drawn Lassie."

"Very funny," Melanie said.

"Well, you are a fabulous dog trainer."

"Because I know animals respond to positive reinforcement," Melanie said.

"So do people," Maggie said, and set a hand on Melanie's. "Seriously . . . those are great. Don't look so worried."

"But it's so . . . strange that I, of all people, could draw something so good," Melanie said.

"I agree," Maggie told her, and that was when Melanie realized her friend was as weirded-out as she was by the whole thing.

They both had their day jobs, but it sometimes seemed that the Alliance, which operated totally beneath the regular radar of humanity, was the most defining force in their lives, one that made them react to even seemingly innocuous events with immediate suspicion. They dealt with the curious, from the slightly uncommon to the absolutely bizarre, which made sense, most of the members being rather unusual themselves.

Their titular head, Lucien DeVeau, lived in New Orleans, where it seemed they most often gathered, since New Orleans seemed to attract the peculiar and mysterious. Then again, Melanie reflected, Los Angeles, where she was now living, could be most unusual itself. Back home, most of her friends were in relationships — married, for the most part. Lucien had a wife he adored, Jade, who of course was part of the Alliance, too. For Melanie, it was like having a big family, but she hated being a third wheel, and it did sometimes feel that way when she was back home.

California had become her place. She was used to standing on her own here, at least on a day-to-day basis.

Tonight was supposed to have been just a nice evening out. Maggie had a houseful of children and a boutique that was thriving. Melanie's life was much easier in one sense — no children — but she was extremely proud to be considered one of the finest trainers in the country now, and she traveled extensively to train show dogs, working dogs and just plain pet dogs. She had an affinity for all animals, not just dogs, and she had always seemed to have a special gift for working with them, from hamsters to horses. Training the unruly German shepherds of an A-list movie star had first brought her out here, and she had been determined to carve out a life for herself.

So far, it had been a fine life. And now and then she got really lucky and her friends came out to see her.

She had found her niche. She had a great job. She loved the animals she worked with, and they loved her.

In her own mind, at least, she didn't do half so well with most human beings. She was lucky to have very good friends despite that, though she wasn't quite certain she considered all of them to be *human* beings. Maggie, however, was definitely very human.

Maggie's home had always been New Orleans, but at least four times a year she took a much-needed break and traveled out to L.A. to spend a few days with Melanie. Her husband, Sean, was a great guy, a police lieutenant working the French Quarter, and though he was very busy himself, he was also a great father. His day job was very important to the Alliance, but he enjoyed getting quality time to bond with his brood when Maggie headed west.

Sometimes a few of Melanie's other friends joined them when they got together, but tonight it was just the two of them, and

Melanie was glad of that.

If she hadn't already felt completely unnerved by the drawings, her friend's reaction would have alerted her that something weird was going on. Maggie was taking the drawings very seriously; Melanie could tell by the way her face had drawn taut and her eyes had darkened.

And Maggie always *knew* these things.

Maggie was a beautiful woman, with deep auburn hair and green eyes; she was down-to-earth and one of the most socially conscious people Melanie had ever met. She adored her own four children and especially loved five-year-olds. They were perfect people then, she had told Melanie once. Old enough to go potty, dress themselves and eat fairly neatly, but too young to have learned hatred or prejudice, and still willing to believe in the word of the adults around them.

"What about six-year-olds?" Melanie had asked her once.

"By that age they start questioning everything you say," Maggie had warned her.

Dogs to Melanie were like five-year-olds to Maggie. They offered up unconditional love. Many were incredibly bright. Most wanted to learn.

Bad dogs, she believed, were like most bad

children: created by those around them. But then, that was a personal opinion.

And she was very aware that she was thinking about dogs and children because she was so upset that she had suddenly become an artist.

"How curious," Maggie said suddenly.

"Well, yes, we've established that," Mel said.

Maggie flashed her a smile before growing somber once again. "Think about it. You drew a waterfall. Water. The wind. Blowing wind — or air. Fire. And what seems to be an earthquake. Earth, wind, fire and water."

"Remember Earth, Wind and Fire? Great group," Melanie said.

Maggie flashed her a concerned frown.

"Mel . . ." she began, then paused.

"What?"

"What the hell is that?" Maggie asked suddenly.

"What?" Melanie asked.

"Can't you feel it?" Maggie asked.

Melanie looked up. They were seated by a gold-filigreed mirror, and she caught sight of her own reflection. She was surprised to see that she looked so wide-eyed, so lost. She wasn't normally uncertain of anything.

It was the drawings, she knew.

She studied her own reflection: wide blue

eyes, hair so blond that her friends teased her about looking angelic. Fair skin. She was tall — even sitting she still somehow looked tall — and that seemed important suddenly. She carried her five-eleven with assurance, and that usually outweighed any suggestion of fragility because of her china-doll coloring.

But at that moment . . .

There was something in her reflection.

Dread.

"Feel it?" Maggie repeated, and tapped a finger on the corner of the cocktail napkin where Mel had drawn an earthquake.

"It's happening *now*," Maggie said.

And then Melanie *did* feel it.

The earth was trembling.

It had started off subtly. Still, she should have felt it, but she hadn't, not until Maggie brought it up.

But it was true. It was happening, slowly at first, barely there.

And then it increased.

Suddenly everyone in the restaurant began to feel it.

People started to talk all at once, panic rising in their voices.

"What the hell is that?" a gruff, heavy-set man demanded.

"Look, the glasses are all shaking!" a

woman cried.

A rumbling sound started to rise over the softness of the dinner music playing in the background.

Dishes suddenly crashed to the floor.

"Earthquake!" someone shouted. "Get under a door-frame. . . . Move!"

Maggie and Melanie just stared at one another.

Because it was true. The rumbling had risen to the decibel level of a freight train rushing through the night. The chandeliers were shaking, the tinkling a strange counterpoint to the roar that was continuing to rise.

A statue near the doorway fell over with a crash.

A young woman let out a terrified scream and jumped to her feet, her chair crashing to the floor. The man with her dove beneath the table.

The woman, in a blind panic, went running toward the entrance.

"Oh, my God!" Melanie said, horrified. "I've got to stop her!"

Maggie caught her arm and tried to stop her.

"Get under the table," Melanie told her, then repeated the warning at the top of her voice as she raced for the door and the young woman who had run right out into the danger of smashing glass and crashing cars.

Outside, it was mayhem. As was so often true with quakes, one side of the street, was a mess. Her side looked almost untouched. In the street itself, cars were crushed and piled everywhere, horns blaring. People were running blindly, shouting in panic. Melanie saw the woman who had raced from the restaurant. She was standing like a deer caught in headlights, right in the middle of the road. Melanie hurried after her just as a Volvo, trying to avoid the crashed car in front of it, nearly plowed into her.

Melanie grasped her by the arm and realized that she was in shock.

"Get back in the doorway . . . come on!"

She dragged the woman back toward the restaurant, where a busboy, standing in amazement by a support beam, reached for them just as a massive planter started to tumble from the terrace above them.

"Help her, please!" Melanie shouted, shoving the woman into the busboy's arms, then turning to leave. He caught her arm, dark eyes concerned.

"Where are you going? Things are still falling. There could be aftershocks. Please, get back in here!" he shouted to Mel.

"I'm all right," she told him. "I'm . . . uh, emergency personnel," she lied. She should have felt bad. He was rising to the fore in the midst of disaster, concerned about others.

But she couldn't stay.

And she couldn't explain what was tearing at her.

She had drawn the earthquake. And then it had *happened*.

She felt responsible.

She told herself that earthquakes were common in California. This wasn't an anomaly.

But this time . . .

She couldn't help it. She felt responsible.

Alarms were going off everywhere. Glass was shattering, sirens blaring.

Outside the restaurant, Santa Monica Boulevard, with its beautiful shops and quaint air of sophistication, was a disaster. The earth was still rumbling. And then it stopped. Everyone seemed to freeze for a split second, as if time stood still. Another rumble came — along with renewed screaming. A smaller rumble followed a second later, and then everything went silent, unmoving. Melanie had been through a few tremors before, and she knew this wasn't the "big one" scientists had been predicting for years, but it had been a strong shake, and it looked as if it had been centered south of them. Looking around, she could see that most lights in the vicinity were gone, but a glow just a few streets over told her that at least part of the city was probably up. She thought about how capricious quakes could be as they spread out from the epicenter, crushing one block and leaving another with crystal curios still standing in their places.

Here, glass and masonry and more lay strewn everywhere.

Some people were staggering around in a daze, others were down, some cut, some screaming. Then came another blast of breaking glass.

This time, it wasn't the earth taking vengeance.

It was a group of hoods.

How anyone had recovered quickly enough from an earthquake to start thinking of looting, Melanie didn't know.

But just as natural disaster brought out the best in some people, it brought out the worst in others.

She saw a group of six thugs making for an antique jewelry shop. They were an odd group; two were preppy looking, in cardigans and button-down shirts, another wore a tie-dyed T-shirt, and three were in hooded sweatshirts. It was Wall Street meets Haight-Ashbury meets Harlem.

A moment after they disappeared inside, she heard a cry and went running toward the shop herself. There was a fissure right in front of the doorway, with steam escaping, and for a moment she thought that it took on substance and oozed from the ground, coalescing into something large and dark, elusive and ever-changing as it emerged from the miasma. . . . It was just steam, she told herself. And indeed, as she stood there, it rose and dissipated, just like steam always did.

Another scream startled her from her bizarre reflection.

She knew both Mr. Delancy, the proprietor, and Viv Larson, his salesgirl, and the minute she stepped inside she saw them being attacked.

"Stop it!" Melanie shouted.

Given the mayhem on the streets, she was surprised that they not only heard her but, to her amazement, turned to look at her.

"Lookit the little snow queen, trying to stop us, Bo," one of them said. He had a scraggly beard, scaly-looking skin, and an odor that drifted all the way over to where she stood in the doorway.

Bo was apparently the tall, broad-shouldered black man — wearing a tie — who started to laugh as he came toward her.

"Let's take the little snow queen here into the back. The old guy, he's no use. But we got ourselves two little chickees, and with the world goin' to hell, everyone will be far too busy to notice a few screams from the back room. Get her, Nicky. Go on and get her."

The scaly-skinned thug started toward her.

"Don't even think about it," she said quietly, and took a single step toward him. "You're going to let those nice people go and get the hell out of here. And I suggest you do it really quickly, because the police will have things under control in a matter of minutes."

All six men began to laugh.

Okay, so she doubted herself that the police would be in control that quickly.

"Melanie, go. Run," Mr. Delancy croaked.

"Nicky, just grab the bitch and shut her up," Bo snapped.

Nicky started toward her again, and she got ready to take him on.

Suddenly another voice sounded from the doorway. "Hey!"

Melanie turned to see a man standing

41

there. He had striking features. The kind of face that would have been at home in a Van Dyck painting. Like a cavalier. Tall and lean, with long, very dark hair. He was in jeans and a tailored shirt, hands in his pockets, like a man who had just been out for a casual evening. As she had been.

He was certainly brave enough, she thought. He didn't look like the type who could race in like a movie hero and fistfight his way through a crowd. His features, however, were set in an expression that made her feel that he might be extremely useful in a fight.

"What's going on here?" he demanded.

"Hey, dude," Bo said. "We're just conducting a little business, so why don't you run on home and leave us to it?"

"Hey, *dude,*" the new arrival said, "you need to let these people go. Now," the man said calmly.

Bo ignored him as he wrapped his long fingers around Viv's neck. With his other hand he scooped some jewelry out of a showcase that had smashed glass everywhere.

As he pocketed the jewels, Viv stared at Melanie imploringly.

"I'm out of here. Nicky, you guys, handle these jokers," Bo said, then turned to leave through the back alley, dragging Viv with him.

Nicky grinned, a malicious twist of his lips.

The man by his side picked up a nineteenth-century rum bottle and cracked the neck on one of the showcases, squaring his shoulders and staring toward the door with amusement in his eyes.

Mel saw one of the men halfheartedly strangling old Mr. Delancy as Bo left with Viv, and she wasn't certain what to do.

"I've got this. You call the police after the one with the girl," the stranger said to her, as, with an almost casual air, he started past her. The man with the broken bottle stepped forward with amusement, as if taking the newcomer down was going to be like swatting a fly.

"No!" she cried, moving closer.

But to her amazement, the newcomer moved with the speed of lightning.

So fast, in fact, that she wasn't sure exactly what she saw.

One minute the thug was coming for him, grinning as he prepared to take on the stranger, and the next . . . he was on the ground, in the fetal position, groaning, and the stranger was heading for the man attacking Mr. Delancy.

She tore past them, through the back

door, ran through the alley to the street and looked around. Everyone she saw appeared to be in shock.

Melanie ran up to a man in a waiter's shirt who was standing by a car, staring in shock at the pole that had crashed down on it. She tapped him on the shoulder. "Did you see a tall black man, dragging a woman, come by here?"

"Pardon?" he said, looking at her as if she had just woken him up.

She heard a scream from down the street and recognized the voice as Viv's.

"Never mind!" she said, as she raced away down Santa Monica. Everyone she saw seemed lost. Even the cops, trying to control the panic, wouldn't be any help now. They were in the midst of Bedlam, and even if they understood her if she tried to explain, she wasn't sure they would care about one woman when it seemed that the whole world had gone mad.

She kept running.

Bo could move amazingly swiftly, considering the fact that he was dragging someone along with him and was running through a crowd.

She nearly fell over a man who was sprawled on the ground in front of a T-shirt shop. A newly purchased sub sandwich lay squashed atop him as people rushed past, trying to get away from the chaos.

Struggling against the rush of people who seemed as crazed as stampeding cows, she tried to get him to his feet.

"Are you all right?" she asked, knowing that all the while, Bo was getting away.

"Guy . . . decked me. He had a girl . . . she was screaming . . . I tried . . ."

She actually shook him to get him to focus, then felt guilty. He'd been one of the good ones. A decent human being. He'd tried to help.

"Listen to me. I need to find that guy before he hurts that girl. Are you all right now? Can you stand?"

"Yeah, yeah, I'm fine. Lady, don't you go getting involved. You'll get yourself killed. Get a cop. Tell him that bastard kept going down Santa Monica. Like toward the cemetery."

"Thanks."

"Don't you go after him. He's an animal!" the man called as she ran in the direction of the cemetery.

"Thanks! Take care of yourself!" she yelled back and kept running.

Near the cemetery, the world seemed far more quiet. There weren't any restaurants and bars near the entrance, only a lot of manufacturing. The cemetery itself was gorgeous and a huge tourist attraction by day. People loved celebrities, dead or alive. Sometimes, at night, they showed old movies on the outside walls of the mausoleum. The living picnicked on an expanse of grass where no interments had yet taken place. It sounded bizarre, but Melanie thought that if she'd been a star and interred in the mausoleum, it would be kind of cool to know that her living celluloid self might still be enjoyed right outside. The owner believed in the living recognizing the dead, but also finding life and peace among them; the Mexican Day of the Dead was celebrated there in a big way.

Because of its distance from the heart of the tourist area, there had been fewer cars in the area, and apparently no collisions. The pavement was ripped and buckled, but there was only one car parked, and no one near it. All the businesses were closed.

Residents, if there were any, remained inside.

The street lamps were all tilted at odd angles, and none of them were lit.

The world was very dark.

She kept running, listening as she did so, heading toward the entrance to the cemetery. Then she paused, standing still in the

46

darkness.

The noise — the sirens, the car horns, the screams and shouts of the people caught in the congested tourist areas — seemed to fade. She wasn't sure where her quarry had gone.

Viv, scream, make a noise, she thought, then listened hard.

Then she thanked God for the darkness and all but flattened herself against a wall as two of the sweatshirted thugs raced by her, so close that she could have reached out and touched them.

They were headed not for the main gate of the cemetery, she realized, but for a street nearby.

She rushed after them and was in time to see them scaling the wall outside a business attached to the cemetery whose sign boasted Mortuary Monuments. Beneath, in smaller letters, it advertised Residents' Discounts!

Melanie looked at the wall.

She hadn't dressed for climbing.

Oh, well.

Despite her silk halter top, linen pants and low-heeled sandals, she jumped, then dug for finger- and toeholds, and crawled over.

The darkness on the other side was almost total.

In the shadows, it appeared as if she had

entered a bizarre realm of the dead. Everything the place offered was displayed in the large, walled-in yard.

And this being L.A., where the dead were often far more famous than the living, the wares tended toward the elaborate.

Marble angels with folded wings greeted her in their forlorn wait to stand guard over the dead.

The monuments, most of them lying askew in the aftermath of the quake, were arranged along a series of winding paths. There were huge marble sarcophagi, along with angels, cherubs, saints and crosses, along with simpler headstones and plaques. Melanie was certain none of them were cheap, but for those in the agony of loss, eager to honor those loved ones who had gone before them, price was undoubtedly no object.

She shivered suddenly, as she felt an odd chill in the air. For a moment, she thought she was in the realm of the damned, hell itself, as if the earthquake had opened a rift in the fabric of the world and tumbled these silent monuments into a more fitting world.

She used her hands to guide her in the dark, her eyes drawn to marble angels that lay open-eyed and eerie against weeping cherubs.

She had never been here before, and she tried to gauge her progress through the narrow alleys of this bizarre kingdom of stone.

She heard a thump and went still. Someone had just entered the yard behind her, and that someone was moving silently, stealthily — and steadily — in her direction.

From somewhere ahead she heard a sound, like a gasp, followed by a choked-out scream, feminine and terrified.

Viv.

She hurried in that direction, then froze, as a shadow — dark, tall, moving like the wind — rushed up on her heels. She barely had time to dodge to one side, and even so, he nearly touched her as he raced by.

She followed as quickly as she could and found herself near a display mausoleum, an example of what the wealthy dead could attain. Stained-glass windows caught what few streaks of moonlight there were and cast a not-quite-earthly glow. It was strange, but beautiful, with gargoyles reminiscent of Notre Dame sitting above the hardwood door, behind an iron railing. Bas-relief saints carried the splendor of the stained glass on their shoulders.

The mysterious man who'd brushed past her in the dark was nowhere to be seen.

The mausoleum door was open to the night, and a match flickered within, casting enough light for her to briefly glimpse the three men and the lone woman inside.

Nicky, bleeding, his eyes blackened, was arguing with Bo.

Who still held Viv.

"Let the girl go, Bo. You've got the diamonds, so let's get out of here before that killing machine comes after us!"

"Asswipe!" Bo raged. "The girl is mine, and there's plenty of time now for a little fun. You want to run like a dog with your tail between your legs, fine, get the hell out of here. How the hell you were beaten by that scrawny fucker, I'll never know. Now quit whining like a two-year-old. We've got the goods *and* the girl, and this is a fucking *empty* tomb in the middle of nowhere in the middle of the night after an earthquake. Who the hell is going to find us here? What the hell, you chicken-liver. Fuck you, run!"

Nicky never had a chance to reply.

Something dark loomed out of nowhere, blocking Melanie's view into the mausoleum.

Then Nicky came flying out, as if he were a sack of dry leaves tossed into the wind, and crashed to the ground in a motionless heap.

Melanie burst into a run when she heard another terrified shriek tear from Viv's throat.

But as she neared the mausoleum, Bo and the stranger who had appeared at the shop suddenly came bursting out of it together, locked in a deadly tangle of arms and legs, nearly knocking Melanie over.

She ignored them, aware that there was still another man in the tomb with Viv.

"I'm sorry," he was saying to the terrified woman. "I'm sorry, but I have to . . . I mean, you're a witness," he told her.

He truly sounded miserable.

Too bad.

Melanie attacked.

He had a knife out, intending to stab Viv, who had been pressed back against the empty sarcophagus displayed in the would-be tomb. She was desperately clutching the marble.

Melanie threw herself straight at the attacker's back. He howled, grabbing at her and taking his attention off Viv.

"Run!" Melanie commanded the other woman, who wasted no time before obeying.

The thug was huge. Heavily muscled. He dislodged Melanie's hold, and she leapt away from him as he swiped at her with the knife. She needed more room to maneuver, she realized.

The second Viv was out the door, Mel backed out of the mausoleum herself, the thug following her.

She could hear thrashing around her, and realized Bo and the stranger were still locked in deadly combat.

This time, when the man with the knife made a leap for her, she caught his arm and nearly broke it. The knife flew from his grasp, and he shrieked in fury, lunging toward her again.

She sidestepped, but he rallied, charging her like a bull.

Again, she used evasive tactics, and he went crashing into the arms of a winged cherub.

She turned around, ready to finish him while he was still staggering from the impact, but as she started to move, Bo's massive body suddenly came flying through the dark night air, landing before her in a heap.

A broken heap.

He groaned, barely alive.

His friend ran at Melanie. This time, she stood her ground, feeling the night, feeling the rush of wind as her attacker ran at her.

She started to spin, raising an arm, and as

he neared her, she struck.

He went flying back, stunned and shaking his head, like a boxer who had been at the wrong end of a strong right hook.

He started toward her again, but this time he never reached her.

The stranger stepped in front of her, reached out and grabbed the man, and spun him around. He hardly seemed to be expending any effort, but as she watched, her attacker was lifted, tossed high into the air and left to fall.

He crashed down on top of Bo, who cried out in agony.

Melanie found herself staring at the stranger and realized she had been right all along. He *was* good to have around in a fight.

His midnight-dark hair was tousled, and beneath the strands that lay over his forehead, she saw that his eyes were dark as coal. His face was so chiseled that it belonged on a bust of a Grecian war hero.

And he was barely breathing hard. "Are you all right?" he asked.

"Are you?" she demanded in return.

He grinned crookedly and nodded.

"The shop owner?" she asked. "Mr. Delancy."

"He's fine," he told her. "And the girl?"

"She ran."

"The streets are still chaos."

"She'll be fine. There really aren't that many Bos out tonight."

"Don't kid yourself. There will be," he said.

She nodded, becoming aware of sirens in the distance again.

In the distance . . . and coming closer.

She stared, assessing him. "Who *are* you?" she demanded.

He inhaled, arched a brow slowly. And his wary grin deepened.

"I have a better question," he said softly to her. "*What* are you?"

The sirens were almost deafening now. They took another heartbeat to stare at each other, then turned and ran in opposite directions.

2

He was there again.

Among the dead.

The maze of paths through the catacombs was becoming familiar, though he remained at a loss as to why he found himself walking those paths again and again.

He did not fear the dead. He pitied them and, in a melancholy way, in these dark regions of his mind, he envied them. He knew there was more to what the subconscious mind saw than the world accepted. And it wasn't the dead who frightened him but the living. The living had free will, and free will allowed for choices, for good and evil. The good offered no harm to others, indeed, would reach out to help another. The evil flourished on the pain of others; they were selfish, seeking their own pleasure above all else. Evil could be minor, manifested in such things as shoplifting and petty theft. That demonstrated the evil of selfishness, but no one was physically harmed. True evil found expression in so many ways in so many societies. He was certain that throughout history, certain inquisitors, witch-finder generals and their ilk, sanctioned by cross and king, had been genuinely evil. They had enjoyed their tasks.

Evil shouldn't be lurking here, in this strange dream world where the long-dead lay in peace.

And . . . it wasn't exactly evil that he sensed. It was more a warning against evil, as if the dead in this dank place in the earth had somehow escaped the bounds of their shrouds to sense a growing disturbance in the earth.

As he walked, smelling the earth and mold, the musk of time and bodies long forgotten, he mocked himself. For one thing, he was dreaming, and in dreams, the message might be real but the evil was imaginary. For another, he did not believe that the earth itself could be evil. Evil lived in the heart or the soul. It was made manifest by those who reveled in its cruelty.

But as he walked, he felt the dead, felt their pain, and he imagined that there was a wind here, and that the wind was the whisperings of the dead. He knew that he was once again walking toward the light ahead, that the light was drawing him. When he reached it, he would once again see that strange stone tomb, and the light would surround him. In the maze of tunnels that stretched out in every direction, candles would glow from sconces set in the walls. Legions of the dead rested there.

He knew he would come upon the mysterious woman, and he would try to go closer, closer . . . and see what lurked beneath the hood, what visage lay hidden there.

Only once had he shared his dream, and seeing the face of another, he had been stunned. The other man had been so real, as if they had both stumbled upon the path like wandering tourists, only to startle one another. He had awakened from the dream that night startled and disturbed.

Tonight he looked down the corridor, but he was alone.

And he was approaching the center.

The wind that was not wind rustled, carrying the voices of the dead. He heard the strange clicking sound as the skeletons began to rebuild themselves.

One, bearing an ancient shield beneath the tattered remnants of his shroud, struggled to rise. The bony face stared at him sightlessly. The brittle finger bones clicked as the corpse attempted to point at him. The skeletal jaw moved, and the wind seemed to form words. Shakespearean words.

" 'Thou shalt beget kings, tho' be none.' "

So far, he had done no "begetting" of any kind, he thought. He stared at the skeleton, and he did not fear it.

The wind seemed to guide him again, and he moved toward the light. But this time, before he could reach it, the earth beneath him rumbled and rose. He nearly fell. Around him, a shelf in the rock crashed down, corpses shattering to dust. The rumbling was growing worse, and the ground began to undulate wildly . . .

He awoke, sitting straight up in bed. At his side, his wife, who knew him so well, jerked up, as well. "Lucien?" she said quietly.

"There's been an earthquake. Somewhere."

"There are often earthquakes somewhere, my love," she said, yawning. But then she bolted straight up, as well. "Maggie! . . . Maggie is out in L.A. visiting Melanie, and they have earthquakes there all the time."

He turned on the television, clicking the remote until he found one of the 24/7 news networks.

In moments he realized that his dream

had been true . . .

The quake registered 4.0 on the Richter scale. Definitely not the big one, but strong enough to cause some serious scattered damage. Centered south of L.A., it did more damage in the Anaheim area than anywhere else. Certain sections of Los Angeles and Orange counties never even lost power, while some areas would be looking at two to three weeks before all public utilities were restored. Thanks to satellite communication, Melanie was able to draw up that much information on her cell phone immediately, even as she made her way back home.

She was deeply relieved to reach Maggie by phone with equal ease and hear that her friend had taken her car and headed for her apartment to wait for her. Melanie lived in Los Feliz, bordering Hollywood, in an apartment she could reach either from the street or from her small storefront, where she sold high-end pet supplies.

Since she had been through a few minor quakes before, she had decorated accordingly. She didn't have glass knickknacks on her shelves, nor had she hung many things on the walls, in either her apartment or her shop. When she reached her apartment —

where, she had to admit, she'd gotten a bit carried away with an astrological theme — she found that her books were strewn across the floor but she'd suffered no other damage. Maggie wasn't in the apartment, so Melanie ignored the books for the moment and walked through to the shop.

The lights were on; she hadn't lost electricity. When she'd first moved to L.A. she'd rued the fact that she didn't have plate-glass windows looking out on the street; now she was glad. Amazingly, she hadn't lost a single windowpane. Peering through her chintz curtains, she could see that other buildings around her hadn't fared so well; many of her neighbors were out sweeping up broken glass.

The corkboard she kept on one wall for posting notices and pictures had fallen, and Maggie was busy collecting the collars and leashes — plain and designer, big and small — that lay scattered around the room.

"Earthquakes!" Maggie said with a shudder.

Melanie grimaced. "At least so far I haven't heard that any deaths have been reported."

"So far," Maggie said quietly.

"Hey, you live with hurricanes. That's the way it is. There is no actual paradise on

60

earth, you know."

Maggie set a rhinestone collar on the counter and stared at Melanie. "Okay, so — what happened after you ran out like a crazy woman?"

Melanie righted the bar stool she kept behind the counter and sat down. "I don't know, exactly," she admitted.

"The way to tell a story is from the beginning to the end, you know," Maggie commented dryly.

Maggie took a deep breath. "Okay. We were out for the evening when the earthquake hit. I went outside to —"

"You're already neglecting something," Maggie pointed out.

"What?"

"You suddenly becoming Rembrandt."

Melanie shook her head and waved a hand in the air, dismissing her artwork. "I heard someone screaming from Mr. Delancy's jewelry shop, and there were six guys there attacking Mr. D and Viv Larson, the salesgirl, and then . . ." She paused and shook her head, as if trying to make sense of everything that had happened. "Then this guy showed up, and he . . . well, he must have had some kind of martial-arts training or something, because I've never seen anyone move that fast. Anyway, he went

61

after the guys beating up Mr. D, and I chased the guy who took Viv. I followed them to the cemetery farther down Santa Monica, and when I got there, the guy showed up again. I mean, it was weird. He was tall enough, and well built, but I have no idea how he took on all six of those creeps."

"You know what they say. Disaster brings out the best and worst in people."

"Yes, but . . ."

"But what?"

"He survived. And I still don't know what he was doing there," Melanie said.

Maggie picked up a broom and started sweeping. "Melanie, don't you think he was pretty surprised to see you there, as well? I mean, how many women who look like you turn out to be good in a fight?"

"Lots," Melanie said with a laugh. "This is Hollywood, remember?"

Maggie didn't laugh. She didn't even smile. She just stopped sweeping and stared at Melanie. "Well, was he . . . ?"

"Like me?" Melanie asked softly.

"Yes," Maggie said flatly.

"No, I don't think so. I mean, I know he wasn't."

"You're certain?"

"I think so."

" 'I'm certain' and 'I think so' are not the same thing," Maggie said. "It's very strange," she continued gravely.

"Maybe he just studied kung fu or something. It's not so strange — maybe."

Maggie stopped sweeping to wave a hand in the air. "I don't mean just your stranger helping out. I mean the whole evening."

"Honestly, an earthquake in California isn't strange," Melanie said.

Maggie let out a sigh of exasperation. "Not the earthquake. The drawings."

"They were doodles," Melanie said uneasily.

"Museum-quality doodles."

"Well, they're gone now," Melanie said.

Maggie placed a hand on her hip. "No, they're not. I took them with me. And I'm going to show them to Lucien. If anyone can figure out what's going on with you, it will be Lucien."

"Lucien is in New Orleans," Melanie pointed out.

"No, Lucien is on his way here. I just talked to him."

"Is he — flying in?" Melanie asked.

"Of course he's flying in."

"But the airport —"

"Suffered no major damage. Limited

flights will begin arriving tomorrow around noon."

"You're kidding. After all this?" Melanie asked.

Maggie nodded. "As you said, an earthquake in California is nothing out of the ordinary. Your TV is working just fine, and a few local stations never even went off the air. Of course, one of them has been airing some kind of psychic who claims that this was just a warning. That the real quake is coming and it will be Armageddon." Maggie rolled her eyes, then managed a smile at last. "The end of the world as we know it. He says this was a prelude to the cataclysm of 2012, as foretold by the Mayans."

"What?"

"Are you telling me you've never heard of the Mayan prophecy?" Maggie asked.

Melanie felt edgy and impatient, but mostly because Maggie seemed to be taking everything so seriously. "Sure, I've heard of it. For some reason they decided the world will end in 2012."

"It's not that simple. They based their calculations on a bunch of factors — the ancient Mayans were brilliant astronomers and mathematicians. They said we're going through a cycle, a twenty-six thousand year evolution, and that culminates on the winter solstice, December twenty-first, 2012. It wasn't just the Mayans who thought so, either. Other societies had similar prophecies, including the Egyptians, the Etruscans, the Navajo and the Apache — and if you look at them closely, you can see hints of the same thing in Druid, ancient Semitic, Celtic, Norse, Greek and Roman beliefs."

"The Egyptians worshipped cats, you know," Melanie reminded her.

"You know, lots of people think cats rule," Maggie said lightly. "But getting back to my point, the Hindus also speak of the stages of life, and the end of one of the stages coincides almost exactly with the Mayan beliefs."

"I would think, when you're dealing with hundreds of thousands of years, someone might have miscounted somewhere along the line," Melanie said, her tone dry. "Seriously, Maggie, do you actually believe all this?"

Maggie shook her head. "I was speaking with Jade — she called me before I had a chance to get hold of anyone, including Sean, back home. Lucien dreamed there was a quake right as it happened. He and Sean are going to fly out here, and Jade's already working the Internet for everything it's worth. But I didn't get all my information from her. I've read a lot about this over the years. I find it fascinating. I was reading an article on the different roads men take to arrive at the same place. In every religion there's a supreme deity, though often there are other gods and magical, even divine, beings. In Christianity you have angels, including one very bad angel — the devil, who has his own demons to control — and other beliefs have demonic beings, too."

Melanie stared at her blankly.

"It's fascinating, really," Maggie told her. "You, of all people, should see that."

Melanie flushed. "There's good and evil in life, we all know that. There's a spark, or a soul, in all people, and some of those people are good and some are evil, and it doesn't matter if they come from the U.S., Canada, Europe or Timbuktu, any more than it matters if they're male or female, black, white, yellow, red or polka-dotted. I know there are things in this world that can't be explained, but . . ."

Maggie smiled slowly as Melanie's voice trailed off. She said firmly, "You drew the four elements."

"And you called Lucien, and told him that he had to come here because of something I drew on a napkin?"

"I told you — Lucien *knew* the minute

the quake occurred." She turned away, suddenly sweeping with new industry.

The way Maggie was behaving was scary, Melanie thought. Like Lucien, it seemed that Maggie simply *knew* things.

"Maggie?" Melanie asked. "What's up?"

"I don't know," Maggie said. She stopped sweeping and stared at Melanie again. "Okay, I'm concerned. Jade said that Lucien hadn't been sleeping well."

"He never sleeps well," Maggie said. "I . . . we never sleep deeply."

Maggie shook her head. "He's been having dreams."

"About what?"

"He hasn't really told her. But she thinks he's worried. It's just . . . Lucien having nightmares, you drawing weird things on cocktail napkins. And then a quake," Maggie said.

"I think that Lucien is . . . informing some of our other friends before he comes," Maggie said. "I think something . . . *big* might be afoot."

Melanie knew that Maggie wasn't referring to just any friends. She meant that Melanie had somehow started something that would require the presence of many members of their loosely knit group.

The group they called the Alliance.

"It's important that we find out if this does all mean something, don't you think?" Maggie asked.

"I was just sketching," Melanie said. But her protest sounded weak even to her own ears, and she felt an odd mix of both anticipation and dread.

"Tonight, that man you saw? He wasn't one of the Alliance?"

"Definitely not. I would know."

"Then for all we know, he's part of what's going on. It will be good to have Lucien and Sean here."

"Sure. It will be great to see them, no matter what," Melanie agreed, then picked up a bag of dog food and put it back on a shelf, trying to behave normally.

Just what the hell was going on?

And who the hell was the tall dark stranger who had come to the rescue, just like a modern-day knight in denim armor?

Whoever he was, he was not like her, but there *was* . . . something about him.

It had seemed easy enough to Scott when he had been chasing the lowlifes who had decided to use the earthquake as an excuse for robbery, and attempted rape and murder.

But after the burst of energy he'd expended disappearing as the cops closed in on the mausoleum, the walk home seemed to be a long one. It was bizarre the way one block showed so much damage, while the next appeared almost as if nothing had happened at all. But ever since he'd made L.A. his home, he'd become well acquainted with earthquakes and their aftereffects.

As he made his way down Santa Monica, he stopped occasionally to help people. He managed to help a guy lift the end of his Mini Cooper off his front porch, and he moved a broken gargoyle that had landed on a woman's steps, imprisoning her in her house. People were still out on the streets, but as he walked along, it seemed that they were already coping better with the crisis. Lights from streets with power cast a pale glow over streets that had none, neighbors were out helping one another, but mainly people were just standing around talking, trading information from cell phones with Internet capacity and calls to friends in other neighborhoods as to what had happened in the rest of the city.

As he turned toward his own neighborhood off Sunset, a woman came running toward him. "Sir, do you have a phone?"

"Sure," he said.

"Do you have service?"

"I do," he told her. She was in her forties, and attractive, but her features were filled with pain and fear — some of it that her request might be rejected.

"If I could — I can pay you."

"Please," he said, and handed her the phone. She glanced at him gratefully and then began to punch in a number with shaking fingers.

"Tommy?" she said. He heard the male voice on the other end. Tommy had apparently answered. Tears streaked down the woman's face, and as he listened to her side of the conversation, he realized that she had reached her son, who was attending a local college. He moved a few steps away and let her talk as long as she wanted.

It wasn't as if there was anyone waiting for him at home.

She finished her call and handed the phone back to him, tear tracks still wet on her face but a smile on her lips. "Bless you," she told him. "Thank you. Thank you so much!"

"Not a problem," he said, smiling as he took his phone back. "I'm glad to hear that Tommy is okay. There hasn't been a single fatality reported."

She nodded. He could tell that she wanted to care about the rest of the world, but she was just too relieved that her son was alive and well to think about anything else.

"Only child?" he asked her.

"Yes."

"I'm so glad he's fine," Scott said again, then offered a casual wave as he started walking again.

Strength wasn't everything, he thought, as he kept heading toward home. It never had been. An oldie went through his head. Dionne Warwick, he was pretty sure: *What the world needs now is love, sweet love.*

It was corny, but it was still true, and never more so than tonight.

There were undoubtedly more bad guys out — a natural disaster like this one was sure to bring them out of the woodwork. But on his way home, he was encouraged to see that the best of mankind seemed to be on show.

Just as he had the thought, he saw a man — bearded, and wearing jeans and a ragged denim shirt — standing in the middle of the road. He was wearing a homemade placard and shouting, "Death is upon us! The bowels of hell are waiting. Repent, sinners, repent! Scorn music, dance, drink, sex and drugs, for the end is coming. Hellhounds will rip out your throat, and demons will slice your flesh and gnaw on the in-

71

nocence of your infants. Repent!"

People were simply walking past him, ignoring him for the most part. But then the prophet of doom ran right up to a young woman. "Repent!" he roared, spittle flying from his lips.

Scott paused, then started to walk toward her, in case she needed help, but she only smiled and managed the situation herself.

"Repent? I'm in the church choir, where I sing for God, and guess what? I think he likes my voice," she said, and walked on by.

The fire-and-brimstone preacher leapt in front of Scott. "Repent! The bowels of hell will burst open, and you will face the death-spewing demons of the deep!"

He reached out to touch Scott, then flinched and drew back. His silence struck Scott as more disturbing than his diatribe.

"I think the Lord and I are good," Scott said, and hurried quickly on. He could feel the man watching him go and winced, afraid the man would start shouting about the Oracle.

But the man remained eerily silent.

In another minute, Scott turned onto his own block. His new design shop was right on Sunset, but he'd purchased a town house down a side street. The lights were out on his block, but the houses were all standing, though there was some broken glass on the sidewalk, and a couple of small trees were down.

He paused one last time to help a man drag a palm tree off his car, then moved on. As soon as he was inside, he turned on the large Coleman lantern the neighbor had suggested he should go out to buy. The guy had been right, and Scott mouthed a silent thank-you.

The pale glow from the lantern displayed his new living quarters in a surreal light. Simple, sparse. He could probably use a few throw pillows or something, he thought, as he looked around the living room. But the place was gaining some character. He'd done some posters for rock bands over the years, and he had several up on the walls. The sofa was an old chesterfield he'd found on eBay, and the throw rug on the hardwood living room floor was a Navaho design. His workstation was an old oak bank desk with tiered files in a lighter wood. The room was finished out with a rocker, TV, end tables and a few photographs — himself and his folks, more family, his friends. For some reason, he'd blown up a picture of himself, Zach and Emory, taken earlier on the night when they'd gone to the rescue of the couple being attacked in the alley, the night

73

that had changed his life. The kitchen, which opened onto a small den, was pretty much bare. On the counter, he had a coffeepot and a can opener. The range — which so far he hadn't even used — had come with a microwave, which had come in handy. He couldn't be bothered cooking, because he spent a lot of his time — when not getting the new business going, because superhuman strength had not come with a superhuman income — staring at the computer and trying to ascertain just what had happened to him. And not only what, but *why?*

He strode through to the kitchen, grabbed a still-cold beer from the fridge and returned to the chesterfield to sit. The situation that had plagued the back of his mind since he'd started his long walk home returned to haunt him.

What the hell had really happened out there tonight?

Who was she, and more importantly, *what* was she?

She was tall, just a few inches shorter than his own height, but slender and angelic in comparison to his own dark appearance. She was a stunning woman who would have looked great strutting a catwalk, modeling the latest fashions. Her hair was rich and lustrous, but pale. Her eyes were light blue, he was pretty certain — but emphasized by strikingly honey-toned brows and lashes. Her bone structure was delicate, but she hadn't betrayed a blink of fear as she faced down a gang of street thugs, completely confident that she could win.

Had she also touched a dying man's hand in an alley and been told that she was Capricorn?

He would probably never know.

He returned to his ongoing examination of his own powers. He was fast, and he was strong. Once he had literally pulled his door off its hinges, an expensive annoyance, but in the end a — good thing. It had taught him that he had to be careful. But, he had to admit, despite his old friends looking at him a bit strangely now, he had found a certain satisfaction with what had occurred, and he'd taken advantage of it. He'd always gone to the gym now and then, and he'd loved playing football and tennis. But since that night, he'd taken up yoga, karate and kickboxing, trying to learn to harness his mind, agility and strength.

Oh, yeah, he was fast. But the platinum-blond beauty had disappeared so quickly that she might have flown away, even disappeared into thin air.

He stretched his legs out on the coffee table and stared at the laptop on the desk, realizing that it still had battery power. He rose slowly, walked over and sat down, then pulled up the site he'd been looking at before he'd gone out. The words swam before him for a moment. Since that night in the alley, he'd been studying astrology, hoping it would take him somewhere, help him to understand Capricorn — and the Oracle.

And the dream. The dream that had recurred several times since then. . . .

That first time had been the most bizarre, though, when another person had been there, as startled to run into him at the juncture of the corridors as he had been to see someone else inside his dream.

So many times he had lain awake at night, staring up into the darkness, trying to make sense of what had happened. His whole place in the world had been changed that night.

A man dying in an alley.

A command to find the Oracle.

And a tall, seemingly very real stranger, suddenly joining him in a bizarre dream.

No matter how real he'd seemed, the man must have been part of the dream. Logic told him so.

Now, tonight . . .

So was the blonde another Capricorn? Or maybe another earth sign? Or maybe she was the Oracle who was supposedly looking for him. Right. She was looking for him about as much as she was looking to contract the bubonic plague.

He leaned back as he hit a link to a recent article. The header read: The Oracle and the Zodiac: Earth, Wind, Fire and Water — and the Puzzle that can Save the World from the Darkness of the Solstice in 2012.

He bolted forward and started to read.

While armchair sleuths and psychics dabble in old Mayan prophecies, finding what they choose in Sumerian, Greek, Indian, African, Asian, Norse and other legends, a mysterious Roman blogger states that the ancient capital may house the answers to the importance of 2012. Reference is made to cities beneath other cities, to a hell below the earth, kept under control by the basic goodness of the human soul, and the ability of the Church and other religious institutions to give man the strength he'll need in the upcoming battle for our world. News has leaked that a quiet convent sheltered near the decaying remains of one of the earliest churches holds prayer services daily for the survival of mankind. Sister Maria Elizabeta, one of the convent's most respected nuns, has denied that the sisters pray for anything other than human souls, but admits that those souls they pray for belong to all the inhabitants of the known world. "If the earth is to end," the sister has been quoted as saying, "then all the peoples of the earth must join to fight evil, by whatever name they call it. The earth, our home, has always been volatile. Earth, wind, fire and water are the elements we need to survive, yet they may come in such torrents as to deluge us, not so much with their power over life and death, but with their power to touch the human soul." Is she speaking in riddles — or, better yet, in parables? Follow the link below to read the blog and decide for yourself.

Rome.

Sister Maria Elizabeta.

His dreams, with skeletons stacked up underground. Catacombs?

Scott hit the link. Words written in Italian popped onto the screen, along with whimsical, medieval drawings. He stared at the words blankly, then spoke aloud impatiently.

"What kind of idiot are you? You need an

Internet translator."

But when he went to hit another key, the battery gave out.

He continued to stare at the dead screen, three words at the forefront of his mind.

Sister Maria Elizabeta.

He told himself that he was crazy, but he knew he wasn't. He had been searching desperately for understanding, and at last he might have found someone who could provide him with answers.

The woman was a nun, he told himself. Of course she wanted the world to come together in peace.

But she had spoken of earth, wind, fire and water.

A nun. In Rome. Where there were dozens of catacombs.

And if he didn't do something, he was going to lose his mind for sure.

Why not?

He pulled out his phone, flipped it open and whispered a prayer of gratitude that he'd kept it charged.

3

Melanie dreamed of being in a strange grotto. Stone, covered with lichen, cool, with a sense of being deep in the earth. There were shadows, dark and looming, and there was a sound like something dripping. And in the distance, a glow, beckoning her.

There were paintings on the walls, frenzied drawings of the cruelties of war and the excesses of victory, the revenge those who had won took on those who had lost. There seemed to be lines carved in the stone, but when she looked, they weren't lines at all, but something dripping down the face of the stone. She blinked, and saw that it was crimson. It was as if the ancient walls were crying tears of blood.

There were holy drawings between those images of war and brutality, oddly peaceful despite the chaos around them. Halos of light above kneeling saints, angels singing cherubically. A lion slept at David's feet, and a cross glowed, the ray of illumination that spared the catacomb from the darkness. Knowledge streaked through her like lightning. She was in a catacomb. A place where the dead lay rotting beneath their shrouds.

Was she, too, clad in a shroud, lying in a niche in the wall, one with the rows of the dead who had been buried in corridors beneath the earth for centuries?

Of course not, because none of this was real. She was dreaming.

She couldn't remember the last time she had dreamed so vividly. Perhaps once, in a different time . . .

She realized she was afraid, and she was *never* afraid.

Suddenly a silhouette appeared in the glow ahead. It loomed large, a shadow snaking along the glistening walls with their tears of blood. She wanted to shrink away from that shadow, to pretend that she was only the detritus of time, dust to dust, ashes to ashes.

But at the heart of that dark figure, there seemed to be a light. Something that was warm and strong. She dared to open her eyes, dared to look. She felt a sense of flesh and blood, bone and breath, a living being, one who had come to offer comfort, perhaps, and hope.

"I am here, waiting," it said.

Which was ridiculous, Melanie told herself. Shadows didn't talk. But this was a dream; the shadow could do whatever it chose, and apparently it had chosen to be there in that place of death and decay, the light in the darkness. But the shadow had form, human form. The whisper was melodic, a soft, feminine voice. The shadow was cloaked, wearing some voluminous garment that swallowed it whole.

The shadow looked like a nun.

"I am the Oracle," the shadow said. "I am waiting. I know you will come, and that we can make it to the light."

The figure faded away, then, leaving Melanie in the darkness, aware of the pungent smell of everything that came from the earth and then returned to it. The scent of mold teased her nostrils, that deep earthy scent that smelled like death. And she felt a growing heat, like the slowly simmering threat of brimstone from the bowels of hell.

Melanie jackknifed into a sitting position, shaking. She panicked at first, looking around, then realized she was in her own room, in her own home, with Maggie sleeping in the guest room down the hall.

She reached over and turned on her

bedside light. Her hands were trembling. The scent of the dream seemed to hover for a moment, but she hugged her arms around herself, and then it was gone.

She was tempted to cry. . . . All she wanted was to live as normal a life as she could, but this . . . bizarre drawings, dreams of hell and nuns promising salvation.

"I'm turning on the television and watching a totally ridiculous sitcom rerun," she announced, as if someone could hear.

Then she turned on the television, and let canned laughter filled the room.

A mile away, Scott was immersed in a dream, as well.

He was standing on a hill, and he could feel the wind ripping around him. There was dirt beneath his feet; he felt the grime between his toes. He was wearing sandals, and some kind of a . . . skirt? And when he moved his head, he realized that he was wearing a helmet. Not only that, he was holding a massive spear.

He heard moans, and above the moans, screams of agony. When he looked around, he saw them.

Human beings, being herded along in single file between the rows of crosses that bordered the road. The crosses rose to the sky all along the path, and each one held a burden of dying flesh. Men and women dying in agony, and nearby, his fellow soldiers sweated in the sun as they nailed another man to a cross.

"Stop!" he roared. But no one heard him, or maybe they just ignored him. He saw the face of the man being nailed to the cross, and it was the face of the old man who had died in the alley.

"Be strong, Capricorn, be strong," he said, his voice hoarse with agony.

"Stop!" Scott raged again, grabbing one of the soldiers, tearing him away. The others, stunned, looked around, seeking to fight an enemy they couldn't see.

"I am gone now. It is up to you to find the Oracle," the old man said. "Tread the ancient road, and go to where the battle must be won."

The face changed and became a woman's. She was old, older than time itself, it seemed. But she had brilliant blue eyes, and she smiled toward heaven even as a nail was being driven into her wrist by one of the soldiers as the others stabbed at the wind.

"You can see me now, and you can see the way. Come to me," she said.

Her face shifted, and then the old man was there again. But he was dead now; he'd been too old, too weak to endure the torture of the nails, the loss of blood.

Scott howled in rage and frustration, then threw out his arms, and the soldiers fell away.

The back of his hand began to throb and he woke in an instant. He was sitting up in bed, and he had just slammed his arms against the wall.

He looked around in the shadows and the darkness. A groan escaped him. "I guess I *am* Capricorn. I *will* find the Oracle. I *will* find the way," he said, then realized he was speaking aloud. What the hell. It was bad enough that his whole life had changed and his days were a torment of hoping that he would discover a reason why, but his nights were worse.

He was beginning to hate going to sleep.

He sat awake, wondering what the dream had meant, or if it had meant anything at all, other than that he was still spooked by that night in the alley. Maybe he was just going mad. Getting really philosophical, was there a point to life at all? Or was he, along with everyone else, just organic matter that had developed until it had to believe in more for the sake of sanity?

He smashed his pillow — better than the wall, at least — and lay down again.

It was hours before he slept.

"I know I need to start all over again. Calming my darling down and letting her know how much I love her. She's just a pile of quivering, quaking nerves," Judy Bobalink declared, cradling Miss Tiffany to her chest.

Miss Tiffany was a "designer dog," a peek-a-poo, bred from a Pekingese and a miniature poodle. Mel knew that Judy had spent a great deal of money on the dog, which was, in Melanie's mind, a cute little mutt. Judy Bobalink reminded Melanie of a designer creation herself. Once upon a time she had been a beautiful young starlet. Fortune had not fallen her way, though, and now she was a character actress — actually, a very good one. But she was sixty, with bleached-blond hair that fell to her waist, pretty blue eyes and massive fake lashes. On the screen, it worked. In person, she was a bit like a photo out of focus. She had given up on the possibility of family for her career, and Miss Tiffany was everything to her.

Miss Tiffany *was* quivering in her owner's arms — but Melanie had seldom seen the dog do anything but.

"So, can you work with her this afternoon?"

"I'm sorry, Judy, but I really can't. I have

friends coming in to help me fix some damage, but I can . . . talk to Miss Tiffany. Honestly, it isn't me she needs now. She doesn't have any behaviors that need to be modified, she's just nervous after the earthquake. She needs *you*."

Judy looked crushed and unconvinced. "Oh. It's just that I was so excited to see that you were open. So many places are closed because of the quake. And honestly, we get those little quakes all the time, and this wasn't really *that* much bigger. It was more like a warning of something more, don't you think?"

A warning? Melanie wasn't sure that the earth knew anything about warning people or that the plates beneath the earth's crust did anything more than react to natural stressors.

"Well, we're always open on Saturday, so I figured I'd give it a few hours. But you know how it goes. I'm sure many places are closed because their employees live in areas that were harder hit. Anyway, I can't keep Miss Tiffany for you, Judy, but let's talk to her for a minute. Hand her over, and listen to the way I reassure her," Melanie suggested.

Judy complied, and Melanie held the little dog and talked to her gently, telling her that the quake was over, that everything was okay. The dog had no idea of what she was saying; it was the soothing cadence of her words that made the animal pay attention and finally wag her tail tentatively. Melanie gave her a few treats, and the little tail began to wag so hard it created a breeze. Judy gushed over the results, but Melanie waved a hand dismissively. "You just need to use positive reinforcement, and it doesn't have to be food. Dogs are affectionate creatures. Miss Tiffany loves you, and she takes all her cues from you. Make sure *you're* calm and she'll be calm, too."

Just as she handed back the dog, Judy gushing at how marvelous she was, Blake Reynaldo, LAPD, walked in with Bruno.

Blake was a big cop. Bruno was a big dog. He wasn't a shepherd or a rottweiler, though. He was a basset. Low to the ground, but massive, Bruno could pull with such strength that Blake had once fallen flat while walking him. After that, Bruno had come in for training. When he looked at Melanie with his soulful eyes, his intelligence shone through. Bruno was the kind of dog who just needed to learn that his master was the boss, and Blake needed to learn to be that boss, establishing his credentials not with swearing or anger, but with a steady stubbornness to match

Bruno's own.

"Hey, Blake," Melanie said. "How's it going out there?"

"This morning, not so bad. Last night, a zoo. We got through with no fatalities. Damage is in the millions, but manageable. But the looting last night was savage. A lot of cops are still out there, but it's been quiet enough that those of us who were out there tackling the looters last night were actually allowed to go home when the new shift came on." Blake Reynaldo was a seasoned cop. Nearing sixty, he had put in all the years he needed to retire, but he said he wasn't ready yet. He wouldn't retire until they kicked him out, he had once assured Melanie. Stocky, strong — almost like Bruno — he was armed with over thirty years of street savvy. He wasn't married, and he spent his free time creating programs for local toughs, putting his time and money into coaching neighborhood baseball teams and sponsoring "art days" when his players spent an afternoon at a dance recital, classical concert or art show, with the intention of showing them how different approaches to movement, rhythm and perception helped with sports. Sometimes a bad baseball player even became an artist or guitarist. There was a method to Blake's madness, and Melanie loved him; she was sure that he had kept a lot of kids from going down the wrong path.

"So what ~~you~~ brings you and Bruno in?" Melanie asked.

"Dog food. I would've had to knock on your apartment door if you hadn't opened today. I had some breakage. Don't want to take any chance of Bruno getting glass slivers in his dinner. I threw away his old dishes, and the coffeepot fell on the bag of food with enough force to split it open, then broke. Bruno is my friend — hell, Bruno is my best friend. Can't go taking any chances."

"Oh, no! You'd never want to take a chance," Judy said. She smiled at Blake. He smiled back. "Well, I'll be on my way. Thanks so much, Melanie." She headed for the door, then turned back to Blake. "You're a very good master," she said.

"Thanks," Blake called, watching her leave.

Melanie wondered if she might be able to build a romance between the two of them. She needed to throw a few more bowwow parties, when her clients brought their dogs in for treats and playtime, then socialized over wine, soda and snacks.

Blake turned his attention back to Melanie. "So where were you when the lights went out?" he asked.

Melanie dragged a fifty pound bag of dog food over to Blake, then set two big new bowls on top of it. "Those are on me — I'll put the food on your account," she told him, then said, "I was out with my friend Maggie. She's in from New Orleans. I think you met her last year. We do a weekend now and then. She leaves the kids at home with her husband and comes out here to do grown-up things."

Blake nodded, then pointed a finger at her. "I heard about you, young lady. What am I going to do with you?"

"I don't know what you're talking about," she told him.

"I think you do — not that I'm objecting, mind you. But what did you think? That just because there was a quake and a lot going on, we weren't going to investigate every incident? We have six beat-up street toughs with rap sheets a mile long in the lockup now, waiting for arraignment. They claimed that you — and some long-haired guy — beat them up."

"What?" Melanie set her hands on her hips. "They . . . said it was *me?*"

"Don't *what* me. L.A. is big, but we're a bunch of neighborhoods. A tall platinum blonde named Melanie who must be a local because Mr. Delancy knows her? All roads lead to you, Mel."

"They were attacking Mr. Delancy!" she said indignantly. "They abducted Viv, and God knew what they intended to do to her."

Blake laughed. "I'm not saying you beat them up without provocation. We followed up, and Mr. Delancy told us that you saved his skin." He wagged a finger at her firmly. "But here's the point. I'm assuming you've taken a lot of jitsu-karate-kick-em-up or something, but Melanie, you can't go taking the law into your own hands — you could get hurt. These gangbangers carry knives, even guns. You may have the best kick in all L.A., but if they shoot you, it's no help."

She flushed. "I'm okay. Honestly."

"That's the point I'm trying to make. You may be okay now, but that's just 'cuz you got lucky. What about next time? You're a civilian. A kick-ass civilian, but no cop."

"Blake, Viv and Mr. Delancy might have *died*. I had to step in."

"I'm grateful to you, and *they're* grateful to you, but no more," Blake said firmly. "You think I haven't heard about you showing up to help out when muggings are going on? No more, and that's that. And who's the guy, by the way?"

"What guy?" Melanie asked.

Blake let out a frustrated sigh. "Tall, dark hair, stronger than he looks. Who was he?"

"I don't know," Melanie admitted.

"Come on, Mel. He's not in trouble. I just need to tell him the same thing I just told you about vigilante justice and ending up dead."

"Honestly, Blake, I don't know, I swear. He just showed up. I've never seen him before."

"If you say so," he said skeptically. "But if you see him again, I want to talk to him," Blake said. "Before he gets himself dead, too."

Dead, too.

Melanie froze for a moment, but Blake didn't notice. He shook his head and went on, "And suppose you killed someone, saving someone else? People have gone up on murder charges for that, you know."

He hadn't meant anything by that turn of phrase, she told herself, then let out a breath. "I still say we can't turn a blind eye to violence."

"Missy —" Blake began, but the door opened then, the little bells above it jingling.

Against the falling afternoon sun, she could see the silhouette of a tall man in a leather motorcycle jacket. He stepped inside, but she already knew that Lucien DeVeau had arrived. She had known him forever, and it was easy to recognize his silhouette. Strange, she thought. She would know the silhouette of the man she had met the night before just as certainly. His height, his lean build, the way he had of standing . . . she would recognize him a mile away.

"Hello there, my friend," Lucien said, smiling at Melanie and nodding an acknowledgment to Blake.

"Lucien!" She hurried around the counter to give him a hug, then turned quickly to make introductions. "Blake, this is my old friend Lucien DeVeau, from New Orleans."

"Hello," Blake said. She could hear the curious pleasure in the tone of his voice. Blake was always trying to set her up with someone.

He suddenly arched a suspicious brow that silently asked, *Tall and dark — is this the guy from last night?*

She shook her head at Blake, then said aloud, "Lucien is married to my good friend Jade."

"Nice to meet you, Blake," Lucien said.

Blake cocked his head to the side. "So what are you? Old college friends?"

Melanie laughed. "Something like that."

"Well, friendship is good," Blake said.

Melanie thought he sounded disappointed that Lucien wasn't a romantic prospect, not to mention that he wasn't the mysterious stranger from the night before.

"Always good to know a cop," Lucien said. "And be friends with one. Have you met Mel's friend Maggie? Her husband, Sean, flew out here with me, and he's a cop back home," Lucien said.

"Cool, I'll have to meet him," Blake said.

"Yes, you will," Melanie agreed, then pointed to the dog, "And that's Bruno," she told Lucien.

"Hello, Bruno," Lucien said.

"Have you seen Maggie yet?" Melanie asked him.

"She and Sean . . . are off somewhere together. She sent me here. She said you'd probably close up early."

"Yeah. I have a couple of college kids who usually run the shop on Saturdays, but after the earthquake, I called them this morning and told them to tend to their own problems," Melanie said.

"And since there was an earthquake, I think it's okay if you close now. What do you think?" Lucien asked.

Lucien wasn't being rude, but Blake Reynaldo could take a hint *before* it was a hint.

95

"Nice to meet you, Lucien. See ya, Melanie." Bruno let out a deep, soulful wolf as if echoing his master's words. "Melanie, don't forget what I was saying to you, you hear?"

"I won't forget, Blake," Melanie assured him.

He left, and she turned to see Lucien staring at her firmly. "So?"

"Come on," she protested. "You just got to California. What's the *so?* Maggie's more concerned than I am."

"I understand you're suddenly drawing like a pro."

"I can't believe Maggie encouraged you to come out here because of that," Melanie said.

"After I dreamed that earthquake, I planned on coming before I ever talked to Maggie. Let's go someplace where we can talk. Maggie and Sean can meet up with us."

"All right, there's a place just down the street. I'm pretty sure they're open. We didn't suffer much damage around here."

Ten minutes later, they'd been served drinks and Lucien had put a call through to Sean to tell them where they were. Lucien was looking at her very seriously and Melanie knew that what she was feeling was dread. He was here because of the Alliance, of course.

All the members of the Alliance led normal lives — or fairly normal, anyway — and they were scattered around the country. But when something was really wrong, Lucien stepped in. He was powerful; he'd lived through a lot, learned a lot, and his senses were as well honed as his physique. And right now she didn't like the assessing way he was staring at her at all.

"Nice neighborhood," he said casually. But Lucien was never *truly* casual.

"I love it," she assured him. "I have a grocery store just across the street, great neighbors and nice customers."

He leaned forward suddenly. "A good life," he assured her. Then he asked her abruptly, "Why are people staring at me?"

"What?"

"People keep looking at me."

Melanie laughed. "Well, this neighborhood does border Hollywood, you know. You're tall, dark and handsome. They're probably trying to figure out which show you're on." She leaned closer. "Our waiter just did a spot on *CSI*. The woman over there is on a soap. And the young guy over there, known as 'The Ponceman,' is a major leaguer with a show on the Internet."

"Great, I thought we were going for

privacy," Lucien murmured.

"Trust me, we'll be plenty private here. It's a neighborhood hangout. People may stare, but they leave you alone. They may look and whisper, but if you're not Clooney or Pitt, they go right back to their own conversations. But what do we have to talk about that's so private?"

He arched a brow to her. His look asked, *What in the world* wouldn't *we need to keep private?* He shook his head and looked down at the table, then stared at her in concern. "You're doing it again," he said.

"What?"

"Sketching," he said.

She froze. She looked down and saw that she had indeed been drawing again. She didn't even remember taking a pen from her purse, but now she stared blankly at the picture she had created.

She had sketched a road not three blocks from her apartment. In her drawing, the ground was practically exploding. A terrified woman looked on with her mouth open in a scream, and others wore detailed looks of absolute panic on their faces.

"Do you recognize the area you've drawn?" Lucien demanded curtly.

"Yes, yes, it's down about three blocks," she said, still stunned at her own artwork.

He rose and grabbed her arm. "Let's go. *Now!*"

Scott couldn't leave until the following night. For some reason, flights to Rome were heavily booked. Summer, he figured. Schools were out. At least he had enough miles to upgrade to first class, and since he was tall, it was damned nice to have the legroom.

He called his three employees to tell them to take care of their own problems but, if everything was all right, report for work on Monday. He only had three employees, but they were all good, young designers who didn't mind doing the physical work of running the presses as long as they were able to get some creative work, to build up their portfolios. He took extra time to brief Kevin Ostrom, his office manager, about everything that might come up during his extended absence. He would try to check in periodically while he was away, but with Kevin in charge he felt confident that things would run smoothly.

Since he had the time, he went to the office to check the damage and found that all his heavy equipment had stayed put, and he'd suffered only one broken monitor and a smashed printer. Whispering a little prayer of thanks, he wrote a note to Kevin to see that the monitor and printer were replaced; he had insurance, so all Kevin had to do was arrange for pick-up.

He had just finished writing the note when he felt an aftershock that shook the place like a fun-house floor. It wasn't severe, but he heard screams and stepped outside to see what was going on.

A block down, the earth had shifted, spewing up concrete and heaving a ruptured gas main to the surface. People were running, some shoving others out of the way, some trying to help those who needed it. He saw a kid of about nine just standing in the street, staring at the broken pipe sticking up into the air.

Scott tore off down the street. First he grabbed the boy and delivered him to a teenager hurrying away from the disaster. The teen stared at him; dumbfounded. Long-haired, wearing an oversized T-shirt, he didn't look mean, just young and confused. "Get him out of here," Scott commanded.

The teen stared at Scott blankly, then nodded. Grabbing the younger child, he ran.

The area was clearing, but any second now the gas would explode, and there was no telling how far the rain of devastation would extend.

Scott raced for the pipe. He grabbed one end, feeling almost overwhelmed by the smell of the escaping gas. He found the other end of the split pipe. He wasn't sure that he could do anything, and his sense of self-preservation was kicking in, screaming at him to run like hell himself. But he didn't. Somehow he forced the broken pieces together. He strained, and felt the tendons in his neck popping. His fingers threatened to snap just like the metal, which had been weakened by the first quake and now had twisted as it split.

He had to straighten out the metal to get the pieces together. It seemed impossible, especially with the seconds ticking by. But to his amazement, though his fingers were bloodied, he managed the task. He forced the pieces together, then wondered what to do next. He couldn't stand there and hold them together forever.

Then he heard someone shout the news that the utility company had been informed and the gas had been turned off.

Sweat was dripping down his face. He gritted his teeth and steeled himself to the task. Someone with the right equipment would come; they had to. No matter what that dying old man had somehow done to him, he couldn't hold the pipe much longer. How much gas was still compressed in there? Should he let it leak out slowly?

Scott was startled when he heard movement behind him. He turned to see another man reaching out to grasp the jagged metal.

He almost dropped the pipe. He was sure his jaw gaped.

It was him.

The man from his dream.

That was impossible, of course. He just thought it was the man from his dream. He'd probably seen the guy's picture somewhere and put him in the dream. Because logic dictated that people — strangers — simply did not walk into each other's dreams.

Yes, they did, and logic be damned, because the man recognized him, too. He saw it in the man's eyes, in his shocked expression.

With impressive dexterity, the man grasped the pipe, not allowing any shift that could create friction and a spark. "I've got it," the man said. "You can let go. Help is coming."

Scott stumbled back. Every bone in his body seemed to ache. He stared at his bloodied hands, and then at the stranger.

He knew him. Damn it, he knew him.

"Are you . . . Earth? Or, uh, the Oracle?" Scott asked quietly.

"What?" the man asked, looking as him as if he must be confused.

"Are you . . . the Oracle? Are you . . . an earth sign?"

"I'm afraid . . . not," the man said, shaking his head, but studying Scott.

He, too, had dark hair and hazel eyes. But he thought he saw more. The man's eyes had a streak in them, like a glint of gold. There was something about him that was . . . different. Scott didn't know how he knew — maybe certain of his senses had been heightened, as well — but he was sure of it.

Just as he was sure the man would stay until the problem was solved.

But the man wasn't the Oracle. Of course not. It had been a stupid question. Scott had held the hand of a dying man in an alley, and now he was searching for some hidden agenda that didn't exist, believing in the ranting of an old man who'd lost all sense of reality as the light faded from his eyes. And just because this man was strong and looked like the man from his dream . . .

Scott suddenly realized that he had to get the hell out of the crowd. Someone might recognize him, people might question him.

Worse, the press might get hold of what had happened and make him out to be a freak or something.

He turned around and started walking quickly — not running, because that would have drawn attention — just walking with long strides down Sunset, where he could disappear into a crowd before doubling back to get home.

Then, just as he reached the crowd, he saw her.

The tall blond beauty with the Jackie Chan soul.

She saw him, too.

Their eyes met. Hers were huge and beautiful — and questioning. And he saw something in them that he hadn't seen the night before. A trace of . . . dread.

His fists clenched at his sides, and he wanted to scream.

Who are you?

But then he heard a shout from the crowd. "There he is! That's the guy who stopped the gas from exploding!"

A hazmat crew was coming around the corner, and sirens were blaring again. He whirled and saw that the tall man with the hazel eyes was moving aside as fire-suited workers moved in to take his place. He seemed intent on getting away from them as quickly as possible, too.

When Scott turned back, the blond beauty was gone, and people were pointing at him. He ran this time, hurrying down the street and plunging around a corner as fast as he could, hurrying for his own place.

Bursting into his townhouse he was startled by the sound of a voice. "Ladies and gentlemen, we are strong, we are survivors, and so is tonight's movie. It's a Marx Brothers classic, and it will be playing as planned at the Hollywood Forever Cemetery tonight, so get there early, bring your blankets, your coolers and your best foot forward."

Scott laughed and leaned against his door. The radio had been on, and now the electricity was back on. What irony that the first thing he heard was an ad for a film screening on the wall of the mausoleum at the very cemetery where he and the mystery blonde had saved the other woman.

He walked on into the bathroom, where he washed his dirtied and bloodied hands, rinsed them with peroxide, and then wrapped them with gauze, hoping they wouldn't bleed through.

After that, he went over to his computer, glad that it was back up, and started to study sites on modern and ancient Rome.

When his phone rang, he answered it absently. "Hello?"

"Scott!" To his surprise, he heard Zach's voice on the other end.

Zach. Once his best friend, now someone from another life. It seemed such a strange interruption. As if a filmed showing of *The Wolfman* had been replaced with *Heidi*.

"Hey, buddy. How's it going?" he asked, forcing himself to sound casual and friendly.

His eyes were still on the computer screen, though. There were two churches just outside Rome that dated back to the early centuries of Christianity. He clicked on a link, waiting for Zach's reply.

"I'm in town — just came in," Zach told him.

"You're kidding — most people put off a trip when there's been an earthquake," Scott said.

The link gave him nothing but another link. He followed it.

It led to a blog. Someone had made a trip to Rome and strayed from the usual tourist regimen to view one of the ancient churches. He'd found it fascinating, one of the most interesting places the man, identified only as 20Roma12, had visited. The description said that the church had been built in circular fashion but with twelve separate alcoves, each with an altar. Each alcove had a mosaic — some of the tiles fading, others chipping — portraying the torture and death of a particular saint.

"Well?" Zach asked.

Scott winced. He hadn't heard a word his friend had said.

"Sorry, bad connection," he lied. "What did you say?"

"I said, I think I'm in love."

"That's great. But why are you here?" Scott asked.

"She lives in L.A. I met her while we were all here — you must remember her. Or maybe you don't. I guess the only thing we all remember for sure is the alley."

No matter what the hell I do, I can't *forget the alley,* Scott thought.

"We were barhopping. We met a lot of girls," Scott reminded him.

"Yeah, well, it turned out this one, Suki, was on that dating site I'm on. And I didn't tell her who I was — I mean, that we'd already met — online. I guess she thought I lived out here. Anyway, I e-mailed her last night as my online self, asking if she was all right, and she was talking about going to some weird movie in a cemetery thing they do out there. So I hopped the first possible flight, and here I am. Thing is, I can't find any info on this movie thing — it isn't in the guide book I have."

"Um, yeah, I just heard an ad saying they still plan on doing it tonight," Scott responded absently. He was half listening and half reading.

It was one of the most unusual places I have ever seen, and I have traveled widely over many years. It seemed to me as if I'd walked into a different dimension; it felt as if the walls were alive, as if they were haunted by hundreds of years of souls. I was humbled and yet comforted, as if I had found a sanctuary. And as I stood there, I also felt as if I were waiting . . . for what, I don't know. In that church, I felt suddenly as if there were a great purpose to my existence.

"Scott, are you there?" Zack asked.

"Yeah, yeah, sorry, I'm here. But, I'm leaving tomorrow," Scott said. "I'm going to . . . a design show in Rome," he lied.

"Oh. Well, would you do me a favor tonight, though?"

Inwardly, Scott groaned. But he should be glad that Zack had called him; it gave him an opportunity to reconnect with the life he had once known, at least in some form.

"What?"

"Go to that show with me tonight, would you? Like we're just going to see it, and then I can 'happen' to run into her. I'll pack for you, I'll sweep up glass at the shop, whatever," Zack said.

"I'm already packed, and the shop is fine. But, yeah, sure, I'll take you to the cemetery. Why not?" Scott replied. "Where are you? I'll pick you up at six — the line starts forming around then."

He got Zach's info, hung up and finished the last of the blog.

I have never felt such a sense of the spiritual; if there is a link between the past and the present, the dead and the living, this is it. The church stands near the catacombs, and it's as if the dead speak in the whisper of the wind, uttering a prophecy in a tone of foreboding — an oracle, if you will.

4

"That was him!" Melanie told Lucien. "The man I told you about. First he shows up to stop robbery, rape and murder — and now he stops a gas explosion. Lucien, do you know him? Is he one of us?" She wasn't accustomed to being afraid, and she told herself she wasn't afraid now, but she knew she was lying. Because after all the awful things she had faced in the past, now she was afraid. Why? The man didn't seem to represent a threat of any kind, and he certainly wasn't perpetrating any evil.

She and Lucien hadn't headed back to the restaurant; they were hurrying toward her apartment instead.

"No," Lucien said at last. He was staring ahead, and when he spoke, he sounded very deliberate. "No, he is not one of us."

"Who is he, then? *What* is he?" she demanded, hurrying to keep pace with his long strides. Lucien always *knew*. He could see through to anyone's soul, and he could sense what good — or evil — lurked within any man or woman. And he always recognized their own kind.

"Lucien!" she pleaded.

He slowed his pace, looking back.

"He is definitely not one of us," he said with certainty.

"Then . . . *what?*"

"I don't know," he admitted.

"But you saw him! That kind strength isn't *normal.* And he was in pain. You could see he could barely stand it, but he stayed."

"Precisely." They had reached the steps to her building. He paused with a foot on the first step and placed a hand on her shoulder. "That blast could have taken out an entire block. It could have killed dozens of people. I admit, I've never seen anything like it before, but whatever he is, he's here to protect humanity. You don't need to be frightened."

"I'm not frightened of him," she insisted.

Lucien arched a brow and offered her a slow, questioning smile.

"I'm not, really. As you said, he seems . . . well, *good,* for lack of a better description. What I'm afraid of is . . . *why?* Why has he suddenly appeared, just when I've suddenly . . ."

"Become an artist?" Lucien asked.

She nodded.

He was silent for several minutes. She knew him well, and she could see that something was definitely disturbing him. "I don't know — what the connection is. We'll have to work on that, won't we? Let's go in and call Maggie and Sean. They might have heard something on the news and be worried about us."

"Oh, no. Do you think a news crew —"

"I didn't see one, but you can be sure they're on site by now," Lucien told her. "Come inside. We'll discuss it when the others get here."

She stopped again, staring at him. "Lucien, you came here . . . because of a dream. Maggie said Jade told her."

"Great. You three talk too much," Lucien said. "Let's get back to your mysterious stranger."

"Lucien, are you sure you don't know anything about him? You haven't seen him before?"

"In the flesh? No."

"You've seen a picture of him?" she asked, startled.

"No."

"Then . . . ?"

"I saw him . . . in a dream."

"In a dream?"

"Can we go in, please?" Lucien said firmly.

They were finally about to enter the apartment when Blake Reynaldo rounded the corner with Bruno. "Hey, folks. How are you doing after that last trembler?" He frowned, seeing Melanie's face. "Is everything all right?"

She quickly smiled. "Fine, Blake. How about you?"

He grimaced. "I'm handing out fliers. For your friend — Judy." He handed her a sheet of paper. "You should come. We're trying to get the community out."

Melanie glanced at the notice he'd handed her. It was a flier suggesting that everyone should come to the movie at the cemetery that night, show their true California style and take a breather after the stress of the quake.

"I knew I could count on you to support the community," Melanie said, and this time her smile was for real.

He smiled back. "So come on. Bring your pals. Hey, I tell you what, don't worry about anything. I'll bring the blankets and the cooler. You just bring your friends and show up."

"Oh, I don't think —" Melanie began.

"We'll be there," Lucien said.

113

She stared at him, and Lucien grinned. "Why not? It will bring the *neighbors* out."

She tried to keep her voice pleasant. "Do you know how many people live in Los Angeles?" she asked him.

"Millions," Blake answered helpfully. "But this is pretty much a local thing. It's really a lot of fun."

"I take it Judy is going?" Melanie asked.

For a big old-time cop, Blake Reynaldo sure could blush. "I told you, she's the one who asked me to hand out the fliers."

"We'll see you there, then," Lucien said, then stooped to pat Bruno, who wagged his tail.

"Okay. I'll look for you around six. I'll be in line by then. If I miss you there, I'll claim a piece of grass up close to the 'screen,' " Blake assured them. "Just make sure you're there by seven, okay?"

"We'll be there," Lucien promised.

Blake smiled, said goodbye and walked away to hand out more fliers.

"What's the matter with you?" Melanie asked the minute Blake was out of earshot. "I don't want to go to a movie. I want to have a drink — a big, tall alcoholic drink — and pretend I don't draw things like earthquakes before they happen. Or convince myself that it's some kid of a fluke, or —"

Kind

114

"Come on in and I'll explain."

"You're back!" Maggie cried, as soon as Melanie opened the door. Behind her stood Sean Canady, her husband, tall, graying a bit now and yet better looking with each year that passed.

Melanie smiled at Maggie and stepped past her to give Sean a warm hug. In New Orleans, the Alliance numbered at least twenty people now, but it couldn't have existed without Maggie, Sean and Lucien, and she was so glad that they were all right there with her now.

"Hey, Munchkin," Sean said. He insisted on calling her by that name, even though she was tall. He'd once said that she looked like a fairy — just a tall one — and a nickname had been born.

"Hey, you," she said huskily, and drew back.

"Where's the refrigerator, Mel?" Lucien asked. "I'm parched."

"In the kitchen — where people usually keep refrigerators," she told him.

"It's stocked?" he asked.

"Of course," she assured him.

"Lucien," Maggie called to him, "it's a good thing your back was toward the first camera on the scene. We saw what happened on the breaking news, but luckily

115

they didn't start filming until just as you were walking away."

"I figured the cameras would come," Lucien said, walking back into the room with a glass of cherry soda.

"Looks like you averted a disaster," Sean commented.

"Not me, the guy before me," Lucien said lightly. "Melanie, where's your computer?"

"Over there," Maggie said, answering for Melanie. "I have it up and running. I've been searching on 'ghost drawings.' "

"I do not have a ghost drawing through me," Melanie protested indignantly, staring at Lucien, who seemed to have forgotten the bombshell he had dropped on her. He had drained the bottle of soda and kept his own attention riveted to the computer.

"Lucien knows the mystery man from last night," Melanie said to Maggie.

"I do not know him," Lucien said.

"Excuse me. He saw him in a dream," Melanie corrected.

"Oh?" Maggie said inquiringly.

Sean groaned, running his fingers through his hair.

"I don't think Melanie's drawings have anything to do with a ghost," Lucien said, as if none of the rest of the conversation had taken place. "Melanie, when is your birthday?"

She was startled. "Excuse me? You already know how old I am."

"The day. It's in August, isn't it?"

She knitted her brows, wondering what on earth he was getting at. "Yes, it's August thirtieth."

"Virgo," Lucien said. "One of the earth signs."

"What, are you buying me a present with a birthstone?" she asked with a lightness she didn't feel.

"When I went to help him, your mystery man asked me if I was earth," Lucien explained. "Earth — not air, water or fire."

Melanie sighed. "Okay, he's super-strong and has a thing for the zodiac. Where on earth does that get us?" she demanded. "Um, no pun intended."

"Look around, will you?" Sean suggested.

Melanie winced. She had a flair for the dramatic and maybe even a retro taste when it came to décor. She'd done her ceiling in cobalt-blue, and a friend had painted the night stars for her — all the constellations that made up the zodiac. With the lights on, it was restful, but with the lights off, the glow-in-the-dark paint made the sky appear real. Despite that, the zodiac was just something that she enjoyed thinking

117

about, not a passion. She also had a Celtic cross on one wall, and a large tapestry depicting the Lady of the Lake in her bedroom. She liked being surrounded by things she enjoyed, and she enjoyed the hard sciences, like astronomy, just as she loved old tales of the Druids and fairy tales like "Sleeping Beauty." Her ceiling was simply part of her love for all things intriguing and whimsical.

"I decorated the ceiling three years ago," she said stubbornly.

"My point is, whether we believe in signs or not, even the most ardent skeptic gets a kick out of reading his horoscope now and then," Lucien said.

"Fine. Now what's the story with the dream?" Maggie demanded.

Lucien winced, paused with his fingers on the keyboard and then swung around, staring at them all. "Okay, I've been having the same dream for months now. I'm deep in the earth, walking through a catacomb." He was quiet for a minute. "I'm heading for a light in the center — and somehow I know I'm in one of twelve corridors that lead to it. I can see someone there, but not who it is."

"The mystery man?" Sean asked.

Lucien shook his head. "No. I only saw

Melanie's mystery crime fighter once, the first time I had the dream. He seemed so real, as if we were having the dream together and were both focused on finding that light and the person standing in it."

"Going to the light is . . . usually associated with near-death experiences," Maggie said nervously.

Lucien managed a smile. "Not in this case. There's a cloaked figure standing in the light. I try to see who it is, to reach it, but I haven't gotten there yet. The last time I had the dream, a skeleton rose up and pointed at me and said, 'Thou shalt beget kings, tho' be none.' "

"What?" Maggie said.

"I have no idea what it means," Lucien admitted.

"Maybe I do," Sean said. "Think about it metaphorically. Maybe it means that you're the . . . catalyst, the connection, the messenger. You'll show the way."

They were all silent. Lucien studied him, then smiled slowly. "No wonder you're a good cop. Maybe that's exactly what it means. Anyway, there was an earthquake in my dream, and I woke up and knew there had been a quake somewhere . . . and it was here. As is this man."

"Back to the computer," Sean suggested.

Melanie watched as Maggie and Sean flanked Lucien's shoulders. "Hey, there's an interesting article," Maggie said, pointing. She read aloud, " 'Is the world really small these days? Or has it always been? Greek and Roman gods, goddesses and astrology in relation to the Mayan doomsday prophecy.' "

"Try the link," Sean suggested.

Lucien hit a key. They were all staring at the screen fascinated. There was no room for her. "Well?" Melanie said impatiently after a moment.

As one, they turned to stare at her.

"What?" she demanded.

"According to this piece, written by a professor from Munich, there are legends from many sources that refer to the world ending in 2012. It will take the combined strength of all four elements — earth, fire, water and air — to save the world. Sound familiar, Mel?" Maggie asked.

Melanie stared at them incredulously. "You have to be joking."

Sean stared at the computer again. "That professor has dozens of links under that article. We might as well get started."

Melanie shook her head. "Lucien," she said. "It doesn't make sense. You're the strongest of . . . our kind."

"But I'm not an earth sign," he said. "I'm a Leo."

"You would be," Maggie said, grinning. "King of the beasts and all that."

"Hey! I'm a Leo, too," Sean told her.

"Yeah, but think about Lucien's dream and all that stuff about kings."

"Never mind, let's get to this," Lucien said.

Sean reached over his shoulder and hit a key. Melanie got up and leaned over Maggie's shoulder to see. She was startled when a picture of a church interior popped up on screen. It had been taken just inside the front doorway, but it was heavily detailed and, even on a computer screen, a little frightening. There were scenes of death and martyrdom on all the walls, and the church seemed to have miles of walls.

"Oh, my God," Maggie said. "People went there for messages of *peace?*" She fingered the beautiful gold cross Sean had given her years ago.

"How odd. It's third century, just outside Rome — very near where a very old friend of mine is living," Lucien said, reading the accompanying description.

"A friend? One . . . of *us?*" Melanie asked.

He shook his head. "No, I do know others of us there, but . . . no, I met a nun there once. She found me, actually, sitting by the Fountain of Trevi. I spoke to her many times. She was very wise, but I haven't thought of her for a long time — until now."

"You've seen that church — in person?" Sean asked.

"Yes," Lucien mused. "Yes, I have." He hesitated and then looked at Melanie thoughtfully. "As I said, I met my friend years ago, in Rome. She lived near this church. She's a nun, and her home is a convent. I was at a rather bad stage, and she helped me a great deal. She told me that I would be needed, but more importantly, that I would be a connection." He shrugged and quoted again, " 'Thou shalt beget kings, tho' be none.' Your interpretation is right, Sean. I should have seen the connection before."

"But *you,* as we all know, *are* the king," Melanie said lightly.

Lucien laughed. Then he grew somber. "You're missing the point. I believe this is bigger than we are, much larger than the Alliance." He surfed over to Google and keyed in the words *Sister Maria Elizabeta.*

They were all stunned when a page full of links popped up.

The very first read Sister Maria Elizabeta — Does a Nun Warn of the Mayan Doomsday Prophecy?

"I think she's been calling me," Lucien said. "I think she's the dark figure in the catacomb. She needs my help to get you to her. I was just slow to make the connection."

"Dark forms are often evil," Maggie warned nervously. "What if . . . what if we're being led astray?"

Lucien shook his head. "The earth . . . moved, just as it did when I walked in the catacombs. The earth rolled and woke me, and so is the man I saw in the dream, a man with superhuman strength who's looking for Capricorn, for earth signs." He stared at Melanie. "We have to help him find her."

"Darkness can be evil," Maggie repeated worriedly.

"But she was standing in the light," Lucien said. He rose. "It's time to find our mystery man."

Blake Reynaldo was true to his word. Along with Judy — but minus Bruno and Miss Tiffany — he was among the first in line to enter when the gates to Hollywood Forever opened for the evening's moviegoers.

The line was huge. Maggie balked at the idea of the four of them simply butting ahead of everyone, but no one objected when they went to join their friends. The quake was on everyone's mind, so the snatches of conversation they overheard as they walked mostly had to do with *Where were you when it hit?*

As Melanie walked past, she looked anxiously through the crowd. She wasn't sure why, but she kept expecting to see the stranger, her cavalier, as she was coming to think of him. It was the darkness of his hair — not that he wore it *that* long. But it was long enough that, against the precision of his features, it gave him the look of a long-ago painting.

She didn't have much time to find him. She was booked out the following evening on the only direct flight from LAX to Rome's Leonardo da Vinci Airport that they had been able to find.

At first she had balked at the idea. But her new tendency to draw pictures she couldn't understand — and then pictures that she understood all too clearly — was already beginning to gnaw at her every thought, and she knew that Lucien was right, that it was important for her to find Sister Maria Elizabeta and see whether she knew anything that might help them decipher what was going on.

But as they neared the front of the line,

she wondered what unnerved her most: her drawings or Lucien's dreams.

Or the stranger.

"Hey, one and all," Blake said, greeting them enthusiastically. Judy was quick with hugs, and thrilled to meet everyone. "Oh, good, we're going in," Judy said happily.

"This is really . . . interesting," Lucien commented as they paid their admission and entered the cemetery. "Beautiful and interesting."

The cemetery *was* absolutely beautiful: well manicured, with stunning and varied architecture on display in the mausoleums and individual tombstones. Melanie thought they were near the spot where she and the stranger had taken out the thugs holding Viv. Lucien thought the mystery man had to live somewhere nearby, so she still might find him, she thought.

"Check that out," Sean said suddenly, and walked off. Maggie followed him; Melanie and Lucien followed Maggie. Sean had gone to stare at the pool outside the tomb of Douglas Fairbanks, Jr.

"Nice way to be buried," Sean said thoughtfully.

"If being buried can be nice," Lucien said. "Mel's friends are already up ahead, right in front of the mausoleum wall. Let's join them."

Blake had brought comforters that he laid out on the ground, and comfy pillows to relax on. He had an ice chest, as well, and Judy had brought crackers and all kinds of cheeses, along with wine and soda. She asked Lucien if he liked red wine, and he winced, then assured her that red was his favorite. Music played while people filed in — more than a thousand, Melanie thought — and while Sean and Maggie relaxed, she — eased back on one of the cushions up against the ice chest, then closed her eyes and tried to take it easy, as well. She could hear Sean and Blake discussing police work in California versus Louisiana, and how natural disasters brought both tragedy and reform. When they started talking guns, she ceased to listen, opening her eyes and looking around at the audience.

"There."

Lucien's soft whisper caught her attention, and she followed his line of vision.

And there was her cavalier.

He was with another man and several women, about fifty yards away, near a memorial statue marking the grave of one of the Ramones.

"Hey, Mel. I think we have a few minutes. Let's go see a few graves," Lucien said.

"Maggie, Sean, you want to come?"

"I can show you around," Blake offered.

"I know the cemetery," Melanie said hastily. "I'll show them around."

The four of them got up and started walking, moving casually, just as if they didn't have a specific destination very much in mind.

Scott didn't know what it was about the foursome that suddenly made him think of a shoot-out in the old West. It wasn't as if they were decked out in long railway coats or wore holsters slung low on their hips. Still, "posse" was the word that came to his mind.

In fact, at least from a distance, they looked like everybody else in L.A. One man looked to be several years older than the others — maybe mid forties. He was graying, but straight and powerful, and the woman at his side moved with grace, and her face held a timeless beauty. But it was the other two who held his attention. The first was the dark-haired man he'd met earlier — in person and in his dreams — and the other was the platinum blond beauty he'd fought beside right here in this cemetery.

As they drew closer, it was the dark-haired

man — who hailed him — not by name, of course, but with a friendly wave.

"Friends of yours?" Zach asked, tearing his attention away from Suki for a moment.

"Acquaintances," Scott responded.

The blonde looked embarrassed to be there, but the dark-haired man with the strength to equal his own said, "Out to prove nothing can keep a good Californian down, huh?" he asked.

Scott introduced Zach, Suki and her friends, and then the dark-haired man followed suit.

Scott felt awkward, but apparently no one noticed. As the others talked like old friends, only Melanie Regan stood as silently as he did.

Then, to Scott's astonishment, someone he did know walked over — Officer Blake Reynaldo. "Hey, here's where you all got to! Guess this really is a small world. Zach, Scott, nice to see you again."

"Officer Reynaldo," Zach said, surprised to see the cop in a social setting. As big as he was, Zach looked uneasy. But then, Scott knew that Zach was remembering the same thing he was: the night they had been witnesses to murder — and the night when Scott had become someone — or some*thing* — very strange.

The fact that Blake Reynaldo knew him seemed to be of interest to Melanie Regan. She stared at him, frowning curiously.

"What are you out here for, Zach?" Blake asked. "It can't be the case, because that's still a couple of months down the line. But they didn't get parole, so at least they're not out on the street."

"What happened?" Melanie asked, frowning more deeply but finding her voice at last.

"These guys tried to stop an assault and murder," Blake said grimly.

"We didn't succeed," Scott said, not looking at her.

"No, but think of the other people who might have met the same end if you and your friends hadn't been around," Blake said. "Well, looks like the show is about to begin." He turned to Melanie and her friends. "We'd better get going."

"Sure, thanks," Lucien said. "Hey, Scott, we'll catch up soon."

Scott kept silent, but Zach answered for him. "You guys may not get a chance to see each other again. Scott's taking off on vacation tomorrow."

"Oh?" Lucien said.

It had all been so deceptively casual, Scott thought. Friends out for the evening, just happening to run into a casual acquaintance. But everything had suddenly changed. And now Lucien was staring at him very oddly. "What a coincidence. Melanie is heading for Rome tomorrow."

"Seriously?" Zach said. "That's where Scott is going."

"You don't happen to be on the Delta non-stop, do you?" Maggie asked.

Scott's gaze shot to Melanie's face and stayed there. She didn't look happy. In fact, she looked very unhappy. He felt a smile coming to his lips for some perverse reason. "Yes, that's the exact flight I'm on."

"Quiet, the movie's starting!" someone nearby called.

Melanie came to life. "Sorry, guys. Come on, let's get back. Nice to meet you all," she added politely.

As the others said their goodbyes, Scott couldn't help himself. He caught Melanie's arm. "Are you an — earth sign, by any chance?" he asked her.

She stared back at him. "I don't know what you're talking about," she said.

Whatever else she was, she wasn't a good liar. His smile deepened. "You are, aren't you? I've been looking for you."

"The movie is starting — I have to go," she said, and stared down at his hand on her arm. "Let go. We're in a public place."

"So we are."

She gave him an icy smile. "Don't make me kick the crap out of you, right here in front of all your friends."

He laughed. "Is that a dare?"

"A friendly warning," she told him.

He released her, still smiling. "It's all right. We have a twelve-hour flight tomorrow to get to know each other."

"Sorry, I'm in first class."

"Perfect. So am I."

"Shush!" someone demanded off to their left.

Lucien set an arm around Melanie's shoulders. "Scott, see you when it's over. We'll have a drink."

"Sure," Scott agreed, not seeing any way out of it, and curiosity getting the better of him.

"And yes," Lucien said, drawing Melanie away. "She is an earth sign — Virgo."

Melanie didn't begin to understand her own fear of getting to know Scott.

There was her original question, of course: who or what was he?

The man Lucien had seen in a dream. A dream of the catacombs and the long dead.

A man capable of blinding speed and an extremely effective fighter.

But what else?

The answer to that question couldn't be discovered unless she got to know him. As she watched the images on the wall of the mausoleum, and accepted wine and cheese from Judy, she tried to understand her own dread of what was to come. She had accepted and even embraced what she had thought was her place in the world, all made easier because of Lucien, first, and then Maggie, Sean, Jade and the many other members of the Alliance. But Scott wasn't one of them. Scott didn't know about the Alliance, and he certainly wasn't part of it. She wondered if, for the first time, she was afraid of someone discovering the truth about her — and loathing her for it. Admittedly, plenty of people would loathe her for what she was, but the truth was that they would never find out. And even if they did, they might not believe, and even if they *did* believe, she wouldn't really care what they thought of her.

It was all so complicated. Blake Reynaldo knew there was something different about her, but because he was her friend, he didn't really question it. He accepted her and worried about her, and that was nice. She couldn't really remember her own father, it had been so long since she'd lost him, but he had been kind and moral and strong like Blake, so in a way Blake compensated for a loss in her world. She loved animals, loved her work, and as for going silently to the rescue in small ways, there was no place better than L.A.

Scott — and the drawings she had been doing — seemed to threaten the level of comfort she had found.

There was applause all around; people were rising, talking. The movie had come to an end, and she hadn't really seen a minute of it, Melanie realized.

She looked around. Lucien was already gone. She looked over at Maggie and Sean.

"He's gone off to meet your new buddy, Scott," Maggie said.

"Oh."

It should have made her happy. Lucien would find out who — or what — he was.

Instead, she felt a growing sense of unease. Something had begun that she couldn't stop. She was on a roller coaster, and there was no getting off.

Why me? she wondered. *Why not Lucien, who's so capable, so wise, who's learned so much through the years? Why not Lucien, who already knows the nun in Rome who might have the answers?*

"That was wonderful, and it was so delightful that you all joined us," Judy said.

"Our pleasure," Sean assured her.

"But we'd best be getting on home now," Maggie said.

"So, Blake, you know those guys we met this evening from a police case?" Sean asked, ignoring her hint.

"Yup. Strangest damned thing, and sad," Blake said. "An old couple was attacked by a group of thugs. Scott and two friends of his — Zach, who was here tonight and another guy — were visiting L.A. and saw what was happening, so they tried to help. They got beat up, too — plenty good. But they didn't run. They really wanted to save that old couple. We caught the killers, though, and the trial's coming up in a few months. We'll need all three of them to put those bastards away for murder. He's quite a guy — I hadn't realized he'd moved out here. He's one of the good ones, you know?"

One of the good ones. Blake thought so, and she believed in Blake.

But he'd been in Lucien's dream, a dream of darkness and death.

She felt Maggie's hand on her shoulder. "Time to be getting on home," she said.

"Where'd Lucien get to?" Blake asked.

"Oh, don't worry about him," Sean said.

"He'll find his way."

They'd been packing up as they talked. Now they picked up the ice chest and the rest of their supplies and headed out of Hollywood Forever, along with the throng. People were chatting about the movie, the quake, work, meeting for dinner or drinks, and Melanie loved it, loved to feel herself a part of it.

But after they left Judy and Blake and were sitting in Melanie's car, with Sean driving, the silence between them suddenly seemed heavy with doom.

"You're going to be fine," Maggie said suddenly.

"You know, I can always take some time off from work and go to Rome," Sean said. "I mean, *we* could go to Rome with Melanie," he amended.

"No," Maggie said. "I think this is something Melanie has to do alone. We'll see what Lucien says when he gets back." She hesitated. "I think that maybe . . . well, we may be needed here."

"Maggie, stop," Melanie groaned.

"I wish I could," Maggie said.

Despite the fact that around a thousand people were leaving the cemetery all at once, Scott wasn't surprised that Lucien found him. Zach was preoccupied with Suki and her friends, and he didn't even seem to notice when Scott said that he was going to take Lucien down Sunset for a drink.

He knew a hole-in-the-wall place where the music was live but low-key. Loud enough to keep others from overhearing their conversation, soft enough that they could actually hear each other. Once they were settled in a corner booth, the man finally asked the question he'd been waiting for.

"So, what's your story?"

"Why don't we start with you?" Scott suggested, taking a swig of the long-neck he had ordered.

"What's your role in all this?" Hell, the man had to be wrapped up in it somehow — Scott had seen him long before they had met. In a dream. A dream about catacombs and corpses.

"I'm seeing you and a very good friend of mine following a strange path, and — I'm trying to figure out how the two of you came to be on it," Lucien said.

Scott stared at him. "Actually, I saw you first, long before I ran into Melanie, and I believe that you saw me."

Lucien nodded. "Yes," he said flatly. "I saw you in a dream. But . . . I'm not an earth sign."

"Maybe it all means . . . something else," Scott suggested.

"Maybe. I don't have the answers yet. But I don't think so. I think you're on the right track with the zodiac thing. Melanie is a Virgo. And you are . . . ?"

"Capricorn."

"Another earth sign. Stubborn — if I remember my astrology. Headstrong, ready to batter down walls." Lucien took a sip of the red wine he had ordered. He winced slightly, as if the taste were just slightly off. "So tell me, what . . . are you? Why did I run across you in a dream?"

"It's seriously bizarre, sharing a dream with a stranger," Scott said. He wasn't really surprised by it, though. Since the night in the alley, not much surprised him. It worried him, disturbed him, though. It . . . felt like more than just wading into a fight against some local toughs. It felt like the prelude to something . . . important.

"So?" Lucien persisted.

"You dreamed of catacombs, right? Of skeletons and a light?" Scott asked.

"You saw what I saw," Lucien said vaguely. "And I think it means something important, I just don't know exactly what yet. I believe I'm here to be a catalyst, though. I think I was even warned about it years ago — in Rome."

"Seriously? In Rome?"

"Yes. But enough about that for now," Lucien told him. "I want to hear your story."

"All right," Scott said, wondering why it felt so easy to confide in the other man. "It began not long ago. Several months ago, actually. I was here in L.A., out drinking with friends. We tried to be heroes. Dumb move," Scott said with a casualness he didn't actually feel. "An old couple was being attacked — you heard the cop tonight. My buddies and I jumped in, and . . . something happened to me. Something I still don't understand, except that it changed my life."

"Zach — the guy tonight. He was there."

"Right."

"But nothing has changed in his life?"

"Not that I know about."

"What happened that night? Why have you changed and not him?"

"Like I said, an elderly couple being attacked. The old guy took my hand and . . . well, it was like something in him passed to me. Ever since, I can just about keep the earth on its axis. Big exaggeration. But I'm a lot stronger than I used to be. Crazy strong. And fast."

Lucien leaned forward. "What about the Capricorn thing? Where did that come in?"

"It's what the old man told me before he died, and maybe it's nothing, just the hallucinations of a dying man. But according to him, I'm supposed to find other earth signs, and then someone called The Oracle, and then we save the world. Or part of it. Hell, I don't know."

"What about before?" Lucien asked.

"Before?" Scott said.

"Yeah, any unusual talents, strengths?"

Scott laughed. "Yeah, I was a graphic designer, a good one. I still am. Only difference is that before, I was a normal, happy guy. And now . . ."

"And now?" Lucien persisted.

"Now . . . I'm waiting. Your turn. What do you know?"

"Nothing, really. Melanie Regan is a good friend — and she's suddenly developed an ability to draw."

"Wow. I feel so sorry for her," Scott said dryly.

"She's not happy, either, seeing as she's drawing things like earthquakes — right before they happen."

"So — why is she going to Rome?"

"Simple. She's coming into it from a different direction, but she's looking for the

139

Oracle, too," Lucien said.

"And that's all you know?" Scott asked.

Lucien hesitated. His choice of wine was a deep red, nearly maroon, cabernet. He took a long sip and studied his glass. "All right. There are a group of people across the world who are slightly . . . *different* from everybody else. We have a loose gathering, called the Alliance. We're friends who support each other and fight . . . problems. I think you and Melanie might be the first ones called upon to solve a really big problem that's going to involve all of us in the end." He hesitated again, which struck Scott as strange. Lucien was clearly a confident man, and even he seemed to be having difficulty coping with whatever was going on. "Since the dream . . . I keep having this strange, random thought running through my head."

"Okay. What is it?"

" 'The blood of the pure is toxic to the darkness of evil.' "

" 'The blood of the pure is toxic to the darkness of evil,' " Scott repeated. "Great. As in human sacrifice?"

Lucien shook his head. "No. Definitely not. But I suppose it will all come clear sometime. And maybe it has nothing to do with the problem that you and Melanie are being called upon to solve."

"And do you have any idea what that problem is?" Scott asked.

Lucien arched his dark brows and offered Scott a dry grimace. "The problem? Why, the end of the world, of course. Armageddon. The Doomsday Prophecy."

5

Even before Scott Bryant sat down beside her, Melanie knew that it was going to happen.

Of course he had the seat next to hers.

She stared out the window as he sat down. He didn't speak, as if he were waiting for her to say something first.

"That just happened to be your seat, right?" she asked.

He didn't glance her way as he found his seat belt and buckled it. "No. I asked at the gate, and they switched me here. I told them I had a friend on the flight. I'm assuming we're intending to be friends?"

They needed to be friends, she thought, then wondered how he could behave so rationally when she was finding it impossible.

She let out a long breath. "Sure. Friends."

"I spent a few hours barhopping with your friend Lucien last night, so that makes us friends by proxy or something."

"Barhopping?" she asked.

"No, not really. We only hopped into one bar. But the conversation was definitely an eye-opener."

"Oh?" she inquired.

According to Lucien, he hadn't said much of anything about her to Scott — though he *had* told him about the Alliance and Sister Maria Elizabeta — only tried to ascertain the source of the man's power and what kind of quest he was on. In the end he'd been left with his original belief — that the world was in danger of ending, and somehow both she and Scott had a role to play in averting the apocalypse.

"Lucien thinks that we might be part of an ancient prophecy," Scott said.

"Right. The Mayan Doomsday Prophecy," Melanie agreed.

"What do you think?" he asked her.

She laughed. "I have no idea. I'm trying to figure out how the Mayans and the ancient Greeks and Romans, and a lot of other cultures, all ended up with the same belief that the world's going to end in 2012." As she spoke, she tried to figure out why she felt so on edge around him. She knew she didn't dislike him, so why did she feel so compelled to stay away from him?

She thought it had something to do with the sense of dread that had descended on her the night she first drew on that cocktail napkin. It certainly wasn't anything about the way he looked. He was striking looking, and he even smelled good. The problem was that she *did* like him — she was fascinated by him, in fact — but he seemed to have as much bizarre stuff going on in his life as she had in hers.

But he wasn't trying to run away from it. He was going to face it, whatever it was.

And that only made her admire him more.

Maybe that was it. Most of the time she only let herself get close to those she already knew well. Who knew her well. Who accepted her for what she was.

Scott had made a point of sitting next to her. He wanted to work with her, to be friends. Maybe he even liked her.

But how would he feel, once he really knew her? Knew all the truths there were to know about her?

Right now, though, he wasn't worrying about what she might be; he was thinking about her earlier comment.

"It's a small world, we all know that," he said.

"Yes, *now,* with all the technology we have," Melanie agreed. "But we're talking about centuries ago. The world wasn't so small then. Great civilizations rose in the Middle East, while elsewhere human beings were barely out of their caves."

"True, but maybe there are, and always have been, deeper forces at work," he pointed out. "Natural forces."

"Such as?" she inquired skeptically, though she found that she was smiling.

"Lately I've begun studying all kinds of prophecies and religions. Historians believe that a comet doomed Harold the Saxon during the Norman invasion of England. William the Conqueror won a battle, and then went on to take a country. Why? The people believed they had lost. They thought the comet foretold it. Or what about the people who believed that the black plague was the end of the world — God's punishment on his evil and misbehaving people? There's a problem with that, though. Why would God punish all the innocents along with the so-called evildoers?"

"You're losing me," she told him lightly.

"Like hell," he said with a laugh. "Okay, look at the Greek and Roman gods, and then at Norse mythology. Then, take a look at Judaism, Christianity and Islam. Look at the old Mesopotamian gods, look at the gods of the ancient Egyptians. Wherever you look, religion centers on a supreme being, and then his — or her — helpers, family, whatever, often lesser gods and goddesses. I was born in New Orleans to a Catholic family, a Buddhist might be born in India, and usually faith is simply a result of birth and upbringing. Which faith is right? None of us knows. Faith is belief. And I'll take it a step further, even though I know it might sound a bit weird, since so many wars have been fought over religion. *They're all the same.* It's just a matter of how we see things. The reality stays the same, it's the perspective that changes."

She stared at him. "Maybe you should go work for the United Nations," she told him.

He grimaced. "Hear me out. Perhaps the Mayans and the others had a way of reading nature that we've lost and foretold a danger that really is destined to arrive. Perhaps all the ancient societies were right about the forces of nature — fire, air, earth and water. Did I ever really believe in astrology before? No. Did I have fun now and then reading my horoscope? Sure. But that was then and this is now. I met a man in an alley. I tried to save his life, and I failed, and he told me that I was Capricorn and I had to find the other earth signs and then the Oracle. Since that night, my world has changed. I can only believe it's for a greater cause, so I can try to find that cause, or I can lose my mind. You're a Virgo, right?"

"August thirtieth," she admitted.

"We're both earth signs, then," he said.

"You do realize that this all sounds like a load of bull?" she asked.

"I have nowhere else to go, nothing else to try," he told her.

"Well, you need to follow your road, and I'll follow mine," she told him. "I just . . . I just work better, think better, alone."

"Ah," he said.

"I'm not trying to be mean, honestly," she told him.

"No offense taken," he assured her. "I'll be close, though, if you do find that you need me. Even you must have to admit sometimes that you need someone else."

"I already admitted that — but none of them would come with me," she heard herself say.

"Because they know I'm there," he said. There was a spark in the intense darkness of his eyes, a humorous lift to his mouth. He really was a gorgeous man, she thought, and she looked away. She didn't want to be drawn to such a gorgeous man, one who thought about others, who was intelligent and rational — and forgiving, no matter how rude she might be.

"What if we're all crazy, just making up this scenario?" she asked him.

"Rome is a big city," he said. "But when it comes to prophecies of doom, it might prove to be as small as the rest of the world."

A flight attendant's voice came over the speakers. They were third in line for takeoff. Time to Rome, twelve hours and thirteen minutes.

It was going to be a very long flight.

Scott loved flying first class. The enclosed seats flattened out like beds, he had a workstation, and his own DVD player, and a long list of movies to choose from. His seat neighbor — he couldn't actually call her a seatmate, she was so fully encapsulated in her own little pod — had immediately pulled out a tourist guide to Rome and was studying avidly, ignoring him. Scott hid a smile, because he could tell that despite her seemingly intense concentration on her guidebook, she was watching him.

When dinner came, she opted for the steak, while he went with the fish. The presentation — for an airplane — was pretty good. He saw her wrinkle her nose as she cut her meat.

"What's wrong? Shall I summon the

waiter?" he teased.

"Smart aleck. It's fine. Just — they over-cooked it, that's all."

Scott looked at the meat, which still had plenty of pink in the middle. "Didn't you want it cooked?" he asked her.

She smiled at him suddenly, a teasing glint in her eyes that he found slightly unnerving. On-purpose-unnerving, even.

"Raw works for me."

"And here I would have seen you as the tofu type."

"I'm quite fond of sushi, too," she assured him. "Raw fish."

He realized at that moment that she seemed to be erecting a wall between them. It was almost as if she wanted him to find her strange, as if there were a distance she needed to keep. But when she wasn't trying to build that wall, she was wonderful. Her smile was natural and quick, and her eyes lit up irresistibly. Odd that she had the strength and agility of Bruce Lee when she looked like a porcelain doll.

They ate in silence. Scott found himself wishing that they were in a restaurant — at least he could have broken the silence and asked her to pass the salt. But she actually made a point of putting on her earbuds and listening to music. He reached down into his backpack and offered her his noise-cancelling headphones.

"No, no, it's all right," she assured him.

"Please — I'm just going to watch a movie, so the cheapies will be just fine for me. Please."

She accepted the headphones. "All right. Thank you. The little ones . . . are like pins in your ears." She hesitated. "These are really good ones. You must love music."

" 'Music hath charms to soothe a savage breast,' " he quoted.

"And you're a savage beast?" she teased.

"I don't really know, do I?" he asked her seriously.

She shook her head. "The world is full of beasts. We often characterize them as savage, but in reality they're just living their lives."

He hadn't been expecting that answer. "Okay," he told her. "I can see that. The wolf hunts because he has to eat."

"Something like that," she said lightly.

She gave up on her meal and leaned back. The flight attendant came back and cleared their dinner trays, and he ordered a Jack Daniels and Coke, thinking it might help him sleep.

He opted for a vampire versus werewolf movie from a couple of years ago, and as he sipped his drink and watched the film, he was aware that Melanie was checking out the screen every now and then. He noticed her grimacing at certain scenes. At last he turned to her. "You don't like the movie?"

"Actually, it's not all that bad. Political struggles between the vampires and were-wolves. Kind of a neat concept. Some are good, some are bad, and some go to war. Hey, that's life, right?" she asked.

"Um, excuse me, may I get past you? The restroom, you know."

"Certainly."

"Then I won't have to bother you again."

"You can bother me anytime," he assured her.

"I'm going to come back and go to sleep," she told him. "I really won't be bothering you again."

Right. And I'm not supposed to bother you.

He got up to allow her to exit. She took her carry-on along with her, he noted, not just a toothbrush and toothpaste.

"Thank you," she murmured, and hurried toward the restroom.

She returned a few minutes later and shoved the carry-on back under the seat. She glanced at him and said, "Thank you. All done. Won't be moving again."

He frowned. There was tiny trail of red at

the corner of her lips.

"Did you cut yourself?" he asked.

"What?"

"Did you cut your lip? You weren't shaving off a mustache or anything, were you?" he teased.

He was startled by the surprised look of horror she gave him; it quickly disappeared as she wiped her mouth and seemed to settle a disciplined mask over her features. "Must have scratched myself . . . I don't know."

He reached out and wiped away the smidgeon of red that remained.

"There. Don't worry — I won't tell anyone about the mustache," he assured her.

"I don't have a mustache," she replied indignantly. "Okay, everyone does, but I'm so blond . . . oh, never mind."

She began adjusting her chair, ready to go to sleep.

He leaned back to watch the end of his movie, absently rubbing his finger. It was sticky from touching her mouth.

He watched the screen. One of the vampires sank huge fangs into a victim's neck. Stage blood flowed.

He rubbed his finger again.

He looked over and studied her face. Her eyes were closed, honey-colored lashes sweeping her cheeks, and he marveled at the porcelain perfection of her skin and the delicate bone structure beneath. He examined her lips, generous and sensual, warm red against her fair complexion.

Not the slightest hint of a scratch was in evidence.

Despite himself, he looked around the aircraft. The passengers were all in their seats, watching movies, working on computers, quietly reading or sleeping. The flight personnel walked down the aisles or gathered in the galley. No one looked as if they'd been attacked by a vampire.

Besides, there was no such thing as vampires, and the woman sitting next to him certainly wasn't one. Crazy. His thoughts had been crazy.

Then again, so was his world.

He turned off the DVD player. He wasn't sure if he had seen the end of the movie or not, but it didn't matter. He didn't intend to arrive in Rome already tired. He reclined his seat, stretched out and closed his eyes. Even if he didn't actually sleep, resting would be good.

For a while he thought about the woman in the seat beside him, and he wondered how it would be once they got to Rome. This whole trip might be pure insanity. He wasn't a cop or in any way qualified to hunt down the clues to solve the puzzle that his life had become. But he had to know what was going on. He might be plunging into danger, or entering the world of a cult, demonic or otherwise. He was heading to a foreign country alone, and he knew only a smattering of the language. The only thing he was sure of, thanks to Lucien, was that he was looking for an ancient church and a nun named Sister Maria Elizabeta. He might well not survive; he didn't think that his newfound powers stopped bullets. But he had to go. If he didn't get the answers he longed for, he wasn't sure that he'd ever know peace of mind again.

He drifted to sleep at last, trying to practice some of his small knowledge of Italian silently in his mind. *Per piacere. Per favore. Grazie. Buon giorno. Benvenuti.* Great. He was going to get really far with that.

And then he was back in the catacombs, and though it was impossible so far beneath the ground, it seemed that a fog was swirling. The path was uneven, with jagged breaks, as if there had been an earthquake. Skeletal remains lay scattered about. A hand here, a tibia there, a jawless and gaping skull cast to one side.

He was walking toward the light cast by

the sconces that burned at the entrances to the tunnels. Twelve of them. Twelve months, twelve phases of the moon. Twelve signs of the zodiac.

The earth was no longer ruptured here, but he couldn't escape the feeling that at any moment he could pitch forward. . . .

Into an abyss.

The abyss from which the dark, swirling ground fog seemed to come. It had to be steam and gas, escaping from the earth's center, the cause of the quake, set free as the tectonic plates of the earth shifted.

It didn't matter where he walked, he told himself. He was dreaming. And yet, if he tripped in this dream, would it hurt? Would he bleed? If he fell deep into a never-ending darkness, would he live to wake up again?

The fog was dark, not like the silver mist he was used to. The fog was evil, he found himself thinking. An evil that seeped from the ground. The thought disturbed him. For a moment he was tempted to run. But the light lay ahead. If he went back, he would be heading into nothing but the darkness.

The sound of a wind that couldn't begin to rise. He heard the clicking sound that meant the bones were coming together again. The skeletons were finding a way to guide him. To warn him? Or to send him forward to a worse damnation? He wasn't certain.

A skeleton, its shroud nothing but tatters, rose. He saw the broken face beneath the ragged fabric, saw the jaw that could not possibly work.

But the sound of words came on the wind.

"The light, the light, the light," the skeleton whispered coarsely.

He knew that he would keep walking, would come to the place where the twelve paths met, and that he would see the dark figure there.

He felt a presence behind him. He spun around and was startled to see that Lucien was in his dream again. His expression was grim, but he nodded an acknowledgment to Scott. "Now this is bizarre," Scott told him. He heard his own voice, a whisper in his dream.

"So it is," Lucien agreed. "I didn't know that I would see you here again, but I know now why I am here."

"Oh?"

"Because you cannot falter."

"Then you should be going to Rome me with me."

"I am not the one for that role. But I *am* with you. Helping you. Here."

He strode at Scott's side, and he didn't

falter. "We are reaching the circle," he said at last.

And it was true. They had reached the light again, and the cloaked and hooded figure was there, standing next to the tomb. Scott thought this place might have been a chapel of sorts at one time. The oil lamp sat on that stone lid, the unknown figure standing by its side, like a sentinel.

Come to me . . . for the darkness threatens.

They both watched as the figure lifted its head.

For a moment Scott felt a sense of infinite peace. The face before him was old, very old, crinkled with time, and yet gentled with kindness and wisdom. The eyes seemed to hold the knowledge of the ages and a wealth of love. In his mind, he knew that this had to be Sister Maria Elizabeta, and he was anxious to touch her.

But the dark mist was becoming more prevalent. He turned slightly and he saw a rush of whirling, cloudlike darkness hurtling down all twelve passages toward them.

It was time to wake up.

He heard Lucien's voice, urging him. "Go, go! We've seen, but we cannot stay for the end until the end is changed."

He looked back to the nun, so anxious to reach out and touch her.

But as he looked, the face changed. The kindly wrinkles of a long life lived in the pursuit of kindness were changing, the features rearranging themselves. As if in a movie, frame by frame, but quickly, a mask was created, one of horror, with great gaping holes where the eyes had been and a fire burning within those holes. The lips curled up and inward, like a slash of cruelty against the teeth. The flesh faded and shrank, the cheeks sinking in. A twisted caricature of death suddenly looked his way, and a cackle, like a harsh laugh borne by the wind of darkness and evil, issued from the mouth as the darkness started to swirl. . . .

"Scott."

His name, spoken softly but insistently. He thought at first that he was choking in the dirt of the catacombs, but then he realized that he wasn't choking at all, he was being shaken.

He turned.

Melanie was leaning over him, her eyes wide with concern. He stared up into them, and it was only then that he realized he was on an airplane, surrounded by the living. The man across the aisle was snoring, which might have been the sound of the evil laughter he'd thought he'd heard. A flight attendant was hurrying down the aisle toward them, her brows drawn together in a frown.

"Is everything all right?" she demanded.

"We're fine. I'm so sorry. My friend fell asleep and had a nightmare," Melanie explained for him.

The woman was still frowning. "You can't go saying things like that on an airplane, sir," she said. "This is a new age of flying. We take words very seriously these days."

He stared at her blankly, having no idea what he had done.

"I'm really sorry," he said, as she turned and headed back to the galley.

He stared at Melanie, who was looking at him, but not unkindly. He took note of her eyes. They were so blue. But like Lucien's, they seemed to have a line of gold around the rim. He wondered why he'd never noticed it before.

"What did I do?" he asked.

She shrugged unhappily. "You cried out that death was coming," she told him.

"What?"

"You said, 'Death is coming, death is coming!' End quote. Luckily, most of the passengers are sleeping and didn't notice."

"Lucien was there, in my dream. He told me to get out," he said, wondering what her response would be.

She might laugh, or she might get angry. She did neither.

"Then you needed to get out of the dream. You need to move fast whenever you hear him tell you what to do," she said.

"What is he, then, a psychic?" Scott asked her.

She let out a breath of air. "Something like that," she said. She hesitated for a minute. "Yes, he has amazing psychic powers. He can sense things and read people." She looked at him, aware that he was staring at her. "It's a good thing. He's the head of . . . of our Alliance. He's strong. He has a vast store of knowledge. It's . . . good that he has a connection with you. Actually, he seems to have more of a connection with you than with me."

"Does that . . . bother you?" he asked her.

She did laugh then. "Not in that way, trust me. Lucien has a wife, and she's . . . a dear friend, not to mention brilliant with a computer. We may be calling on Jade before this is through."

We. She had said "we." Maybe he wasn't going to be quite so alone after all.

"So you had the same dream as Lucien, of death and catacombs?" she said.

He nodded.

"I've dreamed of that place, too."

"It's in Rome," he said.

"Sister Maria Elizabeta will tell us more."

Scott hesitated. "Could she be . . . the very evil we're searching to destroy?" he asked.

She stared at him. "I — I don't think so. Lucien would have known," she said. "Why?"

"I saw her face."

"When? Where? In a book?"

He shook his head. "In my dream. I assume it was her, anyway. And she was old and terribly wrinkled, but something about her was so beautiful, I couldn't look away. Then Lucien told me to get out — and she changed. She became a monster . . . a skeleton and a monster, just as the dark rush of . . . something . . . came after us."

Melanie looked forward again, thoughtful.

"I can't believe that's possible. She's the Oracle. We have to believe that she's the Oracle."

"And if she's not?"

"Then . . . I imagine . . ." Melanie began, faltering. She gave herself a slight shake. "If she *is* the evil, then we have to destroy her."

He leaned back in his chair. "My parents will be very angry."

She looked at him again. "What?"

He shrugged, offering her a half smile. "I went to Catholic school. My folks will be

161

really angry if I start beating up nuns."

She leaned back and groaned. "Five more hours," she said, then yawned.

"You can nod off," he told her.

"I won't sleep. I'll watch over you — just in case you start dreaming, too," he assured her. "I swear, I'll stay awake and hold a most devout vigil," he said.

She laughed. "My cavalier," she said.

She closed her eyes and eased back to rest.

He wasn't touching her, and yet he felt as if he were so close to her as to know her very soul.

He leaned back in his seat, hoping that the time would pass quickly. He was anxious to land in Rome.

Was the figure in the dark cloak and hood Sister Maria Elizabeta or the devil incarnate? He had to know. He closed his eyes, not to sleep, but to block out the plane, to try to summon up the remnants of the dream. The place existed; he knew that it did. And the answers to the riddle lay in the earth, that he knew, as well.

He opened his eyes, not daring to keep them closed for long, and was startled to see Melanie sitting up and leaning over the small tray table, holding a pen and frantically drawing away.

"Melanie," he said.

She didn't hear him. He realized then that she wasn't even looking at the paper. She was staring straight ahead.

"Melanie," he said again, this time, more urgently.

Still she ignored him.

He watched her, wondering if he should shake her, do something more forcible to wake her. Then he glanced at the boarding pass on which she was drawing.

He saw the image take form.

She stopped suddenly and lay back down again. Her eyes closed, and she seemed to be sleeping as sweetly as any angel.

Scott picked up the drawing, lest a flight attendant take it away. He studied it for a moment, remembering his own dreams.

Melanie had drawn the doorway to their future — or to their deaths.

6

When she awoke, Melanie found that Scott was staring at her, and she wasn't sure what his expression indicated. Hope? Faith? Even . . . affection? But he quickly masked his feelings and smiled. "Good morning. I'm glad you're awake. I didn't want to leave you alone, but nature is calling."

"Hey," she protested. "I've been half awake for a long time. I heard them announcing that breakfast would be coming through in a few minutes. This is an airplane, you know, not a hospital."

He flashed her a smile, grabbed a toiletry bag from his backpack and left her. She was glad, though, that he hadn't left her alone. She hadn't dreamed, not a second, once she had fallen back to sleep, but it was nice to know that he'd been standing guard. Against what, on an airplane, she wasn't certain. But she was still glad. Despite what she'd said earlier, however, it troubled her that

164

Lucien seemed to have such a strong connection to Scott. And she knew it wasn't an exaggeration on Scott's part, or hers, because Lucien had been the one to tell her that he'd met Scott in a dream. *The* dream.

About the catacombs and the land of the dead.

A few minutes later, Scott returned, looking clean-shaven and refreshed. He ran his tongue over his teeth and teased, "Minty clean."

"I'm going to have to crawl over you again," Melanie said. "I should have gotten out while you were up. Sorry."

"Crawl away," he told her. She caught his eyes, noticed the small smile curving his lips. There was definitely something sexual going on here. To her dismay, she actually felt a blush rise to her cheeks.

She returned just in time not to have to crawl over the breakfast cart as well as Scott, and she managed a reasonably coordinated re-entry to her window seat. The same flight attendant who'd been upset with him after his nightmare let out a sigh as Melanie struggled briefly with her tray. She smiled and thanked the woman anyway.

"There you see the true trouble with our world," he told her, leaning close and whispering.

165

"The flight attendant is evil?" she asked him.

He leaned back, not responding at first except for that slight smile still on his lips. "I said something that scared her in my sleep, and now she thinks there's something odd about me. She doesn't know what it is, so, instantly, she mistrusts me. She would rather put up her defenses than take the time to learn what's going on. Isn't that what we all do all the time?"

"We're on a plane, and you were shouting about death. That's not a good thing to do these days."

"Whatever. Here's my point. Planes aren't evil, men are. People aren't afraid of planes, they're afraid someone evil, dangerous, might be on board."

She paused in eating her cheese omelet. "What about a faulty engine?" she asked.

"Sometimes a faulty engine is traceable to human greed. Perhaps the airline didn't run a full maintenance check when it should have. Or the company that built the plane chose to use cheaper materials."

"And what if everyone did everything right?"

"God does move in mysterious ways," he said with a shrug.

"So your point isn't a point," she argued.

166

He laughed. "Maybe not. Man doesn't create a hurricane or the sandstorms in the Sahara. I do think we're responsible for global warming, but ice ages have come and gone many times throughout the earth's history without our influence. Man didn't create volcanoes, and he still hasn't completely figured out fire. Who knows? Part of the Mayan prophecy has to do with the way the sun and the planets will align — and none of us can change the earth's orbit or control the sun. So maybe you're right and I don't have a point at all. Except that . . . well, at least currently, humankind's influence on the elements has caused calamity. And a prophecy can be self-fulfilling." He looked over at her then. "So — do you believe in God? Allah? Jehovah? Odin, Zeus — a supreme being?"

"I get a choice, huh?"

"We all do."

He was staring at her intently. She concentrated on her bowl of fruit and picked at it with her plastic fork. "Yes," she said simply.

"So do you also believe in Satan? Or Hades? Or —"

"Good versus evil. Yes. And I believe in . . . life. And humanity."

A male flight attendant picked up their trays, after offering them more coffee. Scott

167

waited until he was gone. Then he drew something from his pocket. "I wasn't sure how to tell you about this, but you didn't wake up screaming. In fact, I don't think you were awake at all. But you did do this."

She stared at him, stunned, as he produced her boarding pass. She had drawn over the airline symbols and the printing, and it took her a few moments to separate her pen marks from the flight record and make out what she had drawn.

It was a church standing on a hill. It appeared to be circular from the outside, and it wasn't in great shape. Plaster peeled, pillars were broken, and it bore a look of age and decay. It sat alongside a road, and all along the road were crosses, and she had even drawn the men dying on those crosses. The door to the church stood open, and someone seemed to be standing there, waiting, a dark figure in a hooded cloak. The drawing was unbelievably detailed. She winced; she knew that her fingers trembled.

"You should have wakened me," she said.

"At first I didn't realize you were sleeping," he told her. "You know, I spent five years at school studying drawing and design, and I couldn't do anything half that good. It's amazing."

"You screamed out and I woke *you* up,"

she said, still tense.

He shook his head. "We weren't about to get kicked off the plane."

"They can't kick you off a plane."

"Shot by an air marshal?" he suggested. "Or, more likely, have the authorities waiting for us when we get off the plane. Melanie, I would have been afraid to stop you."

She inhaled nervously. "But . . . the earthquake. The things I draw happen," she said angrily.

"Or happened," he suggested. He pointed to the crucifixes along the road. "This took place two thousand years ago. It's the road that leads to the church. It's a map of the past." He looked at the drawing thoughtfully for a moment. "And our future. This is where we have to go."

"We already knew where we were going," she said dully.

"Your drawings are important," he assured her. "They may be creating a design."

"A design? Of what?"

"I don't know, but it's part of what I do. I don't know what I'm talking about yet. But for either of us to pretend that these things aren't happening and that there isn't a reason we're here, being *drawn* here, is just foolish. We need to follow this path as quickly as possible."

She didn't answer him, because just then the announcement to return their seatbacks to their upright positions and prepare for landing came on in English and Italian, and the entire plane seemed to spring to anticipatory motion. It had been a long flight.

She was eager to get off the plane herself.

Even if she wasn't eager to follow her "map."

He should have known. They waltzed through customs, with Melanie demonstrating a seemingly perfect grasp of Italian. She charmed each person they met. And then, after they'd collected their luggage, he asked her, "Where are we staying?"

She arched a brow. "You came over here without a hotel reservation?"

"I had one, but I canceled it and figured I'd stay at your hotel instead. So where are we staying?"

"Maybe you shouldn't stay at my hotel."

"Oh, no. We need to be near each other. Hey, I could wind up arrested, waking up in the middle of the night screaming about doomsday. You wouldn't want that on your conscience, would you?"

She stared at him with exasperation, but he knew she was going to give in. "You mean Lucien didn't creep into your dream to give you the name of my hotel?"

He shook his head. "No, and I forgot to ask him at the bar."

She smiled, looking straight ahead.

"What? You're not going to tell me?" he asked. "Come on, I've proven to you that you need me."

"You have?"

"You know you do."

"I thought we'd proven that *you* need *me*," Melanie said.

"Maybe we actually need each other," Scott informed her.

Her smiled faded slightly, and she turned to study him with a strange look in her eyes. "Maybe I'm actually worried about you. Perhaps I don't want you getting hurt."

He inhaled a deep breath. "Let's see, me, big tall guy. You, delicate blonde."

"Member of the Alliance, a group of people who have a knack for handling situations like this, and hardly tiny and petite," she corrected.

He started to protest again, but she waved a hand airily and gave him a perfect Valley girl impression. "Chill, dude. I wasn't going to make you take your own cab."

She started walking. He grinned, shaking his head, and followed.

He was glad that Melanie was as well

versed as she was in the language when their cab driver started to explain something about the route he was going to take. *"Permesso, per piacere,"* he said, then went on to talk about an accident that was blocking the street. Melanie replied easily, telling him it was fine, to take the best route he knew.

Scott had been to Rome several times. He loved it; there were few finer cities for an art student to visit. The art and architecture of centuries was layered atop itself, the genius of ancient Rome alongside medieval treasures and the brilliance of the Renaissance. All combined in a city that was vital and vibrant, alive and bustling. Rome had welcomed the modern world with a loving embrace while never forgetting the past. The airport was sparkling and new and navigable; it was easy to catch a cab, and as they rode, he looked out the window and saw remnants of the empire alongside the magnificent architecture of the dark ages, along with the fabulous palaces of the powerful, relics of a time when the country had yet to be unified, and was a conglomeration of duchies and city-states.

"The Seven Hills of Rome," he said, as if to himself.

She glanced at him.

"So you know the city?"

"Somewhat. And you?"

She was staring out the window. "Somewhat," she told him.

"You speak Italian."

"I speak a few languages. But I see that you know a bit, as well."

"Really? How?"

"I can tell when you understand what someone is saying. It's in your eyes."

"Catholic boy. I had some Latin," he told her.

"Ah."

The Eternal City. The Palatine Hill, the Coliseum and the ancient wonders still seemed to dominate the landscape. It was good, Scott thought — they provided a sense of place at all times, even as they reminded a visitor of how much time and history this place held, and the strange workings of society through the years.

They moved through the city, alive with bumper-to-bumper traffic, honking horns and a sea of humanity, and Scott watched as they traversed the Piazza Venezia and passed the enormous monument to Victor Emmanuel, who became the first king of united Italy in 1861. Built in the late eighteen hundreds, it was grand — and definitely a landmark, but he preferred the older masterpieces, the multitude of churches built throughout the centuries, baroque, medieval, rococo — intricate and detailed, almost to a fault.

They drove by the Coliseum, and Scott stared toward the stretch of the Forum beyond. The stray cats of Rome found a home among the pillars, the last remnants of a great empire. They were as common as the tourists flocking over the ruins with their maps and guidebooks. Then he frowned as he looked up at the sun, then back to the ruins. There was the strangest display of light and shadow that day. He thought that maybe the plentiful cats were creating the flitting shadows, but when he blinked and saw nothing, he leaned back in his seat for a moment, thinking that he was really tired. Night-owl flights and time changes always played havoc with his system.

"What?" Melanie asked him.

"Shadows," he said.

"Shadows?"

"In the Forum. Look, it's like they're dancing between the pillars."

She looked, but they were already rounding the Coliseum, and the Forum was fading into the background.

At last they turned down the Via Veneto and passed by the Capuchin monastery. He knew it well. Visitors could visit the very special altars there, built of bones. The brothers had practiced a strange form of art, creating magnificent designs from the bones of their deceased: intricate patterns on the walls, chandeliers of pelvic bones, candles set in skulls, creating chapels and altars where the living could reflect. They didn't fear the dead, or desecrate them; they honored them with their work. He suddenly found himself remembering an epitaph he had read there once, written for the skeletal figure of a long-gone brother, still clad in his brown robes. *As you are now, so I once was; as I am now, so shall you be.*

The taxi came to a halt in front of a small boutique hotel. He knew that Melanie was amused by what she surely thought was his macho insistence on paying the driver. As they got out of the cab, Scott looked up. It was a beautiful building, late seventh century, with winged cherubs adorning the eaves. Scott knew the hotel; he had been in the bar, but he'd never stayed there. It was upscale and private, and he found himself suddenly grateful for the fact that his credit card had no limit. *Don't leave home without it,* he mocked himself. *You never know where trying to save the world — and your own sanity — will take you.*

Apparently Melanie knew the hotelier. He

welcomed her warmly, with a long hug and a rush of Italian so fast that Scott could pick out little more than *bella, mia amica,* and *bella, bella,* once again. Then the man was staring at him — a little suspiciously at first, but then he seemed to warm to him, and he offered him not just a handshake but a kiss on both cheeks. Scott awkwardly smiled and patted the man's back in return.

"Signore Marchetto has a room for you right next to mine. He's rearranging a few things. We need to get an espresso or cappuccino in the bar and give him a moment or two."

"Great," Scott told her.

They wandered into the bar. "Cappuccino?" he asked Melanie.

"Yes, that would be fine."

He ordered, determined to show her that he had some facility with the language. *"Due cappucini, per piacere,"* he said, smiling — idiotically, he was sure. He could also order *una birra.*

She kept her eyes downcast as he ordered. He thought he saw her secretly smiling.

"All right, why do you speak Italian so well?" he asked.

"College. I was here, and I like languages."

"So helpful when you're a dog trainer," he said. "I guess that pays well, though, seeing as you flew first class. Or is Lucien rich enough to foot that bill?"

"That's a rather rude question, isn't it?" she asked.

"Hey, Virgo, we have to get to know one another," he pointed out.

"Actually, dog training can pay very well. And, to answer your other question, Lucien is in nice financial shape. He got into the collectible craze very — *very* — early, anything from art to artifacts, and he's invested well."

"Of course," Scott said. *"Grazie,"* he added, as their waiter delivered their coffees.

"Prego, prego," the waiter said. He smiled at Melanie, barely noting Scott.

Scott sipped his cappuccino, watching her. Finally he shook his head. "You're such a liar."

"Okay, that's *really* rude."

"But true." He leaned toward her. Her deep blue eyes with the golden highlights met his squarely. A smile teased at her lips, and he wanted to scream. He could tell she liked him, but she was refusing to open up to him in any meaningful way. "What is it you're not telling me?" he asked softly.

She shook her head and leaned closer, as well. The soft waves of her hair fell over his hand, and he felt a sudden deep, burning urge to touch her. More, to hold her, to sweep his hands from her breasts to her thighs, to know her completely, make love to her with his hands, mind and body. He gritted his teeth, trying desperately to control his raw thoughts and keep his mind on the conversation.

"Whatever I'm not telling you, I'm not telling you for a reason," she replied, her tone hushed but heated, her face close to his. "I admit that you're caught up in this, but you're not one of us. You're not one of the Alliance." She met his gaze for a moment, then pulled back — as if carnal thoughts had suddenly occurred to her in the midst of her heated argument. A blush rose to her cheeks. "Look," she said, her tone still soft, "please stop. We're here . . . together. You're looking out for me, I'm looking out for you. Let's solve this puzzle and find out if we're both going to wind up locked away for the rest of our natural lives, or at least until the world explodes. Leave the rest of it alone, please." Her hand fell on his, an almost ethereal touch, like a brush of butterfly wings, and yet that slight contact seemed like an ember of fire against his skin, concrete proof that the hint of gold in her otherwise cobalt eyes did indeed come directly from the sun.

He nodded slowly, realizing that he needed to take his time with her, and smiled. "All right. No more twenty-questions."

Before she could respond, Signor Marchetto came in to tell them that their rooms were ready, so they should follow him, and the cappuccino was his treat.

Scott paused as the other man handed Melanie two keys and pointed down the hall. Scott had assumed they would be taking an elevator, or at least following the stairs to the second floor. But as Melanie spoke to Signor Marchetto in rapid Italian — to make sure he didn't catch what was being said, Scott was certain — they moved down a long hallway and made a left. They reached a door, and, to his surprise, Melanie opened it and ushered him in.

At that precise moment he felt as if he had the libido of a high school boy. Hope soared in his bloodstream.

But the door merely led to a pleasant salon, beautifully furnished with eighteenth-century pieces in white and gold that contrasted nicely with the dark wood paneling. There was a room on each side of the living area. She pointed to the left, and he felt like an idiot — and was glad he was the only one who realized just how stupid his thoughts had been. He almost laughed aloud at himself.

"Signor Marchetto is so sweet. He definitely did a little rearranging to get us this suite. I know we're tired — a night on the plane, the time change — but let's shower and head right out."

It was a statement, but it sounded as if she were asking him. He was touched, and the fire in his loins reignited. There was definitely something going on between them, and he was sure she felt it, too.

"Sounds fine to me," he told her.

There was a knock on the door. The bellboy had brought their bags. Scott thanked the man and tipped him. Melanie took her suitcase and rolled it into her room without another word.

When he went into his room, Scott realized that Melanie must have asked for these specific accommodations. The three-room suite faced a rear courtyard with a gate to the street, and each room had a door to the private shaded space. They could come and go unseen, at all hours. She definitely knew the place and he wondered when she had been there before. Students did not usually stay in a place like this, and why would a dog trainer have come to Rome?

He set his suitcase on the long bench at the foot of his canopied bed and looked around the room. It, too, was beautifully appointed. There was a modern bath to his right, but there was also an antique pitcher and bowl on the dresser. The bed itself was huge and set on a low dais, and piled with pillows and covered by an ornate spread.

He found fresh jeans and a knit short-sleeved shirt; it was warm out, and he was sure they would be doing a lot of walking — above ground, if not below. He dug out his sneakers, clean socks and briefs, and headed into the bathroom.

The hotel might be old, but the plumbing was blessedly modern. A powerful spray of delightfully hot water fell from the shower-head, and for a moment he found himself leaning against the tile and just letting it cascade over him, sluicing down his skin to his feet. At first he couldn't help but imagine how fine it would be if she suddenly cast all reason to the wind and suddenly walked in to join him. He could feel the steam rising around the two of them, and almost imagined he could reach out and touch her, elegant and wanton, flesh sleek and vital, slick from the caress of the water. He rued his thoughts, then felt the exhaustion of the last few days weighing down on him. With his eyes closed, he could almost have fallen asleep right there.

He roused himself with a violent shake. He didn't want to sleep. Not now. He didn't want to dream. He wanted to find Sister Maria Elizabeta, and perhaps he even wanted to tread the catacombs of his dreams in life — no matter what horror might arise to greet him there.

He swiftly scrubbed himself, washed his hair and stepped out to towel-dry briskly, hoping that would help him to wake up. It did. The shower had been more restorative than he could have imagined; he didn't feel the time lag or the hours in the plane.

He dressed quickly and headed into the salon. Melanie wasn't there yet. After a few minutes he tapped on her door. No answer. He waited, tapped harder and listened for the spray of the shower.

Then he cursed as he realized that she had ditched him.

Melanie wasn't particularly happy about what she had done, but she was certain that she was doing the right thing. The more time she spent with Scott, the more she was discovering that she cared about him. He was easy to like; he was honest, intense, funny, polite and charming. What was there to dislike? And she was also finding him far more attractive than she wanted to; she needed her distance. But she kept finding herself feeling stirred by the sound of his voice. She had caught herself studying his hands on the airplane, and liking them. Long hands, long fingers, the nails blunt and clean, somehow masculine, somehow sensual. Her heart fluttered annoyingly when he leaned close, and she often felt tempted to lie back and let him solve the problems of the world, while she basked in the security and protection he seemed to offer.

But that wasn't the way it could be. He was strong, but he was mortal. And he had absolutely no idea of just how bad this could get. She might look like a powder puff, but she had a much better sense of what they might be up against.

She'd seen enough through the years.

She had showered quickly, donned jeans and a tank top, tied a sweatshirt around her waist, grabbed sunglasses and put on her best sneakers and run out like a bat out of hell. She was pretty sure he still didn't know exactly where to go, but she did.

The church where she was headed wasn't far from the Coliseum. And not far from it was the Appian Way, where once upon a time, crosses and their bloody burdens had lined the Way. After Spartacus had led his slave revolt, and he and his men had been captured, history held that six thousand men had been executed via the Roman cross. That had been before the time of Christ, but the Romans had not forgotten their favored method of mass execution. Since then, many a martyr — or common thief or murderer — had met his demise upon a cross along that road.

She reached the church, certain that she was in the right place. Santo Stefano's was in the tourist books, though it was off the beaten track. A great deal of work had been done on it in the last years, but it still wasn't something everyone longed to see. *Rotondo*, or built in a circular fashion, it was ancient and majestic — and boasted eight panels depicting various saints' martyrdom. They were grisly images, gory, many seeming to drip with the blood of those who long ago fell victim to torture. Great columns rose in a circle outside the church, and the architecture alone was fascinating.

But she hadn't come as a tourist.

There were actually a few people in the church when she arrived. Apparently the grotesque went over well with teenage boys. She noticed a German family — the mother was reading from a guidebook — with a boy of about thirteen, and not far away, a Spanish father was telling his son, who looked to be a similar age, the story behind the murals. Catholic priests, he said, might be called upon to travel to pagan regions, where they might well meet a fate like those depicted in the bloody panels. Even now, a missionary into the world of the non-Christian must be prepared, and learning how those who had come before him had met their end with fortitude and unshaken faith was important. Melanie wondered if she could have managed to face such horrible torture — and remain true to any faith.

She looked around the church until she saw a young priest hurrying toward the exit. She ran after him. *"Per favore, un momento, padre."*

He stopped, turned back to her, and studied her long and hard. *"Si, bambina, si?"*

She told him that she was seeking Sister Maria Elizabeta. He looked weary, as if he were often asked about the sister.

He shook his head. "She is not here. *Questa e' la chiesa,* this is a church. The sister, she does not live here. She lives at the convent." His English was good, just a little stilted.

"Can you tell me where that is?"

"It would not matter. You would not see her. She prays. All day. She has taken a step away from the world. And when she worships, it is not at this church."

That startled Melanie. She was so certain she had read the signs correctly.

"Please, it's imperative that I see her," Melanie said. "It's a matter of life and death," she said. She prayed she didn't sound overly dramatic. "Please, I swear, I'm not a reporter or anything. I wouldn't hurt her in any way. I simply need to see her."

He studied her for a long moment and then seemed to soften. "When she worships, it is at San Giovanni in Catacombe."

"San Giovanni — in Catacombe?" Catacombe? Like . . . catacomb? She hadn't heard of it. "You mean San Giovanni in Laterano?" she asked, referring to a well-known church, often visited, but not near here.

"No."

The young priest was staring at her. She felt a moment's panic. *He knew.* He knew what she was, knew all about her, and he did not trust her.

"I swear, Father, I come only in peace," she said softly.

He shook his head. "San Giovanni in Catacombe is . . . not well-known. It is farther along the Appian Way. Look to the left when you see *la roccia,* the old stone in the road. The path to it is old, and made of broken stone. Not many go there. It is like this church, *rotondo,* but there are twelve, where we have only eight." He hesitated again. "It is not a place for tourists. Yet it is intriguing, because of the twelve panels."

"For the twelve apostles?" Melanie asked.

"Eleven were martyred, so say the doctrines. San Giovanni lived for many years and wrote the gospel that bears his name, and the *Book of Revelation.* The others . . . they were martyred. The twelfth panel is San Giovanni's, with sun and light atop, and darkness and the fires of hell below. He is the messenger, so the artist believed. You will see, if you go. The church . . . is older than this. It has not seen much repair." He had a beautiful singsong quality to his voice, ending many words with a soft A. He had a gentle quality about him that made her want to cry, or maybe laugh at herself — and give it all up. But she couldn't.

"I will go to the church at Catacombe, Father. Thank you."

"Bless you, child," he said.

She nodded and turned away, aware that he was still watching her. Something occurred to her, and she turned back to him. "Father, Judas Iscariot hanged himself. He

187

wasn't a martyr."

The young priest smiled. "He was a martyr, for the betrayal had to take place. And there are twelve not only for the apostles but because, long ago, twelve was magical. It was the number marking the turns of the moon, the months, and it has been a key number in many belief systems. The zodiac has twelve signs." He hesitated, then shrugged. "Below the church are catacombs, but those are not opened to the public. They can be accessed only by the old stone steps beneath the central altar. The holy catacomb lies at a northward angle to another, deep within the ground. That other catacomb was there in pagan times, and it is there now. It is believed that the pagan altar was there when the church was built, and that it holds a prophecy of what the future will be — an oracle, perhaps. Man's destiny, man's final chance to make his choice between good and evil." He shrugged, still studying her. "That is all I can tell you."

"Mille grazie, padre, mille grazie," she told him.

He nodded. She turned and left, but she knew that he watched her until she was out of his church.

"That bitch!"

188

Moments ago he had been fantasizing about her; now he wanted to shake her. God! He'd been such a fool. She'd been nothing but sweetness and light — all the while planning to set him up and leave him.

He shook his head, half enraged, half smiling at his own gullibility. He had fallen for her entire act. Hook, line and sinker.

So . . .

He thought about his dreams, and he knew that he had to find someone who could help him find the place he was now certain was real.

However kind Signor Marchetto had been, Scott didn't think the man was going to be the one to help him. Still, he had to start somewhere.

He slipped his hand into his pocket for the drawing Melanie had done on her boarding pass. He knew the Appian Way. Not a problem. And though Melanie might not realize it, he knew about Santo Stefano's, as well. It certainly wasn't as frequently visited as the Vatican, but it was written up in a number of tourist books. He would start by heading that way, unless Signor Marchetto could suggest something better.

Absently, he pocketed his key and studied the drawing as he left his room. On his way through the lobby, he paused to speak with Signor Marchetto.

"*Signor . . . dov'e . . . mia amica?*" Scott asked.

"She is in the room. I have not seen her leave," Signor Marchetto said.

"No. No, she's gone," Scott said.

The other man indignantly pulled himself up to his full height. "Sir, I do not know where she is, then. She did not leave through the lobby."

Was the man protecting her? Scott wondered. No, his indignation seemed real.

And she might well have departed via the courtyard. Scott smiled. "Thanks. *Grazie.*"

"*Si, signor.*"

Scott headed out, still studying the drawing, and realized that Melanie's line of crucifixes did not head to Santo Stefano's. It went farther down the road and seemed to lead to a large standing stone. He couldn't read what was written on it. Maybe nothing. Maybe it was just shading.

He went out and hailed a taxi. His driver didn't speak much English, so Scott used his minimal Italian to the best of his ability to ask the driver to head past Santo Stefano's, hoping he would spot the stone when they got there.

He knew they were going the right way

when they passed the Coliseum.

They left it behind, and Scott stared at the pillars of the Forum, watching as the people began to blur into dots. Soon the road became rough stone, and the taxi driver stopped. He turned to Scott and began to rant. Scott didn't understand his words, but from the accompanying gestures, he gathered that the ancient stone road was eating up his taxi's undercarriage and tires, and he didn't want to go any farther. Scott smiled and nodded, tipped the man well and got out.

He stood alone on the ancient stone paving, fields and forests stretching out on either side. The road grew rougher and more overgrown ahead. He closed his eyes, felt the breeze and the warm Italian sun, and just stood still for a long moment.

No great visions came to him.

With a sigh, he stared at Melanie's drawing again and started walking. A little while later he realized that there *was* something ahead. He began to jog, and almost twisted an ankle in a crack between the stones. Swearing, he slowed his pace. And after a few more minutes of walking, there it was: the stone from Melanie's picture. Big and rounded, worn by time, it might have been an oversized grave monument. There were four words on it; they had obviously been re-etched sometime in the not too distant past.

San Giovanni in Catacombe.

A path — most emphatically not one that cars could travel — led off the road. He followed it through high grass, weeds and then a copse of trees. The sun bore down, making him sweat, and he began to wonder if he was an idiot and how the hell he was going to get back to Rome. Then he passed through the trees, and there it was.

It was built of ancient masonry, round, but not as large as Santo Stefano's. The plaster that had once added brilliance and color to the outer walls was chipped and peeling now. There was an entry at the top of a flight of wide stone steps — twelve of them, Scott counted — and columns that had seen far better days. The adornments atop them seemed to be gargoyles, maybe hellhounds of some kind, and he assumed that they were there for the same reason they sat atop many other churches: as guardians against evil.

He left the woods behind him and climbed the stone steps to the doorway. One of the massive wooden doors stood ajar, and he stepped inside.

For a moment, after the bright sunlight

outside, he was nearly blinded in the pale, filtered light within. The church was dark in the way that only ancient structures could be dark; the heavy walls seemed to carry with them a shadow of age and gloom, as if a living darkness now hovered inside them. Then he saw the twelve panels, each with a stone altar before it, a prayer bench and candles. In the center of the room stood a large stone altar, stark and bare.

He thought for a moment that he was alone.

Then he froze. As his eyes became accustomed to the darkness and shadows, he realized that one of those shadows was real.

Just as in his dream. His nightmare.

A shadowed figure . . .

A representative of stygian darkness, betrayal and damnation?

Or the embodiment of light within the horror of a nightmare?

7

His eyes fully adjusted at last, Scott saw her clearly, his figure in a black hooded cloak. Except she was actually a nun, wearing a black habit and a cowl.

And she was staring straight at him.

He walked over to her.

She was very old. Wrinkles creased every inch of her face, but as she smiled at him, there was a bright light in her eyes, and her cheeks seemed suddenly round and rosy. If there was any light in the church, he found himself thinking, it emanated from her.

"Sister Maria Elizabeta?" he asked softly, but he already knew the answer. And she was indeed the woman he had seen in his dream. He almost bolted, remembering how her face had changed in that dream. Was he a fool? Seeking this woman, thinking she could help him — when there might be far more behind the façade than he could imagine.

She spoke to him in barely accented English. "So, you are the first."

"Pardon?" The idea that her gentle face might turn into some hideous mask of evil seemed suddenly absurd.

"You are the first. The first of twelve, the first of the first three," she said, and smiled beatifically. She reached out to touch him, setting her hand on his face as if he were a small lost boy. If he'd had time to think, he might have shrunk away. But he didn't have time to think, and he was glad. It was a gentle touch, and it provided a sense of comfort and reassurance that he'd come to the right place.

"My name is Scott Bryant," he told her.

"Scott," she repeated.

He nodded.

"You are Capricorn," she said.

He cleared his throat. "Well, I'm *a* Capricorn. A lot of people are Capricorns — though they don't all go in for that kind of thing."

She smiled as if she knew exactly what he was thinking . . . feeling.

She linked an arm through his and began to lead him from one gruesome scene to another. "This church has all but outlasted time. Time past, with eternity still ahead. There you have Andrew, crucified by being

195

bound to the stake, not nailed. This is James the Greater. Here he is depicted as having his head chopped off, though some images have him stabbed. Jude — beaten to death. Poor Matthew. Burned, stoned or beheaded, or all three, and so, in his portrait, we see the tortures of each death. Simon, crucified and sawed in half. They go on."

"There's Judas, hanging," Scott noted.

The sister smiled. "In the Gospel of Matthew, it is suggested that Judas betrayed Jesus because of greed. But in the Gospel of John, Jesus knew that he must be betrayed and offered Judas bread he had dipped, so that 'Satan entered into him.' He is here because he was one of the twelve, just as is John, who lived to be a ripe old age and wrote some of our scriptures that we cherish to this day. In my mind, as in the opinions of so many, Judas was a martyr, as well, for his betrayal of Our Lord was part of what needed to be done. Ah, but who can say, my friend Scott? None of us now living was there, and words written on a page are merely transcriptions, perhaps erroneous ones, and may be interpreted differently by different people." She led him onward. "Ah, here is Judas. He had a role to play, a painful one, but he played it well. What needed to happen, did."

"What about free will?"

"There's the real question, isn't it?" the sister said. She drew Scott over to one of the few pews that ringed the central stone altar. "Do you mind? I am even older than I look, and I have been waiting a long time for you."

"Please," he said, helping her down to the pew.

She sat, sighed with the pleasure of easing her old bones, and turned to him.

"Free will . . . Perhaps Judas Iscariot should be among the saints. Perhaps it was his freely made choice to do what was needed. Indeed, maybe the long-ago faithful who built this church believed as much, for they gave him his place among his peers. Either that, or, they simply believed in the magic of the number twelve. They hadn't come far from pagan days, you know."

Her beliefs seemed almost irreverent, at least compared to other clerics he had known, and yet she seemed to glow with faith and . . . *holiness.*

He liked her.

"The world is not always ours to understand," she went on, then winked. "Here is what I know. When I was a girl, I dreamed of the catacombs."

He started at that. "The catacombs?"

"Not those in the city where they now take the tourists. We believe that the catacombs were more than a burial ground. In the old days, when the Roman gods and goddesses were still worshipped with fervor, the first Christians were often forced into hiding. Scientists, archeologists, anthropologists — all have been at work, and every time an ancient relic is found, a new theory of our faith's past is postulated. As to what I believe . . . No one knows, for I do not speak of it. I see my faith as I see it, and in my heart, I'm sure. Each man — and woman — must find his or her own destiny, use his or her own free will. Often the decisions are small ones. Do I give a dollar to that poor fellow with no legs, or do I walk by?"

"What about the poor fellow who passes by and doesn't have a dollar?" Scott asked.

She laughed, pleased with their conversation.

Then her laughter faded. "The man who doesn't have a dollar cannot give a dollar. But the man who does have a dollar should love his fellow man enough to part with it."

"He will — assuming he has lots of dollars," Scott said.

"Ah, a skeptic. Well, Scott, you've been given a dollar. And you have free will. What will you do with your dollar?"

"Look," he said, growing a little impatient. "I'm a decent fellow — I've given lots of dollars. But this isn't about man's kindness or inhumanity to his fellow man. Lord knows — and *we* both know — that too many wrongs have been committed in the name of religion."

"But you're not here in the name of religion. Religion is an organization. Faith is within." Her eyes sparkled. "Catholic, *cattolico* — it means 'universal.' Too often we forget that. Does God — any man's god — live in his heart? And does evil also dwell within, or can it slip in, as John suggested of Judas?"

"You know you're driving me crazy," he told her.

"I tell you these things because you are Capricorn, and you have come at last."

"And now that I'm here?"

"There are others, and we will wait for them to gather, you and I."

"And then?"

"Then the battle for earth shall begin."

They were both startled by a sudden — and completely irreverent — exclamation from the doorway.

"Oh, my God!"

Scott swung around. One sneaker in hand — she had apparently taken off her shoe to knock stones from it — stood Melanie.

She was looking at him as if he were a ghost — or evil incarnate.

He smiled at Sister Maria Elizabeta. "There's a Virgo for you."

The sister didn't rise, but she did smile. "Come in, child. Come on in. I don't know where your third is as yet — the third earth sign is close — but the two of you are here now, so I'll tell you what I can, as much as I know. As to what will come after that, well, this man and I have just decided that free will does exist, so what one does depends on the circumstances, does it not?"

Melanie walked slowly into the church, looking from the sister to Scott. He shrugged, trying to appear casual, certain that he was gloating, nonetheless, at having gotten here before her. Melanie pursed her lips and kept coming. She ignored him as she sat next to Sister Maria Elizabeta and took her hands.

"My friend Lucien DeVeau knew you," she said, speaking cautiously.

"Ah, yes. I knew him many years ago," the nun said. "So troubled then, but . . . not so much now, I think. Or not in the same way. I have seen him in the dreams.

"I knew the time was coming for the gathering before the storm, if you will, and

I sought both of you in my dreams. There is a tremendous power in the mind, you know. One day, scientists may figure it all out . . . or not. The power of the mind lets us do things we might never have imagined when the need is great enough, when the potential loss is great enough. And I feel that we're now facing a grave danger."

"The Mayan prophecy," Scott said.

"*The* prophecy," Maria Elizabeta agreed. "Mayan, Sumatran, Hopi . . . Doomsday, when the planets align on solstice day, has been spoken of throughout time and by many peoples. The prophecy has shown itself in so many ways." She smiled and drew a breath, looking around as calmly as if she were giving them a tour of the church. "The demons of the old world entered into the new. There are the legends of Mut and Baal, and there was Astarte, the goddess of earth and fertility, along with so many more, and all involved with the seasons, the cycle of life. Ancient Syria and the Canaanites also spoke of the Apocalypse. The ancients, the earliest peoples who inhabited this area, knew the power of twelve, and this church is built — as so many were — over an old temple. They looked to the elements, the crops, the harvests and the weather for their signs, their forecasts, if you will. They

201

divided the year, and the year consisted — as most years do — of twelve months, the new moons and the old. Below, there are etchings on the walls, made far before Christ, far before the conquering Romans came. Someday you'll see them. Right now, I will tell you where your part enters in."

"My part. In . . . the end of the world?" Scott asked.

"I most fervently hope not," she replied briskly. "Now, how did Rome fall?"

Scott wondered if she had ever been a teacher.

"From within," Melanie said, puzzled.

"Precisely. The Romans stretched their roads to the far corners of the world as they knew it, but they could not find the power to survive when their empire started crumbling from the rot within. The real sources of weakness — jealousy, greed, fear — come from inside us. The prophecy states that there will not be one single natural cataclysm. Rather, the earth will offer up a series of challenges related to the four elements — earth, air, fire and water. Each of those challenges must be met, and the first of these comes from the earth herself."

"Are you saying the quake in L.A. was part of that? It wasn't that big," Scott protested.

" 'The earth will rattle,' or so it says," the sister told them. "You'll see in time."

"But . . . we're here now," Scott said. "Why don't we see now?"

"We need the three," Sister Maria Elizabeta said, and rose suddenly. "We must have the three. The last earth sign will come. I have seen him, too, in my dreams. But today is not the day. Go home now. Come back tomorrow."

"Home is in California," Melanie pointed out dryly.

The sister smiled. "Go back to your hotel. Better yet, go out and see Roma. Dinner is not a meal here, it is an occasion. Eat well, and rest well. Tonight you will have no dreams. You have already come to the place where you need to be." She bent over suddenly, grimacing and holding her stomach, then sat down heavily.

"Sister!" Scott cried worriedly.

She shook her head, straightening. "The years . . . I've seen many. Too many, perhaps. I am waiting for my time, but first I must be with you until the time comes for me to move on and another to take my place." She waved a dismissive hand in the air. "You've found me, and all of your own . . . free will." A sparkle lit her eyes. "Now go. And come back tomorrow."

Melanie stood, looking at the sister, then knelt and put her hands on the old woman's knees. "Sister," she said very softly, "I'm worried about my friend's safety." She glanced at Scott. "He is . . . a man. So new to — to what is not accepted by the world or seen by the naked eye. Are you sure that —"

"I'm sure," Sister Maria Elizabeta said. "You are what you are, and he is what he is. The world does not revolve around any single one of us, whatever conceits we may harbor. Have faith, child. Have faith in goodness, in mankind, and in all the creatures of the earth." She set her hands fondly on Melanie's head, her eyes noting the little gold cross Melanie wore. She met Melanie's eyes. "You need strength, you need faith, and you need belief in yourself as well as others. *Per piacere,* I need some rest."

She looked old, Scott thought, older than when he had entered the church. He stood, taking Melanie's hand. He was aggravated; she had tried to elude him, and he wasn't sure he entirely believed that she was worried about his safety. "Sister Maria Elizabeta is tired. We have to go now."

Her face was set, but she could see that the sister truly was tiring. She took her hand from his and rose, then leaned down to

204

plant a kiss on the nun's cheek. "Thank you. *A domani.*"

"Sister," Scott said quietly, nodding to her, and headed for the door. He could hear Melanie's footsteps as she followed him.

Scott kept up a brisk pace. "Glad you finally found the place," he called without turning to look back. She wasn't slamming her feet down, but he could feel her aggravation as if it were washing off her in palpable waves.

"Look, I don't think you should be part of this," she said flatly. "You're just — you're just not prepared for this kind of situation."

Scott stopped short, swinging around to look at her. "Oh, and you are? Aside from the fact that I don't seem to have any choice but to be involved, thanks to that damned dream I keep having, I'm not sure I believe any of this yet. Maybe it's one of those 'if you build it, they will come' deals. I'm just not sure we're not all crazy."

She stared at him, sucked in her breath and walked past him. "That's precisely what I mean. You're not ready. You'll get hurt."

He caught her arm. "What? Are you immortal? You can't get hurt?"

She hesitated, staring down at her arm as if an alien being were holding her. Then she met his gaze with her own. "I can be hurt.

But . . . I'm tougher than you think. I've dealt with this kind of thing before."

"You've dealt with the end of the world?"

She tried to pull her arm away, but his hold was too tight. "I told you. There's a loosely affiliated group we call the Alliance. We've . . . encountered various. . . . difficulties through the years."

"Well, you're in a new group now. The Twelve. And I'm one of them, so quit trying to ditch me. Don't do me that kind of favor, got it?"

She stood very straight, staring at him, then shook her head. "You really don't understand."

"Maybe not, but neither do you."

She looked off across the field that surrounded the church. "All right, I won't ditch you again. Meanwhile, we're stuck out in the middle of nowhere."

He reached into his pocket and produced his cell phone. "Call for a cab. I get a signal almost anywhere. I got a cab to bring me out here — well, most of the way — so we can get one to pick us up."

"San Stefano's isn't that far," she said. But she gratefully accepted the phone; she was worn out, too — no matter how invincible she liked to think of herself as being.

"Buon giorno, prego," she said, as someone answered.

Scott listened to her speak, relishing the cadence of her voice, and though he didn't understand the words, he knew that she was being polite and pleasant. He'd been so angry at her, but now he felt his anger melting away as he watched her. He was hypnotized by the sound of her voice. In the afternoon sunlight, her hair seemed to shimmer with an angelic glow, but he found himself thinking of her as anything but angelic. Tall, lithe, her every movement a statement of sensuality. He found himself turning away as she spoke, not wanting to be seduced.

"Grazie," she said into the phone, then snapped it closed and handed it back to him. She stared at him with her huge blue eyes with those fire circles deep within, and she asked grudgingly, "How did you find the right place so easily?"

"I followed your drawing," he said simply.

She nodded and started walking, moving past him. "There will be a cab waiting for us at San Stefano's," she said.

He followed her. A little while later they stood without speaking in front of San Stefano's, and he was glad that he had the phone. Rome was full of tourists and taxis, but there was no evidence of either one here now.

A few minutes later their taxi drew up, and they entered it in silence. Melanie gave the driver the address of their hotel, and then fell silent again as they drove. When they entered the hotel, a new man was on the desk. He nodded gravely to them, greeting them with a polite *"buona sera,"* before turning back to his work.

Melanie led the way to their suite. Once inside, she turned to him. He was surprised to see that she looked hesitant. "There's a place I know near the Trevi Fountain that has excellent food. Would you like to go out for dinner?"

He felt his heart thud, every fiber in his body tightening. "Sure," he said, and despite his best effort to sound casual, his voice was husky.

Then he turned away from her and headed to his own room to change.

Lucien was making final arrangements with Melanie's employees to look after her apartment and the shop when the call came through from Blake Reynaldo.

"You're still there, huh?" Blake asked him.

"Just taking care of a few details for Melanie, then we'll all head on home," Lucien told him.

"So your cop friend and his wife are still with you?" Blake asked him.

"Yes," Lucien said. "Is there something — we can do for you?"

"Yes, actually, there is. Come on down to headquarters and I'll explain. No, better yet, I'll come to you. No reason to make the rest of the world think I'm going insane. I'm assuming you're still at Melanie's?"

"Yes. What's up?" Lucien asked.

"Well, first, I had the tapes from the broken gas pipe enhanced."

"Oh?"

"Don't even try sounding surprised. You're in this deep, and you know it. Along with Melanie and Scott Bryant."

Lucien shrugged. He felt Sean and Maggie staring at him.

"I tried to help," Lucien pointed out.

"Yes, you did."

"But there's more?"

"Oh, yeah. And I'm hoping you can help."

"How?"

"I don't who you are, or what you're really doing out here, but I'm hoping you can make sense of something for me."

"Well," Lucien said carefully, "I'm certainly always willing to help law enforcement."

"So I hope," Blake said. "We've been questioning the men we picked up after the quake, the ones who went after Mr. Delancy and his salesgirl. And here's the thing. Most of them never actually met each other until after the quake. They claim they just ran into each other in the street. One guy is actually a college professor in Seattle. And guess what they all said?"

"What?" Lucien realized that Maggie and Sean were standing almost on top of him, frowning, trying to hear the conversation.

"The devil made them do it?" Sean asked Lucien.

Blake heard Sean's words.

"Not the devil. Some demon named Bael. But I'll explain more. I'll be there soon. Oh — there's something else. The quake didn't cause that gas main to break. There were saw marks on it."

Blake hung up.

Lucien hung up, too, looked at the other two, then excused himself and strode for the door.

"Lucien!" Maggie called. "Where are you going? He's coming here, right?"

"I'm going out for a pack of cigarettes," Lucien said.

"You don't smoke," Sean told him.

"And it's not good for you," Maggie

210

reminded him.

Lucien paused at the door and looked back dryly. "What? I'm going to die young?"

He turned and left.

Dust to dust. What was created of dust . . .

Could rise again in a black mist of darkness and evil.

The Fontana di Trevi, beautiful and world-renowned, sat at the center of a small piazza. They could see the fountain and the milling tourists, all laughing and throwing coins, as they sat down at their window table at the Ristorante Inferno. Melanie loved the restaurant; she hadn't been back in three years, but it was just as she remembered it, small and intimate, and run by Signor and Signora Fiorelli. They welcomed her as if she had never left Italy, or as if they had seen her just the week before. She introduced Scott, and they greeted him in turn like a long-lost son.

Signora Fiorelli smiled and gushed, and rattled off praise in speedy Italian to Melanie. He was a beautiful man, so straight, so tall, a face a sculptor would love.

Melanie smiled and nodded, then agreed in Italian that yes, he was a very fine man.

Scott did his best with his limited Italian, and the friendly couple brought them wine, delicious bread to dip in olive oil, and small starter plates of antipasti followed by pasta plates. It wasn't until they brought the main course, bistecca con verde, that they left Scott and Melanie alone.

"Wow. I've eaten many meals in Italy, but never quite like this," Scott said.

Melanie shrugged. "You need to try the small places, where the locals eat."

"Without you here to order, I could end up eating fish livers or something."

Melanie laughed. "How do you know you're not?"

He cast her an evil glare, and she laughed. He turned to look out the window at the piazza again.

"It rakes in about three thousand euros a day," Scott mused.

"What?"

Scott grinned. "The Fountain of Trevi. This place has been the constant site of a fountain, even before its more-or-less present design, dating from the sixteen hundreds. When Rome fell, the invaders destroyed the aqueducts, and the Romans were forced to use local well water or, worse, the river, filled with sewage. The poor Romans, used to bathing in fresh, clean water at a time . . . when the rest of the world seldom even thought of bathing — or thought that bathing could wash away the soul." He leaned close to Melanie. "This fountain is mostly the work of Nicola Salvi, a depiction of Oceanus riding the waves in a shell, set against the Palazzo Poli." He grinned self-deprecatingly. "Hey, I was an art student."

"So — have you thrown three coins in the fountain?"

He grinned. "Of course."

She liked his grin. It held both confidence and humility, a reflection of the man, she thought.

"And you? Have *you* thrown three coins in the fountain?"

"No."

"Horrors! You're lucky you were able to return to Rome," he told her gravely.

She had to laugh. "That superstition changes constantly. Once it was two coins, then three — two over one shoulder and the third over the other. Anyway, are you sure we're *lucky* to be in Rome right now?" she asked.

He turned in his seat, and she found herself fascinated by the aquiline structure of his face, the vivid darkness of his hair and eyes. He stared out at the massive fountain at night, the dancing water illuminated by the lights. All around the fountain, children played, laughed and called out — in a variety of languages. Lovers sat together, staring into the water. An Italian baritone was singing a ballad for someone, the scene charming and innocent. Deceptively innocent? he wondered.

Scott turned back to her with a rueful smile. "Yes, we're lucky to be in Rome. No one knows what the next hour will bring, much less the next day, and at least we're here in one of the most beautiful cities in the world."

She was startled to realize that she had reached out to set her hand over his, startled by her strong desire to touch him, and by the fact that his warmth and something of his life seemed to seep through to her in that touch. She blushed and would have drawn her hand back, but his grin deepened as he laid his left hand on top of hers.

"Okay," she said, "it's a beautiful place, the food smells wonderful, and we've had a long flight and a long day. Time to chill, and then get a good night's sleep."

He was more pleased than he should have been at her gesture of intimacy. "So where are you from originally?"

"Where did I grow up?" she asked.

"That, too, but where were you born?"

She hesitated.

214

"Is even that a deep, dark secret?" he asked her.

"Dublin," she told him. "I was born in Ireland. But I've been in the States a long time. That's where I went to school."

"Irish, huh? You might have been Norse. You look like a Viking. Not that you have a red beard, or anything," he teased. "Tall, blond and beautiful, how's that?"

"It will do. And Dublin was founded by the Norse, so maybe I do have a few Vikings in my background."

"Have you been back to Dublin?"

"Sure. It's lovely. The land of leprechauns," she said. They'd ordered a nice burgundy, and she sipped it, loving the taste even though it seemed to be missing something. But she smiled and drank more. "Tell me about *your*self," she pressured.

"I'm an open book," he told her. "A boy from New Orleans. I didn't go far until I moved to California. I went to Tulane, had good friends, supported the Saints, worked for a guy in Metairie, founded my own business, bought a great house in the Quarter — then sold that great house in the Quarter — and moved to California. My folks still live in the Garden District. I have one sister, and she lives in D.C. with her husband. We fought as kids, get along great now. My mom always says there's no pressure, but she'd cry like a baby if we didn't all get together for Christmas. Your turn."

She smiled. "That's nice, that your mom keeps you all together. What about your dad?"

"He's a good guy. Loves the Saints, good jazz and a fried Cajun-style turkey at Thanksgiving. Your turn," he repeated.

"I lived in New Orleans for a while," she said.

"No kidding?"

"Lucien, Sean and Maggie all live there, too. Sean's a cop, and Maggie has a dress shop right on Bourbon Street."

"Go figure. They say it's a small world, but I lived there my whole life and never met any of them," Scott said. "I've probably noticed Maggie's shop, though. But what about *you?* What about *your* family?"

"My parents have been gone a long time," she told him. "I only lived in New Orleans for a little while. I went to L.A. once for a client and wound up spending a lot of time there, so I moved."

"Where did you grow up? Besides 'in the States,' I mean."

"Here and there."

"A military family?" he asked her.

"Something like that."

Staring at her, he shook his head. "You're certainly full of secrets."

"I'm sorry."

"So tell me more about this Alliance of yours. Is it like a neighborhood crime watch? No, wait — can't be. You're not all in the same neighborhood."

"When something happens and our help is needed, we get together."

"Expensive," Scott noted. "All those air-fares."

"Well, you asked before — rather rudely," she pointed out, "but Lucien *is* rich. Anyway, I thought we were trying to enjoy Rome?"

"We are," he said, and his voice had a deep, husky note that created flutters and a rise of desire within her. It had been a long time, a very long time, since she'd been with anyone, cared about anyone. Dating rules changed; she wasn't sure she knew how to flirt anymore, or what was right or wrong, or even whether any of that mattered when desire ran deep enough. She was aware that he was drawing a line along her hand with the tip of his finger, that it felt like a whisper of air and a slow-burning fire all in one, and she couldn't seem to help herself, she just wanted to get away from the world, to be alone with him somewhere. She longed to touch his hair and find out if it was possible to *feel* the blackness of it, explore his face, lie next to him, naked, and feel the heat of his body against her.

"You really are stunning, and so much more."

"Thank you. Unless that's a line?" she asked him.

He laughed easily. "No line, just an indisputable fact."

"Then you're very kind."

"Facts aren't necessarily a kindness," he told her. "Just take the compliment."

"Okay. Then . . . you're actually very beautiful, too."

"Ouch."

"What?"

"Men are supposed to be . . . manly," he said, grinning. "Handsome."

"You're very beautiful in a handsome, manly way. How's that?"

"Much better. Thanks."

"And very macho," she told him.

"In a good way, I hope," he replied. "I meant that whole Viking comment in a good way, too."

"Right. Vikings were sea raiders who raped, pillaged and murdered."

"And founded settlements all over the world, created beautiful jewelry and believed in valor. Lots of them stayed where they raped, pillaged and murdered, and became upstanding citizens."

She laughed. "If that's a pickup line, it's certainly a different one."

He looked down for a moment, out the window for another moment, and then he finally looked at her again, as if he had made a decision. "I'm serious. I admire you very much. I wouldn't dream of giving you a pick-up line."

"You wouldn't pick me up?" she asked, surprised by how badly the thought hurt. Almost like a stake to the heart.

He leaned toward her. "Only a dead man wouldn't want to sleep with you, and I think maybe, given the chance, even the dead would rise to the occasion. I don't want to look like a fool, so I really shouldn't say this, but . . . every second with you, all I want is another second with you."

She stared at him, stunned.

The earlier flutter became a whirlwind inside her, and she wondered if they were flirting, if this was the beginning of something wild and abandoned, if *his* thoughts were running in tandem with her own. It was crazy, of course. *Can't shake him, might as well sleep with him. . . .* She mocked herself. The world might be ending, or they might meet their demise in the process of averting that end, so they might as well indulge?

Except that she could feel herself starting to care about him, and she didn't want to just go wild and crazy with him. She wanted more.

She knew that she was smiling, that they were leaning closer to one another, touching, flirting, as if this were an actual first date. She knew that he was honest, and that he had been so all his life. She knew that he wanted the night, this night, to follow through on every fantasy she'd begun to indulge. She was glad of the meal, the wine, and the walk they would take in the piazza before returning to the hotel on this night in which exhaustion seemed to have faded with the light of day.

His fingers curled around hers. "No pressure," he said very softly. "Honest to God, no pressure. We're in this together. I don't want you running from me again."

Running . . .

She'd been running for years, and it had never mattered. Until now.

Until him.

She raised her head to smile at him, to speak. To tell him that she was equally drawn to him, that she didn't know what it meant, because she normally didn't fall head over heels or give in to seduction, or even loneliness.

But she never spoke.

Her smile faded.

A tall blond man was standing just outside the window, staring in.

Straight at her.

8

For the life of him, at first Scott had no clue
as to what had happened.

They had been getting close. Not so much
in the words that were being said, though
they had actually exchanged a bit of personal information. It had been in her smiles,
in the fall of her eyelashes, in the laughter
in her eyes.

It might have been a normal date.

Then something about her changed. And
it had to do with the man in the window.

When he had seen her face go pale — and
she was as pale as alabaster as it was — he
had turned and seen him. The man was tall
and blond — another Viking? He wore his
hair longer than the customary current cut,
and it was the gold of sheaves of wheat. He
had a rugged face, though he wasn't old,
perhaps in his mid to late thirties. He wore
a long-sleeved tailored shirt and jeans, nothing out of the ordinary, so he should have

blended in with the crowd. But he didn't.

As Scott was assessing the blond man, with his peripheral vision he caught Melanie shaking her head in a barely perceptible movement.

He turned back to stare at her. "A friend?" he asked.

She shook her head. "No. Um . . . who?"

He offered her a grim smile. "The big Viking guy standing just outside."

"I didn't really notice him," she said blithely, reaching for her wine glass.

"Like hell you didn't."

"Let's go. I'm getting tired," she said, standing.

He rose, as well. She was leaving, and he didn't want her wandering around without him. *"Il conto, per favore,"* he said to the waitress. She nodded, looking surprised. Dining was supposed to be slow and relaxing. Such haste was unusual.

"I can get it —" Melanie began.

"Macho, remember?" he said, offering the waitress his credit card.

Melanie let him pay, but she seemed fidgety while she waited for the card to be run through. Even when the Fiorellis hurried out from the kitchen to say goodbye to her, she was in a rush. She was warm and polite, but Scott could sense her eagerness

223

to get going.

Out on the street, she headed straight for a taxi stand down the road. He almost had to run to keep up with her.

In the cab, after providing their address on the Via Veneto, she sat back, silent.

"Melanie, who is he?" Scott persisted. He didn't yell, but his tone was determined.

She shook her head. "Look, I'm just tired, all right? Do you realize that we haven't slept in a real bed in about . . . almost forty-eight hours, I think. Aren't you tired? It must be the food and the wine. It just hit me like a ton of bricks. I'm exhausted."

"Melanie, I can't make you tell me anything," Scott said, turning to her in the cab. "But don't take me for a fool."

"All right, I won't," she said.

"So who is he?"

"You can't make me tell you anything — but I won't treat you like a fool by lying to you. That's it. Done. Over. All right?"

They reached the hotel. She didn't even seem to notice as he paid the driver, just breezed ahead of him and headed down the hall for their suite. She opened the door and paused only long enough for him to follow her in. "Thank you. That was a really nice evening," she said stiffly, then turned for her room.

He caught her arm. He didn't care if she protested or not as he drew her back and into his arms. He was suddenly and eternally glad of his height when she looked up at him, blue eyes as magic as crystal with their golden inner gleam, her expression surprised and perhaps fascinated. He gave her a split second to protest, but she didn't.

He cupped her face gently with his hand, his fingers stroking her cheek, marveling at the silken softness of her flesh. He kissed her. His mouth light on hers at first, then with a greater fervor and passion. He savored the feel of her lips beneath his as he pressed on. He felt the instant when she surrendered. Felt the liquid flow of her blood as she leaned against him, her lips parting. He suddenly felt as seduced as he had meant for her to be, mesmerized by the feel of his tongue in her mouth, the explosive warmth that seemed to combust between them. She kissed him back, the tip of her tongue rimming his lips, plunging between. Her body seemed to mold to his naturally, sensual and sleek, igniting a fire so exotic he felt it tear through him unchecked. Her arms went around him, her hands tangling in his hair. They kissed and parted, and kissed again, and he had never known it was possible to kiss so deeply, to feel as if he could merge into a woman's very being.

They broke apart at last, and she stepped away, staring at him. Then she smiled slowly, though it seemed as if a look of pain flamed into her eyes at the same time.

"Thank you," she said. "Thank you for a really wonderful night."

Then she turned and left him standing there, and he found he wasn't thinking of his own sense of loss as it tore through his body, he was thinking of that look in her eyes.

He didn't want to lose her. And at that moment, he was certain that the only way to keep her was to let her go.

That morning he had appreciated the hotel's steaming hot water.

Now he appreciated the fact that he could step into the shower and have it run as cold as ice.

And as he stood under the pulsing spray of cold water, he wondered who the hell the blond man could be. Brother? Ex-lover?

Maybe he was going insane. Maybe he had hallucinated the other man? Maybe all this was nothing but a dream.

But it wasn't. The walk with the corpses had been a dream. This was real.

He was still speculating when he heard his

phone ringing.

He stepped out of the shower, grabbed a towel and rummaged in the pocket of his discarded jeans until he found his phone.

"Hello?"

"Scott?"

"Yes?"

"It's Lucien."

Lucien. He'd given the man his cell number, but still . . . Why call him — and not Melanie?

"What's up?" he asked.

"You've found her, right? Sister Maria Elizabeta."

"Yes. She told us to come back tomorrow."

"You need to ask her about Bael. It's a long story, but I've been talking to Blake Reynaldo, and he and I are on the way to the jail right now. Those toughs you and Melanie took on the night of the quake turned out to be a strange mix. They included a professor, a Hollywood bit player, a cabinetmaker, and — get this — an ex-priest, along with two actual street toughs."

"*What?* They were a bunch of gang-bangers," Scott protested.

"No, they'd never met each other until that night."

"They knew each other's names. Well,

some of them did."

"Doesn't matter. Tell Sister Maria Elizabeta that you need to know everything you can about Bael. We're looking up what we can at this end, but she may know more than we'll ever be able to find out."

"All right. Is everything else back there fine?" Scott asked.

"As of now."

As of now. Not a good answer.

"Hey, we ran into a tall blond guy over here," Scott said. "A . . . friend of Melanie's. Do you know him? Is he safe?" Scott tried.

"Rainier?" Lucien asked.

"Yeah, I think that was his name."

Lucien was quiet for a long moment. "Yes, he's safe. I don't know if he's any part of this, but he's . . . safe. Look, is Melanie all right? I tried to reach her, but she's not answering her room phone. I left a message, but . . ."

"She'll probably call you right back. We just got in a few minutes ago — she's probably in the shower, just like I was."

"Sorry I got you out, then, but so long as you two are all right and on the right path . . ."

"Yes to both. Assuming this is the right path, anyway."

"When it's where you *have* to go, it's the

right path," Lucien said. "Just follow your instincts."

"Sure."

Lucien was quiet for so long that Scott thought he had hung up, until the other man said, "I can't imagine how bizarre this must . . . seem to you. But I think it's real."

"Me, too. And I'll tell the sister what you told me."

"Ciao," Lucien said, and hung up.

Bael. Wasn't he some kind of ancient middle-east demon? Or was that Baal?

He didn't know. Great. The world was ending, he was in a fabulous hotel in Rome, and he was totally frustrated. He stretched out on the bed, fighting the urge to make sure Melanie was all right — or even still there — and stared up at the ceiling.

Cherubs.

Dozens of little cherubs decorated the high canopy above the bed.

Great.

He stared at their chubby little bodies, and prayed for sleep.

It was after general visiting hours at the Men's Central Facility, but Lucien and Sean were with Blake Reynaldo, which meant they were allowed to meet with the man named Bo Ridley. In person, even in a

229

prison uniform, Bo was tall and dignified, with finely chiseled features. Despite his black skin, he looked ashen. He sat across a table from Blake, Lucien and Sean.

"Thank you for seeing us," Sean said easily, ever the cop.

Bo nodded, then shook his head in confusion.

"I don't know what got into me that night. I teach physics," he said.

"Yes, Officer Reynaldo told us that," Sean said. "He said you told him that you'd never met those other men until that night, and that when you woke up — in a holding cell — you were aware of everything that had happened but certain that you couldn't really have done any of it."

Blake was there simply to watch, Lucien realized. He'd already talked to Ridley. Now he wanted to see what they could get from the man.

"Physics. You're a scientist. So what do *you* think happened?" Sean asked.

The man shook his head. "I have no idea, no explanation," he said quietly. "I was on the street when the quake hit. I was right by a fissure, and it seemed like some kind of black smoke rose from it, and then it . . . it was as if — as if it entered into me." He looked down for a moment. "I was feeling pretty bad when it happened. I —"

Lucien leaned forward and interrupted, speaking as quietly as Sean had been. "Mr. Ridley, were you feeling as if you had done something bad already?"

The man looked up instantly, meeting Lucien's eyes, his own expression despairing. "I'd had an affair, and I was afraid that my marriage was about to end. I was completely disgusted with myself."

He fell silent.

Sean prompted him. "And then what?"

"Have you ever heard of those near-death experiences where people say they're floating above themselves, watching their bodies lying on a bed or an operating table? It was . . . like that. Except I wasn't near death. I was just suddenly watching myself as I joined a group of men, as if we were old friends. I even knew their names. And I knew that we had a chance to be totally *savage,* and it was exactly what I wanted. But it wasn't *me,*" he said desperately, as if he didn't really believe it himself and therefore didn't expect them to believe him. "Then . . . well, you know. We broke into the store, robbed it, beat up the old man . . . and I abducted that poor woman. Then that guy showed up and knocked me out. I remember, as the world went black, hearing someone whispering to me, telling me that all I wanted in life was to do the bidding of Bael, that I was a failure and deserved whatever misery came my way. And then it was like that dark smoky *thing* rose from my body, and the cops came and . . . It wasn't me, I swear. I don't hurt people. I — I teach physics," he finished lamely. "Or I did."

The man's life was probably ruined, Lucien thought. He was never going to be able to go into a courtroom and convince twelve of his peers that he had been possessed by an evil demon. Maybe temporary insanity?

Sean was apparently thinking along the same line. "Perhaps you were exposed to poison gas. You need to get a good attorney and plead temporary insanity from gas poisoning," he recommended.

Bo looked at them with a small spark of hope in his eyes, then shook his head. "It must have been my imagination. Or maybe I really am . . . evil at heart."

"I don't think so," Lucien told him. "Have you spoken with the others?"

Bo looked from Blake to Sean to Lucien. "They didn't tell you yet?"

"Tell us what?"

"One of the other guys — Hank Serle — used to be a priest. He hanged himself in his cell. He was clutching his prayer book, and he left a note saying that he refused to be a vessel for a fallen angel." Bo leaned forward, groaning, running his fingers through his hair. "A fallen angel . . . ? Good God. I'm a physics teacher. I *was* a physics teacher. Anyway, I don't think you'll get anything from the others. Two of them really are street toughs — gang members. Isn't that right, Officer Reynaldo? That's what you told me."

"Yes, that's right," Blake agreed. "And you're right, they're not talking. No one is."

They talked to Bo for a little while longer. Lucien asked him more about the whispers in his head, and had him redescribe the black mist that had seemed to enter his body.

When they left the prison and stepped out on the sidewalk, Blake asked,

"All right, you two. What the hell is going on here?"

Lucien looked at Sean, who looked at Lucien.

"Come on," Blake said impatiently. "Tell me what's happening here."

"I don't know," Lucien admitted. "But I do know this is only the beginning. But if you need more help with this, call Sean."

"Why? Where will you be?"

"I think I have to go to Rome," Lucien said.

Sleep that night was welcome, Scott felt. There was cool air rushing over him, thanks to the hotel's very efficient air-conditioning, and the equally cool, clean feel of the sheets beneath him.

And then there was the dream.

She came like a sylph in the night, moving with the sensual precision of a cat, languid and lazy, and yet with smooth purpose. She was one with the shadows, beautifully shaped, full breasts, tiny waist, perfectly flared hips and wickedly long legs. As she walked across the room, his dream was heavy with anticipation, sweet with longing. He barely dared to breathe, and he could hear the thunder of his own heart as he waited.

She reached the bedside and stared down at him. Cascading waves of platinum-blond hair swirled around her shoulders as hypnotically as the waves in the ocean, her eyes were clear and yet haunting, heavy-lidded, and her lips were full and parted. He didn't dare reach out; he let her come to him. In seconds she was lying against him, a sinuous length of fire and sweet enticement, and, then, at last, he clasped his arms around her, drawing her more tightly to him, needing to feel the clamor of her heart, the rise and fall of her breath, even the rush of blood through her veins. . . .

"Scott."

He started awake, instantly bolting up into a sitting position, ready to leap into battle.

He blinked, his eyes adjusting to the darkness. From somewhere outside, beyond the courtyard at the back of the hotel, neon lights cast ribbons of color in the room, red, yellow, green, enough light to show him that Melanie really was in the room.

Really was standing by his bedside.

Not quite naked, not quite moving like a cat. She was in a Tinkerbell T-shirt. Odd, he'd never thought of Tinkerbell as sexual, but that T-shirt was more erotic than the bare flesh of his dreams, because she was real beneath that shirt. He longed to reach out and touch her, but, just as he had in the dream, he held still.

"Are you all right?" he asked anxiously. "What is it?"

She touched him at last, laying a hand on his shoulder.

"I'm sorry if I scared you. Nothing is wrong."

He eased back, puzzled. "Then . . . ?"

Then . . .

It was better than the sweetest dream.

She sat at his side. She looked hesitant, lost . . . vulnerable.

He reached out for her, drawing her down beside him. She lay against him for a moment, and he would have been happy with that. Anything . . . so long as she stayed there with him. Fool. He was in . . . something. Couldn't be love. No one fell in love that fast. But it wasn't just lust, either, because he needed . . . more. . . .

"Hey," he said, and just touched her cheek, stroked her hair.

"Is it all right that I'm here?" she asked.

All right?

He didn't scream his answer, though he wanted to.

"You know how I feel."

"I do?"

"I think I've been pretty damned open."

She just smiled and propped herself up on an elbow, studying his face so seriously that he almost laughed. But he didn't. He just died a little in the gold and crystal-blue of her eyes, the color enhanced by the pale neon ribbons of light that filtered through the curtains. He slipped his arm around her and found her mouth again. She kissed him in return with an urgency that was madly arousing. He drew his hand from the silk of

236

her hair to the perfect sculpture of her breast, then down along her hip, praying for control and patience as he found the hem of the T-shirt. She helped him remove it, then returned to lie against him again, breasts and nipples crushed to his chest, head against his shoulder for a moment before she sought his mouth again. They kissed, wet kisses, heavy, deep, and then his mouth traveled to her throat, down to her breasts, back to her lips again. He felt her fingers digging into his biceps, his shoulders, felt the exotic brush of her nails down his spine.

Again he found her mouth, and he pressed her down into the wealth of pillows, where they lay locked together again, just kissing. When he finally moved away from the kiss it was only to slide along the length of her body, desperate to learn each curve and hollow of her. His muscles seemed to jump and twitch; his arousal was throbbing, burning, and still he made love to her, savoring his own rising fever. He found her belly and was fascinated by the tiny diamond navel ring she wore, then made his way lower to the curves of her hips. He felt her touch on his hair, his shoulders. He eased himself lower, running his hand down the shapely length of her legs, the muscles of her thighs, her calves. He kissed and teased, finding her center, making love with his touch, his lips and tongue. He felt the life in her, the surge, the rhythm of her movement, and he thought he was about to lose his mind with longing. She cried out softly, then whispered his name in the play of erotic light and shadow.

She drew him to her, and in a moment he was inside her. The world seemed to tremble and shake beyond what any earthquake could achieve. She held him as she writhed, and she whispered, she moaned. He held her, lifted her, moved with her, and relished every beat of his own desperate torment until he felt her body shuddering, felt her fall against him, and only then did he allow himself to climax. The earth, he thought vaguely, could be no more volatile.

They fell back together onto the sea of pillows and sheets, damp, slick and still in one another's arms. He didn't release her, and she didn't attempt to escape. The neon lights continued to flicker across the room as he lay silently, stroking her hair.

Several times, words came to his lips.

He swallowed them back each time.

He didn't want to say anything that could possibly mar the moment in any way.

She let out a soft sigh, and he felt her relax

against him. After a while he thought she even slept.

Who the hell is Rainier? he wondered as he stared down at her. *And what the hell is he to you?* He wanted to wake her up and demand answers. But he didn't. Rainier was out there somewhere, but *he* was here.

He closed his eyes, almost afraid to sleep, but at last he drifted off. No images of dark mist and skeletons came to trouble his dreams.

A little while later he shifted and opened his eyes to see her looking up at him. She smiled. Sleek, sinuous and graceful as a cat, she half rose above him. Her hair teased his flesh like a sweet breath of air. She seemed to pour herself over him, leaning low. Her lips teased his chest, his throat, found his mouth, and once again . . . slow, deep kisses became fevered. Her body molded itself to his like a glove, then moved sensuously, rubbing slowly down the length of him.

He was suddenly wide awake.

They made love until dawn.

Then, at last, she yawned and curled up against him, and he fell into a deep, peaceful sleep, resting as calmly as the dead.

Melanie awoke feeling rested and wonderful.

Then reality crashed down upon her. She had no regrets; she had done exactly what she had wanted to do, and he had been everything she'd hoped, imagined . . . dreamed.

But even if the world didn't end . . .

She rose slowly, and was startled to see that Scott was already awake, sitting in a chair drawn up by the bed. He had been watching her with a very serious expression, and she flushed. "Have you been staring at me long?" she asked him.

"I ordered coffee," he told her. "*Americana.* With cold milk on the side."

"Thanks," she said, accepting the cup he handed her.

"Who is Rainier, by the way?" he asked.

She almost choked on her first sip. "Pardon?"

"Lucien called last night."

She frowned. "He called *you?*"

"He tried to reach you. Didn't you see your message? Apparently those thugs who attacked your friends the night of the quake weren't really thugs. Or not all of them, anyway. They didn't even know each other before it began. One guy said something about Bael making them do it."

"That's ridiculous — they knew each other by name!"

"That's what I said. Anyway, Lucien and Sean will be working that angle. He wants us to tell Sister Maria Elizabeta about the reference to Bael. So . . . who is Rainier?"

"He's an old friend," she said, wondering how he'd found out Rainier's name. He must have gotten it from Lucien. "But I don't want to see him now, all right? I don't want any outside involvement until we know what's going on."

Scott lifted his hands, not angry, just perplexed. "Why didn't you just tell me that last night?"

"I guess it just surprised me to see him here. Now. That's all."

Scott smiled slowly. "That was more than surprise. It was . . . dismay."

She rose, trying to appear calm and uninterested, ignoring her nakedness and striding for the door. "Don't worry about it, please. And don't be jealous."

"I'm not jealous. I'm just extremely curious."

"Well, don't be. I'm going to shower, and then we need to get going."

He had risen to watch her. His dark hair framed his face. He really was a cavalier, standing so straight, his shoulders set. She felt a flush sweeping to her cheeks. He didn't understand. She longed to run to him, tell him to screw the world and hold her. But she couldn't.

"There are parts of my life you have to stay out of," she whispered.

"Maybe I can, maybe I can't," he told her. "Melanie, don't lie to me, or to yourself. There's something between us."

"Last night was great. *You* were great," she said, trying to be dismissive. "But . . . I have a different life. And you won't understand, believe me."

She practically ran away then, so desperately did she need to end the conversation.

She stayed in the shower far too long, but she couldn't remember ever feeling such a state of confusion. She cared about him, and she wanted to be with him, but she couldn't be, not in any long-term meaningful way. She might have made an incredible mistake in going to him last night, because no matter how much she wanted to, she could never change who she was.

Or *what.*

Staying in the shower wasn't going to help anything. She had listened to Lucien's message, which was just a repeat of what Scott had already told her, and they did have to get going, because Sister Maria Elizabeta seemed to think their third earth sign would arrive that day. With regret, she turned off the water, dressed in jeans and a tank top again, put on sneakers and tied a sweatshirt around her waist. Her passport was in the hotel safe, so she stuffed some Euros and a credit card in her pocket and went out to meet Scott.

"Let's get going," he said briskly. He set down the newspaper he had been reading while waiting for her and led her out. Once they left the hotel, she was startled to see him walking toward a yellow Subaru Outback.

"That's ours?" she asked.

He nodded. "This thing should handle those crazy stone roads all right. It's not easy getting taxis to go out to the middle of nowhere." She realized she was staring at him blankly when he added, "Sorry, it seemed like a smart thing to do."

"No, no, it's brilliant," she assured him. "I should have thought of it."

"Get in. I may need help with the map."

They ended up having to park the car some distance from the church, and Scott made certain to lock it. "In case the world survives, I really don't want to have to buy the sucker," he told her.

She smiled, and together, they headed for the church.

They didn't see the sister when they

stepped inside.

They did see a man standing by the altar. Melanie's heart sank. When he turned, she realized she had run for nothing the night before.

"Hello, Melanie," he said gravely, then nodded to Scott.

She felt Scott stiffen beside her, felt his hand resting protectively at the small of her back. He would venture into hell for her, she was certain. And she couldn't let him.

Rainier came forward, a hand outstretched to Scott. "So nice to see you again," he told Melanie. His English was only slightly accented with a hint of his native Italian, but then, Rainier spoke many languages extremely well.

"How do you do?" he said politely to Scott. "My name is Rainier Montenegro."

"Scott Bryant. How do *you* do?"

"What are you doing here, Rainier?" Melanie asked, dismayed to hear the desperation in her own voice.

Rainier looked at her, smiling with empathy. "I am a — Taurus, and my presence is required, it seems," he told her. "The third earth sign. Like you, I have been called here, drawn here."

"Are you a member of the Alliance?" Scott asked bluntly.

Melanie stared at him, startled.

"Yes," Rainier said, looking at Scott, clearly intrigued by him.

"Ah! You are all here!" Sister Maria Elizabeta's voice was pleased.

Rainier introduced himself to her, and she . . . sized him up, smiling. Then she reached out and touched his cheek, and Melanie thought that perhaps that touch was the nun's way of being certain that the right people had come to her.

"And so we begin," the elderly nun said at last.

Scott said, "Before we start, Lucien called last night. He said that I was to ask you what you know about Bael."

"Bael?" the nun asked, frowning. The name obviously meant something to her.

She nodded gravely, thoughtfully.

"He goes by other names, as well. The Irish knew him as Balor, a one-eyed king of the Fomorians, a race of giants. Sometimes he is Baal. In my world he is a demon under Satan, a fallen angel. He is the kind of spirit who can enter into others and make them do his evil bidding, cause chaos and hurt others, anything to damage the soul. He was cast out of heaven in the wars against heaven, and he is very dangerous indeed."

"Surely, Sister," Scott protested, "you

245

don't really believe in . . . demons? I mean, that demons are real, that they have substance."

"If you believe in goodness, then surely you must believe in evil," she answered him gravely. "The Church says that hell is the absence of God, but that very explanation gives rise to more questions. Do I believe in evil? Very much so. We have all seen it at work, whether it is perpetrated by man or demon. Why has Lucien asked about Bael?"

"Some thugs in Los Angeles are claiming that Bael made them attack a man and a woman and destroy a shop," Scott explained.

"Lucien is there now?" she asked worriedly.

"Yes."

She nodded. "It has begun. It has begun with the earth erupting and spewing forth the black fog of evil that is Bael's earthly cloak. He hides in the shadows. He can find weakness in the heart, in the soul. He can find a man's lack of faith and exploit it. He can call upon other evil spirits to do his bidding, and a man's life and sanity may depend upon his faith."

Melanie saw that Scott was watching Sister Maria Elizabeta politely but skeptically. He was there in Italy, having followed his dreams and his instincts. But he didn't really believe.

She found that she was more worried about him than ever.

"When one doesn't believe, one is vulnerable," Melanie said to Sister Maria Elizabeta, indicating Scott with a slight tilt her head.

But the sister wasn't to be shaken from her certainty. "It is for you to crush the evil that will spill from the earth. The three of you together. You represent the earth. Capricorn, Taurus and Virgo. This task has been entrusted to you, and the world must pray that you see it through."

"So where do we begin?" asked Scott.

"We must enter the catacombs. Well, *you* must. I am not sure that I have the strength any longer," the sister told them.

"Where is the entrance?" Scott asked.

"Beneath the altar," she informed him with a smile.

She led the way. Scott looked at Melanie, then more guardedly at Rainier, and turned to follow the sister. Melanie followed him, aware that Rainier was close behind her.

She hadn't noticed the trapdoor in the floor, but then again, it wasn't meant to be noticed. The dust of the ages seemed to have settled over it, and when Sister Maria

Elizabeta pointed out the ancient iron ring, camouflaged in a design in the tile flooring, even Scott had to strain to open it. There was a heavy creaking, and pale dust choked the air when he succeeded. He paused, looking at the sister.

"When was someone last down here?" he asked.

She smiled. "Long ago. The church stands here to protect the dead and the tunnels through which early Christians often fled to safety. But remember, it was built upon a pagan temple. Some say that this church also stands here to guard against the evil, ancient and of our world, that might otherwise rise from the earth. You will find one altar below, and many tunnels, and one of those will lead to the place where the twelve hallways of the ancients break off. Perhaps, today, you should simply read the inscriptions cut into the stones below and see what wisdom they hold. But to explore the tunnels, you will need lights. Even with them, it will be dangerous. There have been many quakes and tremors here, as well."

Scott reached into his pocket and produced a slim flashlight. "We'll see you in a while," he said, then turned and carefully followed the ancient stone steps down into the darkness below.

9

Melanie followed Scott down into the darkness. Rainier followed her.

It felt almost as if they had discovered a portal to hell.

Scott's flashlight was surprisingly bright, and in its reflected glow, he glanced back over his shoulder at Melanie. She was looking at Rainier, who seemed faintly amused by what was happening.

These steps led them to a circular room, smaller than the one above them, but similar. The saints were once again shown being martyred on eleven panels, while the twelfth featured Saint John, the light and the darkness. There were sconces set in brackets between the panels, and Scott lit one, then tossed the lighter to Rainier. Between the three of them, they soon had all the sconces burning. An acrid smell filled the air, and she thought that these lights probably hadn't burned in centuries.

The small circular altar room came alive in the glow. They could see that the altar itself was a simple piece, a block of solid rock, with twelve sides.

"Damn!" Scott exclaimed, bending low to read, then looking up at the other two. "I'm not sure what the hell I was expecting, but I don't read ancient Sumerian — or whatever this is. Though I see some Latin over here. I can probably make that out, thanks to Catholic school," he said.

Rainier hunkered down behind him as Scott started translating aloud. "Once the ancients referred to him as god, but to them he was but one of a group of gods, and never *the* God, He whom we hold most dear.

"We shall refer to none as god but *the* God. Bael has been banished back to his place with the legion of demons. In Hell the demons are divided, but none amongst them can bear that man knows they are not He who reigns as true king. Bael is he who died and was returned to them. Death takes all, and the new order will awaken all. Bael is called many names in many languages, but be forever careful and warned, for it is he, the minion of the most damned, Satan, who was of the land and with the land, and he will seek to destroy mankind through the power of the earth. When the planets near alignment at the solstice of the omens, it is Bael who will begin the destruction, seeking to raise what is dust and return it to form, seeking to use the dead as he would use the living. For his power is in trickery. He knows the hearts and minds of men and all creatures of the earth, the beast and the innocent, and he will prey upon the very souls of the unwary." Scott stopped reading. "Wow. That helped a lot. Does either of you read ancient Sumerian?"

"I think," Melanie said, hunkering down beside him, "that there are four 'readings,' if you will, each repeated in three languages. You read the Latin of the first one, this is the ancient Sumerian version, and the third is the same thing in ancient Greek."

"Great," Scott grumbled. "The Latin version of the next one is too worn to read."

"I can read the ancient Greek," Rainier said. He, too, crouched down beside them. "Virgo, she is the ancient mind, the reason, and orderly in all things, and she sees the earth ever for what it is, what it gives and what it must take. She is the goodness of the earth, all that rebuilds and stays steady and strong. She must learn her strength and her faith, and in doing so, she will see what is to be done, what road must be taken. She will accept the truth when it cannot be believed — she will refuse the darkness when it comes."

"That's you, I'm assuming," Scott said. "I can read the Latin over here . . . Taurus. He must . . . plow? Yes, plow ahead with the horns of the bull, for he has learned his power. He will take the road when it is blocked, but he must listen to the reason of others. If he stumbles, he will be supported, for the earth and those of the earth are strong, stronger than the demons, for good is greater. He will hold the line." Scott looked at them in disgust.

"We could have found this in the newspaper's Sunday horoscope."

Melanie ignored him. "I can read Latin, too," she said. "Here's yours. Capricorn. He will nurture, and he will be steadfast. Whatever labor is called for, he will see it through to the end. The earth will rumble, but he will never falter. His strength against all odds will be needed, and he will support the earth, for the earth has been his well, and his logic and reason will see that the battle is not lost in the dream. He will step forward, steadfast, even when he must go forward alone."

"Seriously, the Sunday horoscope," Scott said, then stood and began dusting off the top of the altar. He let out a slow whistle.

"What is it?" Melanie asked, straightening.

Rainier took a sconce from the wall and raised it over the altar. "Yes, what is it?" he asked.

"There's the picture you drew on the plane," Scott said. He reached into his pocket and produced Melanie's drawing. He'd added lines to it, turning it into a two-dimensional map. And there, engraved on the stone of the altar top, was the same map, identical in every way. The stone alongside the road, the church . . .

"Sunday papers?" Melanie asked. He saw the triumph in her eyes.

He was surprised to find that he suddenly felt suspicious. He took her by her shoulders, turning her to face him. "You've really never been here before?" he asked her.

She shook her head. "Never."

She was telling the truth. He could see it in her eyes.

Scott released her and ran his flashlight around the circular room. He could see the long underground corridors that stretched from it, and vaguely, lying on the recessed shelves that lined those corridors, he could see the bones of the dead.

"Perhaps we should start out," Rainier said.

Scott shook his head. "I say we come back when we have some stronger flashlights with us. But what the hell are we looking for, anyway?"

"Maybe we don't know yet," Melanie said. "Maybe . . . all right, I know this sounds crazy, but maybe I'm supposed to draw it first." She smiled. "If I'm reading this correctly, we need one another, and I'm supposed to be the one who figures out our road."

"I dreamed of those corridors," Rainier said.

"So did I," Scott told him dully.

"Bambini?" Sister Maria Elizabeta called from above. Her voice was worried.

"We're coming," Melanie assured her.

"We should follow these paths now," Rainier said.

Melanie laughed. "The bull is impatient to ram something."

Rainier made a face at her, and she smiled, and Scott found himself wondering again just where and when the two had met, and just how far their friendship had extended. He felt an evil rising within himself — jealousy. He gritted his teeth and clamped down on it. Hard. No matter how he felt —

and he wasn't even sure of that at this point — he had no rights when it came to Melanie, and he knew it. Whatever had happened in the past was nothing that anyone could change, and even in the present, she had warned him that certain aspects of her life were hers, and hers alone. He let out a breath. He needed to get a grip.

"We've discovered nothing," Rainier said, sounding frustrated.

"We've discovered each other — and the relevance of Melanie's drawings," Scott pointed out. He, too, was anxious to find out what the hell all this was really about. His head seemed to be swimming; he couldn't forget his conversation with Lucien.

The thugs on the night of the quake hadn't known one another. One man was a professor, another an ex-priest. And they claimed that Bael had been controlling them.

"My children?" Sister Maria Elizabeta called out.

"Coming!" Melanie assured her. She glared at Scott and Rainier, then started back up the stone steps. Scott let Rainier precede him, then looked back as he followed the other man. The sconces still burned.

He stared down at the top of the altar, and he saw what seemed to be a dark shadow falling over the map etched into the stone.

And he thought he heard a whisper in his ear.

Scott.

He looked up. Melanie was just reentering the church above; Rainier still blocked his way.

He almost started back down.

Fool, come down and finish it. I can end this for you, rid you of the Norseman. You want her, and you can have her. You can fuck her and fuck her and fuck her, and never have to deal with him. He can die.

Scott started and swore aloud, wondering if the whisper had come from within his own mind, if he hadn't conjured it along with his jealousy of Rainier. The shadow still lay atop the altar, shifting in the candle-glow. It was almost as if the undulation of light and dark was beckoning to him.

He turned away, feeling ill. He didn't want to kill Rainier. He didn't want *anyone* dead. What the hell had gotten into him?

Think of his hands on her. Think of them sweating and rutting. Think of him where you want to be, of all that he has taken, all that he can still take from you, will take from you. I

*can help you see that he dies for good, that
he is dust that never rises again. Don't you
see the evil in both of them? And the nun, she
has you all fooled. She is evil. . . . Picture it.
Picture her going down on that would-be
Viking, think of what he will do to her,* with
her, fucking, fucking, fucking.

"Hey, hurry up, up there!" Scott said
aloud. What the hell was going on in his
mind? He never used words that were so
coarse, words that changed the nature of
everything.

It was something in the shadows, in the
ancient dust sifting through the air.

Scott climbed out and stood gratefully on
the church floor once again. He closed the
trapdoor, then looked at Rainier and Melanie and started to laugh. They were white
with dust from the catacombs.

"I know the first order of business," he
said.

"You do?" Melanie was surprised.

"Showers," he said gravely.

"But . . . this can't be all there is," Rainier
said.

"It is not," Sister Maria Elizabeta said.
"You have come together, and you have
learned the secret of the altar tablets."

Scott didn't want to argue with her,
although he didn't feel as if he'd learned a

damned thing of any use. Maybe it was all bunk. Maybe he really was losing his mind. Were those whispers in his head nothing but a vile fantasy created by his own sick mind? The thought made him ill, but the voice in his mind was gone, gone as if it had never been.

"So what now?" Melanie asked.

"We'll come back tomorrow with heavy-duty flashlights and some old-fashioned weapons," Rainier said firmly.

To fight corpses? Scott thought.

But the sister nodded, as if she had just heard the most logical thing in the world. "Now that you are together, you are one. And I must rest."

She turned away from them, and Scott realized that she was coming and going via a door that blended into the panel of St. Paul's torture and execution.

"Let's go," Melanie said.

Rainier fell into step with Scott as they followed her. "So Melanie didn't tell you anything about me?" he asked.

"No, not really," Scott said evasively. The tall man at his side might look like a Norseman, but he had the hint of an Italian accent. "Old friends, huh?"

"So she has not explained everything," Rainier said.

Scott felt his temper rising. But he wasn't seeing sexual images in his mind, nor did he want anyone dead. He just wanted to belt the guy.

"Were you two . . . together?" Scott asked, as if it were merely a casual question.

"Together?" Rainier asked. "Oh, no. We are friends, very old friends. No, I meant . . . well, apparently, there are things she still needs to tell you."

Melanie had heard him and stopped. She was staring at Rainier, and her look was both angry — and afraid.

What the hell was going on? Scott wondered.

"A car! Wonderful," Rainier said.

"Where are we dropping you?" Scott asked.

"I'm at a place on the Piazza Navonna, but I'll transfer to your hotel. Where are you staying?" Rainier asked.

He must have seen something in Scott's expression, because he explained, "I believe we need to be close, the better to work together. Melanie can arrange a reservation for me. I'll be along this evening."

"Great," Scott said. Nope, not a single trace of enthusiasm in his voice, but at least there wasn't a trace of rancor in it, either. Still, he was aggravated. This guy was

259

amused that he knew something about Melanie that Scott didn't.

Scott didn't appreciate feeling as if he were the only one not in on the joke — or the dark secret. Whichever it was, he resented not being included.

When they reached the city, Scott drove past the city's ancient landmarks again; the Forum, the Coliseum and the Palatine Hill, where once upon an ancient time the very rich had built their homes.

His eyes were not drawn to the hill, though, or even to the immensity of the Coliseum. He watched the area around the Forum. The idea of living shadows struck him again, though because he was driving, he couldn't really watch. But there was definitely something odd. He wasn't seeing real shadows, just strange wisps of floating blackness.

He glanced at Melanie, who was sitting in the passenger seat.

"Do you see them?" he asked.

"What?" she replied.

"The shadows," he said.

Rainier leaned forward, looking. "Perhaps a trick of the light. Ah, there — a group of our Roman cats, slinking away from that horde of tourists."

A little while later Scott dropped Rainier

at his hotel, then continued on to their hotel. He hadn't realized how late it had grown, but now, he felt a rumbling in his stomach. They'd had coffee, but they hadn't eaten.

"I'm starving. Aren't you?" he asked, and smiled. So far, the world hadn't ended, and Rainier wasn't at their hotel yet. They still had a little time together. Alone.

"What?" She had been deep in thought; now she look at him, startled.

"Food. We haven't eaten, and it's late in the afternoon. Aren't you famished?"

"Oh. Right. Of course."

"We could get room service," Scott offered with a suggestive smile.

"Sure, whatever you want."

She was still distracted by her own thoughts. He was flirting, but she wasn't even noticing. He wasn't sure if he was amused or deflated.

When they reached the hotel, she was still caught up in her own world. He asked her what she wanted to eat, went ahead and put in the order at the front desk, and then followed her to the suite. She had already headed to her own room, but she hadn't closed the door.

He could hear her moving around, but he just sighed and headed for the shower. He scrubbed away the dirt, dust and grime of the catacombs, and then leaned against the wall, letting the water sluice over him. Suddenly he heard a noise and spun around, and to his surprise and delight, she was there. She had come to him again.

This time they made love with the soap and the water slick against them, creating an erotic new sensation. Heat and steam from the water combined with what they created, and they made love madly at first, then with laughter as they slid and slipped against the soapy tiles. At one point, as she clung to him, he felt the feverish touch of her fingers, followed by the scrape of her nails moving down his back. Her lips grazed his shoulder, then her teeth.

She abruptly drew back and met his eyes. He thought he saw a moment of panic in her look, so he just smiled and kissed her again, puzzled. She sighed and moved against him, and in moments they were laughing again, finding themselves just too tall for the small hotel shower.

In the end he scooped her up, and they made love again on the freshly made bed, soaking the sheets, but heedless of any discomfort. When they lay still afterward, basking in one another's arms, he felt a sense of intimacy with her that he hadn't known before. For just a second or two, perhaps, she had let down her wall.

They were startled up by a firm knock on the outer door.

He swore.

"Dinner!" Melanie gasped, then yelled, *"Tra un attimo!"*

They both hopped up and found robes. Melanie rushed ahead of him to open the door to the suite. A young room-service attendant was standing there, looking somewhat abashed. Scott was pretty sure he was apologizing for the interruption with his rushed Italian, and expressing his fear that their food would grow cold.

Melanie must have assured him that it was fine, because a moment later the waiter wheeled their food cart into the salon. He set it up by one of the windows that looked out on the courtyard, and they sat, eating ravenously for a few minutes.

At first they talked about the food. But then, try as he might, he couldn't help himself. He had to ask her, "What does Rainier Montenegro think you should have told me?"

She froze, just for the blink of an eye, then pretended to be incredibly interested in dipping a piece of bread into a mixture of olive oil, garlic and pepper. She finally spoke after she swallowed. "I have no idea. This is absolutely delicious, don't you think?"

She excused herself a moment later and disappeared into her bedroom. That time, she shut the door.

While she was gone, he eased back, sipping red wine. This was, he decided, exactly the way one should save the world.

There was another knock at the door — one knock, loud and firm. He rose, thinking it was pretty rude for room service to have come back so quickly for the table.

But it wasn't room service. It was Rainier Montenegro.

Scott stepped back, hoping his irritation wasn't obvious.

"Sorry, but I think Melanie forgot to get you a room," he told the other man blandly.

"It's all right. I took care of it myself."

"Great," Scott said.

If the man had a room, why the hell wasn't he in it?

Melanie came out of her room, her robe wrapped tightly around her. "Rainier," she said, and looked distraught. "I forgot all about —"

"No problem. It's all taken care of. However, I do hope you have an extra wine glass?" Rainier said.

"Of course," Melanie assured him. "So

where's your room?"

"Right next to yours. Same courtyard exit as you two have," he said.

"Great," Scott repeated.

Rainier looked down as he poured his wine. He seemed amused again, but not in a malicious way. Then he looked across the room at Melanie and made a motion with his fingers, dabbing at the side of his mouth. Melanie looked stricken as she did the same.

What the hell was going on? Scott wondered. He felt as if he had stumbled into a secret society and the members didn't intend to let him in.

"Excuse me," he said, and returned to his own room to dress. When he came back out, Rainier was sitting on the sofa in the parlor, reading the paper. Melanie was nowhere in sight, but presumably had gone to get dressed herself.

"What do you think of this?" Rainier asked, rising and passing the paper to him.

It was in Italian. Scott read very slowly, using context to figure out the words he didn't know.

"There was an earthquake in the Naples region," he said carefully.

"Right. Read further."

There was a captioned picture below the major headline, a photo of a priest, stern-faced and stoic, his hand raised in blessing over a man on the ground. The man appeared to be bleeding profusely. So much blood.

Rainier had apparently decided not to make him suffer and said, "The man on the ground went crazy after the quake. He stabbed several people. Someone managed to get him down, using his own knife against him. He told the police on the scene that he didn't do it — even though a crowd saw him. The priest took it upon himself to perform an exorcism, because the man was begging that his soul be saved before he died. There's a huge to-do over it. The Church must approve all exorcisms, and they don't often do so these days."

"So he was possessed — that's what you think, right?" Scott asked.

"He was a factory worker, a family man. He'd never lifted a hand against anyone before."

"He . . . died?"

"Yes."

Rainier looked intently at him then, studying him for a moment. "There was something down there. Didn't you feel it?"

"Something? As in . . . ?" Scott asked.

He wanted to deny the whisper he had heard. He didn't want to believe it had come from his own mind, from a place in his soul that was far more savage than he'd ever imagined himself to be — and he certainly didn't want to believe that there was really a demon who could slip into a man's body and take over his mind.

"Bael," Rainier said flatly.

Scott shook his head. "Wait a minute. You think the same demon was busy in Los Angeles and Naples *and* here?"

Rainier reflected for a moment, then answered slowly and carefully. "I believe that Sister Maria Elizabeta's church was built to stand guard over the demon Bael, to prevent his reentry into this world. But time passes, demons become little more than gruesome fairy tales. Perhaps he's always found the occasional chance to slip out as a black mist. Or perhaps he has managed to accrue his own minions and *they've* slipped out to act in his name. According to certain beliefs, demons can attack when someone is either full of sin — or believes they are."

"If you're right, then why are we here, when he's already out and doing his damage in the world?"

"Damage, yes. The true horror he could possibly evoke? Not yet. I think our part in this is to stop Bael from escaping in full force."

"And you think he's under the church?"

"You and I — and Lucien — all dreamed of the catacombs, right?" Rainier asked.

"But — that was the sister, calling to us."

"She called to us in the dream, but she was only part of the dream. The dream might be like Melanie's sudden artistic ability — a warning."

Melanie came out, dressed in a summery halter dress that flowed around her as she walked, emphasizing her curves. Her hair was still damp, and she had applied a bit of eye makeup. In short, she was stunning. No one would guess she'd been crawling through a catacomb earlier that day, searching for a demon.

"Shall we take a walk?" she suggested.

"A walk?" Rainier said.

"Why not? We shouldn't just sit here brooding, waiting. We need to buy flashlights for tomorrow, anyway — but for now, let's just take a stroll."

"All right," Scott said.

They probably looked like any group of tourists out to see the sights of Rome, Scott thought as they stepped outside. At this time of day, many of the tourist spots would be closing, but some stayed open longer because it was the summer. They passed the

American Embassy, and then Rainier paused, staring at the church across the street, which held the entrance to the Capuchin crypt.

"They're still open," Rainier said.

"We've all been there before — even Scott," Melanie said.

Ignoring her, Rainier made his way across the traffic, causing several drivers to honk their horns.

Melanie looked at Scott. "Taurus — the bull. Barging onward. We need to keep an eye on him."

Scott caught her hand, watching the cars, and when the street was as clear as it was going to get, they ran together across the street and followed Rainier up the steps.

There was no set charge for entry, but a donation was required. As Scott paid for the three of them, Rainier got into a discussion with a man near the entry. Scott had been raised Catholic; he knew by the man's garb that he was a priest and not one of the Capuchin brothers.

"What's he doing?" Scott asked Melanie, taking her hand and strolling inside to the first altar. He knew the place and found it fascinating, with its juxtaposition of mortality and immortality. Two skeletons in their Capuchin robes were standing in the chapel, while the wall decorations were created from skulls and hips.

"I'm not sure. I believe he knows the Father," Melanie said. "Should we keep going or . . . ?"

"No, we should wait. We need to stay together," Scott said.

He watched as Rainier followed the priest to the nearby gift shop, where he selected a number of rosaries and waited while the priest gave them his blessing.

"Is he that religious?" Scott whispered.

"So it seems," Melanie said.

"Grazie, grazie," Rainier told the priest.

Scott wasn't sure what the priest said in return, but his expression as he spoke was grave. The priest touched Rainier's chest, making the sign of the cross. The two men parted, and Rainier walked over to join them.

"Wear these at all times," Rainier said, slipping a rosary around each of their necks.

"I thought we were fighting a non-denominational demon," Scott said dryly.

"Then you weren't really listening to Sister Maria Elizabeta," Rainier said. "Goodness does not have to do with any one religion, and faith is simply the face we put on what we believe ourselves. Melanie and I are both Catholic, and when I spoke to Lucien earlier, he said that you're from New Orleans, where . . . it's the predominant religion, so . . ."

"What if I'm lapsed?" Scott asked.

"What is lapsed? Faith can return at any time. Besides, it can't hurt, and these carry my friend Father O'Hara's blessing," Rainier said.

"O'Hara?" Scott said. With a name like O'Hara, the priest probably spoke English as his first language.

"Men of the cloth go where they are sent," Rainier pointed out. "And Father O'Hara was taught about Bael, whom he knows as Balor, when he was in the seminary. He recalls the legend in which Balor was captured by a saint long ago and imprisoned beneath the earth. If he were ever to escape his prison completely, the earth would crumble, the mountains fall, and men, like rats in a cage, would destroy their fellow men and then themselves."

"If that's true," Scott said, "if we go digging around in the catacombs, don't we stand a chance of releasing him?"

"I think he is already halfway out," Rainier said. "We have to imprison him again, or kill him if we can."

Melanie stared at the bones of the long-gone Capuchins and shivered suddenly.

"I'm going back to the hotel," she said quickly. Rainier turned to follow her, but Scott looked around first and saw that the priest had gone to stand just outside the door to the church.

Night had fallen, but Father O'Hara was standing against the wall beneath an overhang, lighting a cigarette.

"Go on, catch up with Melanie," Scott told Rainier. "I think I'll look around a little more."

Rainier nodded. In his way, he seemed as protective of Melanie as Scott felt — even though he knew full well that she was capable of taking care of herself and was in fact worried about *his* abilities.

He waited until Rainier was out of sight and then hurried to join the priest.

"Excuse me, Father O'Hara?" he said.

The man started. He looked at his cigarette and grimaced. "I'm sorry. You know me?"

"You were talking to my friend earlier. Rainier Montenegro," he said.

"Yes, yes."

"You two were talking about Bael. Balor."

The priest arched his brows. "Are you a believer, son?"

"I believe that — that there are things in this world beyond our customary comprehension. Actually, Father, I wanted to ask you if you know about something called the Alliance?"

The priest's breath caught for a fraction of a second, before he took a drag of his cigarette to camouflage his hesitation. "Your friends are part of the Alliance," he said carefully.

"How does one join?" Scott asked.

"One doesn't."

"Look, I'm supposed to be hunting down a demon alongside two people who won't let me be a part of their little organization. Am I a fool? What am I supposed to believe in here?" Scott asked, surprised at the passion in his own voice.

Father O'Hara looked at him. "Belief is each man's destiny. We all have free —"

"Will. I know," Scott finished for him, realizing that the man wasn't going to give him any help.

And then he did. He reached into his pocket and drew out a card. "You can find me if you need me. I even have a cell phone. The Church has entered the brave new world."

"I'm asking you for help *now,*" Scott said.

"No, you're asking me about your friends, and it isn't my place to talk about them," Father O'Hara said. "But when you truly need me, you may call on me."

Scott smiled. He liked Father O'Hara. "All right. Thank you."

He left Father O'Hara with a wave and started back toward the hotel. He didn't see Melanie and Rainier, but there were plenty of little shops, cafes and bars where they might have stopped along the way.

He looked up at the sky as he walked. The moon would be full in the next night or so, he realized.

He stopped walking, aware that he had wandered off the main road. He had gone down an alley, though he didn't remember changing direction. He had been distracted by the moon.

Or maybe he had followed it.

He was at the rear of a building. At one time, he thought, it had been a church, though it seemed vacant now, with broken windows and only half a spire remaining. The odd thing was that the walls seemed to be alive with constantly changing shadows.

He wasn't alarmed at first, just curious. Then he heard the chattering, like the whisper of the wind at first, then growing louder, like the call of a flock of strange birds. He searched the sky again, only dimly aware of the light and traffic of the nearby street.

All at once the shadows seemed to swoop down around him, and suddenly he wasn't certain what they were at all. They were huge, black-winged . . . Bats? He heard the sound of high-pitched evil laughter behind him, and he spun around.

A girl was standing there. She had a strange smile on her lips, and her eyes were alight. She was wearing an old-fashioned dress, a torn and tattered garment, and her hair was tangled, part of it tied on top of her hair with a ribbon.

More laughter, this time deep, but with the same malicious tone. He turned again. Behind him stood a man. He wore a top hat and Victorian frock coat, as if he'd stepped off the screen of a Jack the Ripper movie.

The swooping and chittering continued. The black-winged shadows seemed to be everywhere.

Suddenly silence fell, and a crowd stepped out of the shadows, though there should have been no room for them there. They wore various forms of dress, as if they had just come from a bizarre costume party at which "tattered" and even "decayed" had been on the must list.

"Buona sera," the girl said, and she laughed at him again. "Oh, ducky," she added, her

accent decidedly British, "you do look quite delicious."

And then she moved.

10

"I still don't think I understand, much less accept, what's supposedly going on here," Melanie told Rainier. "There have been natural disasters throughout history. The 'big one' is expected somewhere along the San Andreas fault any time now. There are active volcanoes all over the world, and hurricanes and tidal waves have always plagued low-lying areas."

"Natural disasters have always occurred, yes," Rainier agreed. "And they always will. But the thing is, prophecies have always held power over the human mind. And there's no prophecy more common than the one about the end of the world. It's just that we have a habit of thinking that the end will come as a huge cataclysm, not something that occurs slowly. The planets will align and boom — a solar flare will shoot down to earth, bursting it with a single firestorm. I believe in what we're doing, though I don't know what is coming. But I think there's a seepage of evil from the bowels of the earth, and I'm pretty sure that's just the beginning."

A step. She took a single step toward him first.

She ran her tongue around her lips in a lascivious gesture, and saliva dripped from teeth she must have had filed to sharp, jagged points.

What the hell kind of gang was this?

She started to walk toward him. He thought about what Lucien had told him about the gang in L.A., about the man going insane in Naples. Had this entire group gone in some way insane together, a form of murderous mass hysteria?

"Stay away from me," he warned the girl quietly.

To his amazement, she let out another cackle, and then she seemed to . . . fly at him. He had no trouble lifting an arm and batting her away to crash hard against the building.

But he wasn't prepared for the sudden onslaught that followed.

What seemed to be dozens of crazed costume-freaks suddenly came at him, grasping him, tearing at him. He fought them off, using skills he'd never learned but that came to him as if he'd been born with them. Another young woman planted firm arms around him while he back-kicked a man who had leaped on his shoulders. She stared down at him, insanely laughing, then she licked her lips and snaked her tongue over his cheek in a manner far more reptilian than human.

It felt like sandpaper. Horrible. Repulsive.

She drew back suddenly, hissing like the snake he'd just compared her to, staring at his chest, though he didn't know why.

It didn't matter; it was his chance.

He strained, bursting free from her grasp and hurling her away. Despite his strength, he was afraid that he could lose the battle because of the sheer number of his attackers, but then, suddenly, he wasn't fighting alone.

Rainier and Melanie were there with him. He moved like a whirlwind then. When the mob wasn't atop him, his strength was easily enough to keep them at bay. One swing of either arm sent an attacker flying. It was only when they clung to him like flies on a corpse that he struggled. They seemed determined to tear at his flesh, and ridding himself of them once they had taken hold was like divesting himself of glue. One of

the young women grabbed at him, screaming in agony as her hand brushed his chest,
yet not letting go.

"Don't let them — bite you, Scott. Keep
them away!" Melanie cried as she tore away
an old hag who was trying desperately to
sink her teeth into his arm. Melanie didn't
seem to care that the woman was old; she
threw her so high that she fell onto the
broken spire of the ruined church, which
pierced her clean through.

Jack the Ripper let out a bellow of rage
and came at him. Scott shot out his fist,
catching the man in the face. He flew
backwards and was impaled by a bent piece
of wrought iron that had once protected a
church window. He stared at Scott, then
collapsed like a rag doll.

"Scott!"

He didn't have time to reflect on the fact
that he had just killed a man — albeit a man
clearly trying to kill him — because Rainier's voice warned him of another attacker,
this one about to leap at him from the
shadows. Scott ducked as the man's own
impetus sent him flying past, then lashed
out with a kickboxing move, sending the
man crashing against a tree in the shadows
near the wall.

Suddenly Scott heard that strange chattering again, saw the shadows rising above the ruined church and the alley, above the trees that had clung so tenaciously to life here.

Melanie grasped his arm and dragged him back toward the busy street. "Come on, let's go!" she commanded.

"Wait!" he demanded. "What the hell was that?"

"Let's go!" she cried again.

They quickly reached the street, Rainier right behind them. But as soon as they reached the sidewalk, Scott stopped. "Melanie, we have to report this. I was attacked. I killed a man, and —"

"We can't report it," Rainier said. "Oh, hell, Melanie, explain it to him."

"We can't let ourselves get caught up in an investigation. If we were to go to jail . . ." she said, then stared at him, her huge blue eyes entreating. He saw that strange flicker of gold in them, and for a moment he was uncomfortable. He couldn't help caring about her, was certainly obsessed with her. But she scared him, as well. The way she had fought, the fact that she had killed a woman and didn't seem to care . . . her secrets . . . And it wasn't just that at that moment he was a little bit afraid of her, he realized. He was also afraid *for* her. And that

281

made him truly afraid for himself, because he didn't want to lose her.

"Look, Melanie, the police will find the bodies, and they'll investigate. Something happened back there. We could wind up in serious trouble if we don't go to the cops and tell them that we were attacked."

"There's a bar just down the street with quiet booths and a mainly Italian-speaking clientele," Rainier said. "I think we all need a drink."

Over Scott's protests, the other man urged them down the street and into the bar, then found them a corner booth in the back. The canned music was loud, affording them a certain amount of privacy. Scott ordered a Jack Black, neat, while Rainier opted for beer and Melanie chose red wine. Scott downed his first drink in a single swallow, then ordered another. Melanie watched him anxiously.

"Is that what the Alliance does? Kill people — yes, I know they were trying to kill me first — but kill them and then disappear?"

"Only when it's the only way," Rainier said.

"Please, Scott," Melanie murmured.

"That wasn't one person running amok or some gang possessed by black mist or a demon or . . . whatever. That was a crowd of crazy people in costume, and they were out for blood," Scott said, staring from one of them to the other.

"And we handled it. Together," Rainier pointed out.

Scott finished his second drink. "You're just not going to let me past that wall you two are hiding behind, are you?" he demanded.

Scott looked at Melanie expectantly. "I can't," she said miserably. "I've told you that —"

"Yeah, yeah, your life is your life," he said, and stood up. Melanie started to rise. "No, don't worry about me. I won't wander off the beaten path again. Enjoy your drinks — and don't try to follow me."

He left them and started to turn back toward the hotel, then paused.

He headed back to the abandoned church and the alley, instead, unable to believe that he hadn't heard any police sirens while they'd been in the bar. Surely someone — one of the survivors, maybe — must have reported the carnage by now.

But when he arrived, there were no shadows.

And there were no bodies.

"Impossible," he breathed aloud.

He checked the wrought-iron bar, but there was nothing there. No flesh. No blood. Nothing but a small pile of dust.

He bent down and searched. There wasn't even a speck of blood to be seen.

"I *am* losing my mind," he told himself.

But he wasn't. They had known. Somehow Melanie and Rainier had known the bodies would disappear, that there wouldn't be anything left for the police to find.

Tired and disgusted, he headed back to the hotel, went to his own room, crashed down on the bed and prayed for sleep.

Mercifully, it came quickly and hard.

Despite the depth of his sleep, he woke instantly when Melanie came in.

She didn't come right to him. He could sense her standing in the door, hesitant. He knew that she was worried about his anger, perhaps even worried about rejection, and despite the fact that he knew he was right to be furious, he wanted to take her into his arms. No matter what secrets she was guarding, he couldn't bear to see her hurt.

But he held his emotions, his desires, in check and didn't move, only watched her through half-closed eyes.

In a few moments she left the doorway and came to him, sitting on the side of the bed. "You're awake, aren't you?" she asked softly.

He opened his eyes fully and looked up at her. She was still so hesitant.

"Scott . . . you're acting like a child, you know."

That wasn't what he had expected to hear. He shook his head. "You're forcing me to play a game in which I'm the only one who doesn't understand all the rules," he told her.

"What if the rules don't really matter?" she asked.

She looked so forlorn, as if the truth hurt her more than the silence could ever hurt him. He reached for her, drawing her down beside him, and simply held her.

"What if we fail — and cause the end of the world?" he inquired.

"We can't fail," she told him. "We simply can't."

He lifted her chin; she looked as if she were about to start crying.

He was such a wimp, he told himself. It was the time to press his point, to demand to know what was going on with her and the Alliance.

But he didn't. He just held her against him. It seemed like the thing to do at the time, and he must have been right, because

she stayed. And because she stayed, the slow
— building warmth between them began to
deepen until it was unbearable. He ran his
fingers down the length of her arm, then
cupped her chin and kissed her. She kissed
him in return. Slow, deep, long, wet and
arousing. Passionate. Then they were both
struggling to rid themselves of their clothing as quickly as possible, desperate to feel
the fire of flesh against flesh. Hands, lips,
kisses and caresses, were everywhere at
once, until they tangled in the sheets, making love as if the world was indeed going to
end any second, and if they didn't learn
every nuance of one another now, they
would be lost for all eternity. He was staring at her face as he erupted in a staggering, volatile climax, made that much more
powerful because, absurd or not, he loved
her. The whole damned world and all its
secrets could explode, and he would die
happy in her arms. He fell to her side, drawing her against him. He didn't question her;
she didn't offer any answers. He felt the
thunder of his heart ease and the cool air
rush over their damp nakedness, and it was
enough. They were silent, drifting together
into sleep.

When he awoke, he was immediately
aware that she was no longer at his side. He

rose up on one elbow, looking around the room. She had never closed the door to the common room, and now light poured in from doorway, enough for him to see her standing at the wall that separated the two rooms.

"Melanie?"

She didn't answer him. He rose carefully, silently, and went over to her.

She had taken the pen from the bedside table and was drawing on the beautifully papered wall. It occurred to him that they were going to have one hell of a room bill, but he didn't try to stop her. Her eyes were open, but he knew that she was completely unaware of what she was doing.

He moved closer, trying to make out what she was drawing.

It was the church. Sister Maria Elizabeta's church. The sister herself was standing in the doorway, as if she were protecting the church against intruders.

Scott frowned as he peered closer and realized that she was actually protecting the outside world, trying to close the door against an army of bones and swirling dark mist trying to escape the sacred confines of the church.

"Melanie!" Filled with a sudden inexplicable urgency, he caught her by the waist and spun her around to face him.

She blinked, and suddenly she was back in the real world.

"Scott?"

"Melanie, we have to get Rainier, and we have to get to the church. Now!"

She turned and studied her drawing.

"Oh, God."

Scott was already searching the jumble around the bed for his clothing. He separated pieces, tossing her the cocktail dress she had worn, finding his own briefs and jeans and climbing into them. She was just as quick, scrambling around for her shoes, but she let out a cry.

"I need jeans and flats. Wake . . . Rainier and give me two seconds."

He didn't need to wake Rainier; when he banged on the man's door, he found Rainier awake, a light on by the sofa and the pile of guidebooks and maps he had been studying.

"We have to get to the church right away," Scott said.

Rainier didn't question him, only went back for his jacket. "Let's go."

By night, the stone trail that led from the road and turned into nothing but a path near the church was dark, and only the nearly full moon above them kept them

288

from losing their way. Scott took the car as far as he could, then parked. They leaped out in unison, but when Melanie started to run ahead, Scott called her back.

"Melanie, wait. We need weapons. Damn it, one of us should have been a cop. We could use a gun."

"Against the dead?" Melanie asked. She stared at him for a moment, then headed for the trees. Scott and Rainier looked at one another, then followed. They found branches that could be used as spikes or bats, and then hurried onward.

They quickly reached the copse in front of the church, whose stone walls and pillars were pure white beneath the glow of the moon. Sister Maria Elizabeta was standing in the center of the copse. She had taken one of the old wooden crosses that had been hanging on a wall near the altar and was swinging it around, chanting in the moonlight.

So far, her cross and her prayers had protected her. She was keeping the army at bay.

A bizarre army, an impossible one. An army that gleamed in the moonlight, just like the church itself. The soldiers she fought were skeletal remains and little more, bones shrouded in decaying cloth, some with scraps of desiccated flesh still clinging to their bones. They had encircled the sister, many missing an arm, a jaw, fingers, hands.

Scott stopped momentarily, staring. The skeletons had no eyes, but their empty sockets were staring at the elderly nun. They had no muscles or ligaments, but somehow their bones had joined together and were keeping them moving. And no matter how hard she fought, they were closing in on Sister Maria Elizabeta. She swung the cross continuously, catching any skeleton that came too close and sometimes disarticulating it, but at other times only forcing it back.

"They're like zombies," Melanie said. "We just need to smash them hard to make them fall apart."

And then she was rushing in to join the macabre dance of death. Scott flew after her, swinging his branch with a vengeance. Rainier was close behind.

Scott caught the first *thing* that came at him across the rib cage. To his horror, his massive swing just forced the skeleton back around at him. He slammed harder, and that time hit the skull full force. It went flying to land in the dirt, and as it did, the thing's remaining bones clattered to the ground. He heard a cry and saw Melanie fighting a skeleton still wearing the shreds of its burial shroud and still bearing the ancient shield and sword with which it had been buried. Bone fingers wielded the sword, slashing the air as it tried to get to her. She ducked each slash with limber agility, swiping at its feet. Scott rushed forward, swinging at the still-helmeted skull. Again the head flew, hitting more of the creatures that were pouring through the doors of the church. They seemed startled and wavered momentarily, then came on again.

"Take its sword and aim for the skulls!" Scott called to her.

She nodded, ducked down to get the sword, then rolled, barely missing a swipe from another skeleton.

Rainier was battling two of the clicking, armor-clad skeletons, ducking each sword stroke that was aimed at him and coming closer to the legs each time. He tackled one, and they went down together. He rose with the sword already swinging, slashing at the legs and feet of the second and several others near him, toppling several. Then he stepped into the crowd, aiming at skull after skull as the bones thrashed and clicked beneath him.

Scott stepped forward and claimed one loser's sword as his own.

"Scott!"

Melanie's cry warned him to turn and duck as a skeleton armed with an ancient water vessel tried to crack his head open. He rose in a swirl of motion, his sword swinging. As he moved, he saw that the circle around Sister Maria Elizabeta was closing in on her. He burst through the army of bones and positioned himself directly in front of her, forcing her back into the shelter of an ancient tree trunk. She sank down to the ground, moaning. He had no choice but to ignore her and give his full concentration to the task at hand, spinning as she had done, aware that he had to take them down one by one, yet prevent the others from coming any closer. He cut one clean in half, but the pelvis stood wavering on spindly legs, while the arms tried to drag what was left of the torso forward, the few remaining teeth, gnashing.

He slammed a foot down on the skull while aiming at the next thing headed his way. He sensed someone near him and realized that Melanie had made it into the inner circle. And next to her, protecting the nun, was Rainier. They were surrounded, but they didn't stop, growing more proficient the more they swung their swords.

Scott slammed his own blade hard against another skull, which exploded in a rush of powder, but against that pale dust, he thought he could see something black and viscous, as well. It seemed caught in the moonlight for a moment, before it sprinkled down to become one with the ground again.

Behind him, Sister Maria Elizabeta was praying again. She was on her knees, her voice slowly beginning to go hoarse. She must have been praying for hours, he thought.

The army kept coming. No matter how many the three of them destroyed, still they came.

Then, suddenly, the sister cried out loudly and the army halted. One by one, as if they had been nothing but wind-up toys that had now run down, they went still.

Then, with a tremendous roar, they fell. Dust to dust. Only scattered antique weapons and a few disjoined pieces of bone remained to testify that they had ever been there, a skull, a pelvis, an arm, a disarticulated hand.

Scott stood still, gasping for breath. He looked up and saw that though the moon was still glowing in the sky, the pink tinge of dawn had arrived. The sun was showing in the east, just creeping above the horizon.

His lungs hurt, his muscles hurt, but more than that, his *heart* hurt. Turning at last, he saw that Melanie and Rainier didn't look that much worse for wear, certainly nothing like he felt. Melanie was hunkered down next to Sister Maria Elizabeta, and Rainier was kneeling at her back, ready to support her.

Scott remained where he was, wary, his sword still clutched in his hand. His fingers were filled with tension; he had to release his grip slowly. He looked at the sword. Like everything else around them, it was covered in bone dust. It was old and bent. But as battered as it was, it had withstood the battle.

The Romans had forged steel that would outlast the ages.

What had been a patch of grass and flowers in front of the church now looked like the garden of a haunted house, planted with bones instead of blossoms.

"Scott!" Melanie called. "She can't breathe!"

He turned around at last, and hunkered down with Rainier and Melanie.

"We've got to get her to a hospital," he said.

The old woman shook her head emphatically.

"Help me back into the church," she pleaded, trying to sit and leaning heavily on

Scott. He helped her up, but when she started to fall, he swept her into his arms. She was so tiny, so light inside the voluminous habit, he marveled.

"We've got to get you to a hospital," he insisted again.

"No, no, please. Just take me into the church. I can't leave now. My time is coming, but I must be in the church when it does. Melanie, *cara bella,* follow that path. . . . It will take you to the convent. Get Sister Ana. She will come. She will know what to do."

"I agree with Scott," Rainier said. "A hospital would be the best thing."

"No!"

The sister was so emphatic that Scott was afraid they would do her further damage by trying to force her against her will.

He looked at Melanie. "I'll carry her into the church. Do as she says, as quickly as possible."

Melanie nodded, looking stricken. She didn't waste time. She turned and ran. Rainier walked ahead of Scott, kicking skulls and the fragile scraps of decaying shrouds out of the way. Inside the church, Scott set the sister down on a pew near the altar. The secret door to the crypts lay open, and it looked as though the earth itself had exploded past it.

The sister motioned toward the trapdoor, and Rainier hurried over to close it.

"I thought I was still strong enough," the old nun murmured. "But I was wrong. I could not stop myself. He . . . called to me, and I opened the door. . . . I let them out."

Scott stripped off his jacket and made a pillow of it to set beneath her head. She clutched his hand. "Stay with me. Please."

"I'm here," he assured her. "I'm here."

Even in the strengthening light of day, the odd and overgrown path that led from the church to the convent seemed dark to Melanie. Not that darkness actually bothered her, only the shift and flow of the shadows. She was on edge, thinking that any second another skeleton would jump out at her, and she regretted not bringing a sword. She wasn't sure why the light had caused the creatures to crumble, or maybe it had been Sister Maria Elizabeta's invocations.

She was hurrying so quickly that she tripped over a root and fell facedown. Swearing softly, she started to push herself up, then froze instead.

She had fallen on top of a collapsed skeleton, her own face mere inches from its bone-white skull. As she stared at it, she thought she saw something dark lurking deep in the eye sockets.

She heard a strange rattling sound coming from the skull. It grew and became a laugh like the sound of dry leaves rustling. "As I am now, so shall you be," the skull said, though she was certain the jaw had never moved.

Just as she rolled away, rising to her feet in the same motion, with a strange swoosh the skeleton's bones seemed to knit together and it began to stand. Once it had been clad in a grand robe, and the putrid remnants of that robe still clung to its bones as it towered over her.

"You!" A bony finger slowly stretched toward her. The laughter came again, hoarse and cruel. "You think that you can save anyone? Such a fool you are. Darkness still lurks in your heart. You were born of evil blood, and you are not fit for any decent man. How could you keep such a thing as love growing? Love is like a flower, and flowers are nurtured by the sun and the light. And you are evil. You are darkness."

She stared at it, thinking how impossible this was. This skeleton *knew* her.

"Murderess! Foul creature!" it cried, and then the skull let out a mournful wail, as if it were crying.

297

She blinked, but it was true. Tears of blood were forming in the eye sockets and running down those hollow cheeks.

"How many have you killed? Do you cry at night? You know how to ease that pain, how to remove the knife that twists in your heart at all times. You have no life, no life, no life. . . ."

"I have a life!" she cried, aware of a sudden twisting pain within her, as if her own body were attacking her.

"You think you kill only when you must, but you are wrong, and you should do the world a favor and die. Let it happen. Let your soul float down to the fires of the damned, and there you will find release."

Shaking, clacking, laughing hoarsely again, the thing took a step closer.

"You can't love, and you can't *be* loved. You are despised. You are like a snake in the grass, a rodent, a roach. You are vile. You are loathsome."

The skeleton jerked suddenly, and straightened its aim at her with its extended arm. "You think there's a God who will hear you? You, you, you, you, you . . . ?"

She felt faint, dizzy, terrified, and yet almost ready to welcome whatever punishment or execution the skeleton offered. She felt as if she'd been drugged, hypnotized, and that she couldn't prevent the evil in her from taking over, from giving in.

"You are a killer who deserves to die. And why not take the wretched man with you? It would be so easy. Take up your sword and kill, and when the blood sluices over you, you will feel again. Slice his flesh, let his blood fill you. Or die now, by your own hand, like the coward you are. I know what you are, and soon others will, too. And then you will be despised, hated, loathed, as the evil toxin that you are. I know, I know, I know. . . ."

It knew her fears. It recognized the pain that filled her. She could feel the anger and the hatred — the self-hatred — creeping into her as if it were part of the air she breathed, air that carried with it the fresh scent of blood, the scent of . . .

She curled her fingers around the rosary she still wore around her neck.

"I'm *good*," she managed to whisper. "You're wrong. I know that — my soul is clean."

The cackling stopped. The skeleton missed a beat. Then it seemed to gather its thoughts and spoke again.

"In your dreams. Who will ever believe that you — you! — are in any way a being that is good?"

It was speaking, but its voice was weaker. She had to pull herself back together, had to fight this thing.

"I know what you are, I know you are evil. I know what you are, what you are!" it said.

"And I know what *you* are. You're nothing but a trick of the mind. You're the essence of greed and need, envy and evil," she retorted.

It began to shrink back.

"Melanie?"

She shook with relief when she heard his voice. Scott's voice. How long had she been standing there, facing that thing, letting it talk to her? It was moving again, getting ready to impale her with its sharp-boned arm.

"Melanie!"

She came back to life, jumping backward as Scott came tearing past. He wasn't armed, but he didn't need to be. With his bare hands he grabbed the creature by its bony shoulders and hurled it to the ground, then stamped as hard as he could on the skull.

Dust. Fragments of bone. Nothing else was left. She stared at the remnants of her enemy and saw the black mist that seemed to seep from those shards — and from her — before wafting into the ground.

Scott took her by the shoulders then, staring into her eyes.

"My God," she breathed. What would have happened to her without Scott, ever the cavalier, always rushing in, ready to die to save her.

"Are you all right? Did it hurt you? Melanie?"

Bone, she thought. The creature that taunted her had been made of bone and yet . . . not. It had been animated by something viscous from the earth, something evil, possessed of the power to slip into the dead . . .

And the living.

"My God, I'm sorry!" she cried. "Sister Maria Elizabeta, how is she? Oh, God . . ."

Scott didn't take the time to answer, only gripped her hand and started dragging her at a run along the path to the convent. They threaded past small trees, dodged bushes, pushed through bracken, and then at last they saw the old stone walls of the convent before them. Scott banged on the heavy wooden door, and, in a moment it opened.

There were several sisters there, crowded behind the one who had opened the door. "Sister Ana?" Scott asked, and the nun nodded. "Sister Maria Elizabeta is ill, and . . . she wants you. She won't let me take her to

301

the hospital."

The sister at the door turned, speaking in a dialect Melanie didn't understand. From somewhere a black bag was passed to her. Then she pushed by Scott and Melanie, and hurried along the trail back to the church.

Scott was still holding Melanie's hand, and he pulled her with them as they followed Sister Ana. The nun was not young — she looked to be in her seventies — but she moved with determination as well as speed, and it was difficult to keep up with her, with the bracken slapping back at them as they hurried in her wake.

When Sister Ana reached the place where the skeleton had accosted Melanie, she paused for a minute and looked back at them shrewdly, then started moving again.

As soon as they reached the church, Sister Ana fell to her knees next to Sister Maria Elizabeta, who still lay stretched out on the pew. Sister Ana spoke again in that dialect Melanie couldn't follow, then reached into her bag and produced a tiny pill, which she slid beneath the older sister's tongue. Sister Maria Elizabeta closed her eyes, lying very still.

"She's . . . ?" Scott began weakly.

"She's resting," Sister Ana said, her English just barely accented. "For now, you must leave her be." She looked all three of them up and down. "You can come back later and seek what you need. But now, it is time for you to leave so she can rest." Her eyes fell to Scott's chest and the rosary he wore, visible in the open V of his shirt. "You will need more, but she has planned for that. Go now. She is the general, and you are her army. She has been weakened, but her soul is very strong. Give her time. She will be well."

"She'll need more than a morning," Scott said. "Her heart . . . has she suffered a heart attack?"

"She will live, and she will be strong for as long as she is needed. Until the changing of the guard. Please. The other sisters and I will care for her. Right now, you must go."

Scott took Melanie's hand again. Followed by Rainier, they walked out the front doors of the church.

For the first time, there were other people there. The sisters. In their black habits and carrying brooms. They were sweeping up the bone dust, but they paused, bowing their heads slightly in acknowledgment, as the three of them left.

"How do we know how long to stay gone?" Scott asked.

"I say we come back by full noon," Rainier

303

said. "When the sun is highest."

They reached the car and drove back to the hotel. Melanie leaned her head against the window and wondered if the evil thing — essence? demon? — had been able to get into her head because in some way she truly was evil herself.

She felt Rainier place a hand on her shoulder in comfort, though she knew he had no idea what had happened. When they reached the hotel, she offered the two men a smile. "I wonder what people think? This is the second time we've shown back up here looking filthy, so let's go through the courtyard this time. Gentlemen, I'm off to shower. And to sleep. I'll get a wake-up call for eleven."

She quickly left them, hurrying down the hall. She headed straight for her shower, discarding her clothing as she walked, suddenly anxious to remove anything that had been touched by that skeletal army.

In the shower, she let the steam swirl around her. She scrubbed her hair, thinking how ironic it was that she was cleaning up only to go right back into the land of dead.

She didn't want to hear the echo of the voice in her mind, and she tried to drown it out with the pounding of the water.

But it wasn't enough.

I know what you are. I know what you are. . . .

Evil.

11

Scott saw that the door to Melanie's room was closed, and he respected her obvious need for distance. As he turned toward his own door, he found himself trying to understand the look he'd seen on her face when he had come upon her facing the last of the standing skeletons.

Horror.

But why?

There had been a time when he might have been paralyzed by the concept of a reanimated skeleton, but since that night in the alley — the night of his Becoming — as he thought of it — he wasn't easily daunted. Just last night, dozens of bizarrely dressed people had appeared in an alley to attack him, and that now seemed only one more part of the strange journey. Melanie had faced everything he had and probably more. She'd gone after the attackers the night of the quake like a pro, without even blinking.

She hadn't even wanted his help. She'd entered the fray in the alley as if she were a seasoned soldier.

But today . . .

He didn't understand. He wanted to. He had ached to see her looking so horrified, so filled with . . . self-loathing. . . .

He got out of the shower and donned clean clothes, anxious to see if she had emerged from her room. She wasn't there, though she must have made a brief appearance, because Rainier was sitting there, a stack of maps, guidebooks and texts at his side, a cup of coffee in front of him, and a pensive look on his face. Scott sat next to him, and picked up something called *The New Testament Guide to Angels and Demons.*

"There's a difference between demonic possession and the influence of a demon, did you know that?" Rainier asked him, then mused, "I wonder how ancient demons really are?"

"I don't know, but the Bible says angels existed long before man, and demons are fallen angels, so I assume they were around before men, too."

Rainier tossed him another book. It held quotes from the *Torah,* the *New Testament,* the *Koran* and many more ancient texts, including several written by the Canaanites.

307

"As far as I can discover," Rainier said, "the trouble with demons is that we let them in. They're jealous, so once they're here, they hate us and want what we have. There are also a lot of references in there regarding prophecies and how we make them self-fulfilling. The Mayans were waiting for the return of Kulkulcan — and instead they got the Spanish invaders, who they looked on as gods, leading to their own destruction. Their prophecies and calendars run in cycles, and every twenty years a new cycle begins. Pretty much every society believed in a supreme being — even in polytheistic societies, there was one god above all the others. Which corresponds to our God, and the angels, saints — and demons."

"And, according to my reading, most saw man as a creature with a soul, a life force, that would live on, or live again, in one way or another," Scott added as he leaned back, lacing his fingers behind his head. "I grew up Roman Catholic — with a little voodoo thrown in here and there. I'm one of those weird people who still really loves ritual, I guess. But, even as a kid, I couldn't fathom why a child born in Africa or Asia, who had never heard of Catholicism, would go to Hell. My assumption is that we really *are* one people, and we just see some things in different ways. So the way to fight a demon, any demon, old or new, would be with the ritual of our own beliefs. The prophecy isn't that the Christian world will face Armageddon, but that mankind itself will face the Apocalypse."

Rainier nodded, smiling at him in agreement. He stood up suddenly. "Let's take a drive."

Scott straightened, frowning. "What about Melanie . . . ? I'm not sure we should leave her alone. She seemed a bit . . . off."

"She'll be all right. She's stronger than she knows herself. And we won't be more than half an hour," Rainier assured him.

"Give me a minute."

He walked to Melanie's door and considered knocking, but cracked the door open instead. She was on her bed and appeared to be sleeping. Good. She needed the rest.

"All right, I'll just leave her a note, letting her know we'll be right back," Scott told him.

"We can pick up a few things while we're out."

"All right," Scott agreed.

They drove first toward the Palatine Hill. As he navigated the heavy traffic, Scott found himself marveling anew at the beauty and character of Rome. Ancient ruins everywhere, interspersed with the legacy of the Renaissance, the Baroque, the Rococo. Following Rainier's directions, he turned down a side street before reaching the Forum and the Coliseum. The roads were crowded, but Rainier guided him to a parking lot near a church dating back to the medieval era. Great cherubs guarded gold-inlaid doors, and marble reliefs — St. George slaying the dragon, the Madonna and Child, the Last Supper, and more — decorated the outside of the church. "St. Peter in the Garden," Rainier pointed out, as they headed toward the doors.

"Very nice. Are we sightseeing?" Scott asked him.

"In a way. Just follow me. Another church stood here originally, built in the fourth century. The present structure dates from the fifteenth. Generations of the Montenegro family are buried here."

"Your family?" Scott asked.

"Yes."

The church was active: pews crowded with people at prayer; a young priest lighting candles at the main altar, a simple marble structure. Side altars and small chapels lined the walls to either side.

"My family," Rainier said, as if in introduction. He had led Scott along the row of chapels on the east side of the church before coming to a dead stop at the tomb of Conte Rainier Michelo Montenegro — God's Warrior, according to the inscription in the stone.

Atop the marble sarcophagus that held the remains of the long-dead conte was a sculpture of the man, clad in medieval armor, his sword lying atop his body, his hands folded over the hilt.

What struck Scott was how much the marble likeness of the man in the tomb resembled Rainier.

Scott let out a soft whistle, then stopped himself in embarrassment when he remembered he was in a church. "That's quite a family resemblance. I'd never have taken you for Italian, you're so fair."

"My mother was a Dane," Rainier said.

"Still, it's amazing. So how many great-greats back is he?" Scott asked.

"None."

The reply was so flat that Scott turned to look at the other man in complete surprise. "What . . . ?"

"I have no ancestor interred here."

"Then who *is* interred here?" Scott asked.

"No one."

"All right, family-legend time. Is this go-

311

ing to help us any?"

"I hope so. This sarcophagus, this tomb, was meant for me."

Scott inhaled. "All right — it's not enough that we're battling skeletons and trying to figure out how to save the world, now you want me to believe that you somehow escaped the grave and you're approximately eight hundred years old?"

"Yes," Rainier said.

Scott turned away in disgust and started walking.

Rainier caught up to him with long strides. "My God, man, haven't you figured it out yet?"

"What are you talking about?" Scott asked.

They were passing the basin of holy water. By rote, he paused and dipped his finger in it, and made the sign of the cross on his forehead. Rainier smiled and did the same.

"Why do you keep denying what *might* be when you're already seen what *is?*" Rainier demanded.

Scott crossed his arms over his chest and stared at Rainier. "Okay, you're eight hundred years old. You wear your age damned well."

"Because I am a vampire," Rainier said. "I am a vampire, Lucien is a vampire — and

312

Melanie is a vampire."

Scott stared at him, then laughed. "Is that what your Alliance is? You're a group of lunatics who think you have to drink blood to stay young?"

"No," Rainier said icily. "We drink blood to stay alive. Or . . . undead."

Scott swore. "You know what? Vampires are nasty, smelly beings with bad teeth. They're evil. They have no souls. I hardly think that the task of saving of the earth would fall to beings who are just as bad as the demons they're supposed to be destroying. If you're trying to make me think less of Melanie, you can give it up. There's nothing evil in her whatsoever."

"You fool," Rainier said. "I'm trying to help you understand her."

"This is bull," Scott said angrily. In the midst of everything else that was going on, he didn't need this kind of crap from Rainier. "Right. You're a vampire. Going out in broad daylight. Standing in a church. Crossing yourself with holy water. I don't think so."

"Really? You know so many vampires? They've clued you in to the truth — and not the legend? You — who have battled living skeletons and dreamed of catacombs with a link to Hell — dare to call me a liar?"

Scott didn't know what he thought. Rainier appeared to be serious, but . . . he couldn't be. This was just . . .

Totally insane, but . . . not . . . impossible.

"What do you think you were fighting in that alley by the church the other night?"

"Wait, wait, wait," Scott said, staring the other man in the eye. "You're trying to tell me that you're a vampire — all warm and fuzzy — and those wackos the other night were vampires, too? Make up your mind, why don't you?"

Scott realized he had spoken too loudly when he saw a nun at prayer looked up at him in disapproval.

He shook his head in disgust, turned and left the church. Rainier followed him, stopping him before he reached the car.

"Wait. We need more than flashlights before we go back to the catacombs," Rainier said. "Follow me."

Scott followed. He was so on edge that it felt as if electricity were twitching through his limbs. This was all just too bizarre. Rainier seemed to be a decent guy, except for the part where he thought he was a vampire.

The man was certifiably crazy.

No. He wasn't. He was telling the truth.

Admittedly, there was no way they had all

hallucinated the bone army, or that he had made up what happened the night in the alley when he had been touched by a dying man, or the disappearing corpses from the alley by the church. But that was a far cry from vampires — especially good vampires.

And Melanie a vampire? That was ridiculous. He'd held her, kissed her, made mad love with her, and she was human. Smart, strong, good in a fight — but human.

They walked along the outside of the church until they reached a side door. Rainier tapped on it, and someone opened it just a crack. Rainier spoke in rapid Italian, and the door opened fully. A small, wizened priest let them into a small room holding only a bed, a desk and an open closet that held vestments. A Bible was open on the desk, and there was but a single lamp. This was a man of the cloth who lived simply indeed.

The elderly priest smiled at Scott, and blessed him swiftly, speaking Latin. Then he led them to a door, and opened it, revealing a stone stairway that led to the crypts below.

"Why are we here?" Scott asked. Should he be afraid? he wondered. Was he being lured to the lair of some cult — the Alliance, maybe — so he could be drained of blood?

Could he be drained of blood?

Logically, the answer was yes. He still nicked himself shaving.

At the base of the old stone stairway were iron gates that led to a seemingly endless row of crypts. But they didn't head into the crypts. Instead, the priest opened the door to a storage chamber. He pulled three canvas bags from one shelf and began to fill them with strange odds and ends, including mysterious vials and crosses — all of which looked very old — of wood, silver and gold. Along with the ancient relics, he included a number of flashlights, lanterns, small sharply honed spikes, cigarette lighters, flares and what looked and smelled like small torches doused in oil. When he had completed his task, he spoke so rapidly to Rainier that Scott caught nothing but *chiesa,* church, and the name Maria Elizabeta. And this man was a priest who, like Father O'Hara, seemed to know Rainier well. And Rainier seemed to respect the priest.

Vampire. Right.

With a smile, Scott thanked the priest. He was good at *"Grazie."*

"Now we can go back," Rainier told him.

The bags were heavy. Scott tossed the two he carried into the back of the car, staring at Rainier. "We're fighting a demon with holy water and stakes? I thought that was how you fought vampires?"

"Ritual. The power lies in faith and belief," Rainier said. "I know where we can get guns, too, but I honestly don't think they'd do us much good."

Scott looked at his watch as he slid into the driver's seat. "Melanie should be awake by now," he said. "We should hurry back. It's nearly noon. We need to get to the church and pray that Sister Maria Elizabeta is doing better."

Sean was somewhere with Blake, Lucien was finalizing his plans to fly to Rome, and she missed her children and was anxious to go home, Maggie mused. But Lucien had asked that she and Sean stay where they were, because he was certain that events in L.A. weren't over yet. At least Judy had stopped by to keep her company.

Even though a slow romance seemed to be developing between Blake and Judy — even the two dogs got along great — the other woman still sometimes seemed lonely, so the two of them had met for dinner at the same place on the Strip where she and Melanie had been when the quake struck. They ate, talked about kids, dogs and men, and then headed out.

It wasn't late, but the street didn't seem to be crowded. As they walked down the block toward Judy's car, Maggie paused. The fissure that had opened in the street there had yet to be repaired. Cones and aluminum fences and warning signs surrounded it, but it still gaped in the combined light of the moon and the streetlights. As she glanced over toward it, a sense of unease filled her. She blinked, and suddenly she heard a fluttering in the air and saw a thick stream of black mist rising from the fissure.

"Dogs are the best companions," Judy was saying. "They love you no matter what. But —"

"Judy, we have to get to the car now," Maggie said. "Hurry."

She took Judy's arm, ready to run. But Judy was wearing spike heels, and running was not a possibility.

"Maggie, what's the matter with you?" Judy demanded.

The fluttering sound was growing louder. Then the first of them stepped from around a telephone pole.

He was a young man in his twenties. He was in a casual suit and looked a little bit like a wannabe producer, except that his hair was too long.

And his teeth, when he opened his mouth, were *way* too long.

Maggie felt the second presence circling around from behind them and turned to look. This one was a girl in a slinky silk dress that would have done Carole Lombard proud. Her lips were bloodred but not dripping yet, which eased Maggie's mind somewhat.

The third had apparently been a rapper at one time. He was laden with heavy gold chains. And the fourth was a Valley girl, miniskirt and all.

"Judy, keep behind me," Maggie warned.

"What are you talk —" Judy started to protest, but then the first vampire flew right at them. Maggie had her hand in her purse already, her fingers curling around one of the small stakes she carried at all times. She caught him dead center in the chest and he dropped.

The Valley girl let out a howl of fury and came at them next, teeth bared, fangs dripping with saliva. Maggie pushed Judy behind her and reached for a second stake. The girl ducked, but Maggie grabbed her shoulder and threw her off, then gored her.

The rapper came next, along with the Carole Lombard clone. Two of them. Maggie fought two-handed, catching the rapper in the chest but missing Carole Lombard. The vampiress was almost on top of her when she suddenly stopped in shock and fell.

Maggie turned. Behind her stood Judy Bobalink, one shoe in hand, the stiletto heel dripping with the gory brown blood of the creature. As the corpses began to putrefy and fall to dust before them, Judy started to shake.

Maggie grabbed her. They had to get away. Quickly. She managed to rid the other woman of her second shoe. Then she grabbed her arm and dragged her the remaining distance to the car.

What the hell . . . ? Maggie wondered as they ran.

The fissure in the road seemed to be a conduit for evil to enter the world, controlling those it touched.

Just how many similar fissures were there in the city?

And in the world?

Because of the SUV's strange cargo, Scott was very careful to lock it when they got back to the hotel. He hurried to the suite, Rainier following, and all but threw the door open.

His note had been replaced by one from

Melanie.

Went for coffee; be right back, it read.

"She's getting coffee," Scott told Rainier, then went into Melanie's bedroom. He knew he should have felt as if he were trespassing, but he didn't. He looked around, even checked under the bed. Hell, if she had traveled with a coffin, he would know it, wouldn't he? Just one more reason to dismiss Rainier's claims out of hand.

And speak of the devil, Rainier was standing in the doorway, watching him sympathetically, as if he knew the thoughts and feelings Scott was struggling with.

"Okay, so having to sleep in a coffin filled with one's native earth is myth, right?" Scott asked harshly.

Rainier only walked into the room and looked around for a moment. There was a small jewelry case by the bed. He picked it up and offered it to Scott.

Scott did feel guilty now, really delving into her personal belongings, but he couldn't help himself. He opened the jewelry box and almost dropped it. It was filled with earth.

"Technically, we can get away from it for quite some time, but having some nearby does make sleeping easier. You know — like a baby's blankie," Rainier explained.

Scott closed the box and set it back down on her bedside table. He felt sick — no, beyond sick — as the indisputable truth stared him in the face.

"You want more proof?" Rainier asked softly. "Open the minibar."

Scott stared at him. He didn't want to do it.

He did it anyway.

He saw several bottles of what looked, at first glance, like cherry soda.

He thought of the red drop near her lips when she had returned from the restroom on the plane.

He locked the minibar door and stared at Rainier. "None of this means anything. I'm from New Orleans. I've met lots of so-called vampires."

Rainier stared back at him and shrugged. Then suddenly, and with a violence and viciousness that seemed like a dagger straight through Scott's heart, he changed. His face became a mask made to evoke terror. He bared his teeth and revealed eyeteeth that had elongated and looked like the fangs of a cobra.

As quickly as it had come, the change was gone. If he had blinked at the wrong moment, Scott would have missed it.

They were still standing there, staring at

one another, when the outer door opened. "Hey, where are you two?" Melanie called.

She saw Rainier first, then rushed through the doorway into her room and stared at Scott, stricken.

If he hadn't already believed before, he would have then. The look on her face told him that it was true, all true. He didn't know what he felt anymore, what he should do. He did know that the way he handled this moment would affect the rest of his life.

However long that might be.

Melanie spun on Rainier. "You . . . what did you tell him?" she demanded.

"The truth," Rainier said softly. "He had to know. He has to be prepared."

"But *we're* not even prepared for this," she said weakly, and then she turned to stare at Scott again.

"I'm sorry," she said. "I should have let you know. . . . I mean, you have the right to be . . . to loathe me."

"Loathe you?" Scott asked quietly. "Melanie, I adore you. Nothing could make me feel any different about you."

Okay, he was lying like hell, but he was confused. He did adore her — or the woman he'd thought she was, anyway — so where did that put him? Where did that put any of them? What the hell had happened to the normal world?

She was still just staring at him, her eyes filled with torment.

He kept talking.

"I think I have it all straight. Somewhere along the line, we're all souls. And in death, the same as in life, we're good, bad and in between. And what we are in life, that's what we are in death. And in being . . . undead. So seeing as how we're trying to fight a demon, I think it's very important that we have me — whatever I am — *and* you, with whatever talents you have that I don't really know about yet." Had he made the least bit of sense? he wondered.

Maybe not, because she didn't say a thing in response, just turned to stare accusingly at Rainier.

"Melanie, he had the right to know. I had to tell him," Rainier said.

She nodded finally.

Did he feel the same way about her? Scott wondered.

He walked over to her and set his hands on her shoulders. Her eyes were still that beautiful crystal-blue — with that tinge of gold. He couldn't help wondering if they'd been that way in life, too.

She should have been cold, according to legend, but she still felt warm and vibrant.

He looked into her eyes and still saw her . . . soul? The wonder, beauty and courage that were uniquely her, certainly.

He smiled and he kissed her lips, and she started to cry. He felt the saltiness of her tears. She didn't kiss him back at first, but finally her arms went around him, and if someone had told him that she was Medusa in the flesh and snakes would sprout from her head and kill him if he looked, he wouldn't have cared.

From the doorway, Rainier cleared his throat. "Enough with all the mushy stuff, huh? We need to get back to the church."

Melanie still had a shimmer of a question in her eyes as they broke apart. Scott offered her his most gentle smile. "We're going to do our part to save the world," he said. "And we're going to be together."

She smiled at last. Maybe there was still a little disbelief in her smile, but there was hope, too.

Scott took her hand and headed for the doorway. He was about to exit the suite when he paused, then went back to the table for one of the books he'd been looking at earlier.

"We're going after a demon," he reminded the others. "We need all the help we can get."

Then they then headed out to the car, as if nothing in the world had happened, nothing had changed.

As they drove, Melanie inspected one of the canvas bags they had acquired at the church. As she did, Scott's phone rang, and he handed it to her to answer. She glanced at the caller ID, and answered it. "Maggie?" A pause and then, "You have to try, and you have to get the word out. Have you spoken to Lucien?" Another pause.

"All right. If I can figure out anything that will help, I'll call you right away."

She hung up.

Scott glanced over at her. She was pale again. Very pale.

"Maggie was out with Judy and they were attacked by four vampires who seemed to have come out of a fissure left over from the earthquake. She said that she saw something black, like a shadow, and then the vampires came."

"Is she all right?" Rainier asked.

"Is she a vampire, too?" Scott heard himself ask.

"No, not anymore," Melanie said, distracted. She glanced at him then. "She's the only case I have ever heard about in which . . . someone became totally human again. And Sean never was a vampire. She

326

said that Judy is still in shock. And Lucien is coming."

Imagine that, Scott thought dryly.

"Lucien is on his way here?" Rainier asked.

"Yes, and that's good, but also kind of strange, because he thought his only role was to point me in the right direction. . . . And it's bad, too, because now Maggie is having problems in California," Melanie said.

"Maggie — who isn't a vampire," Scott said.

"But she does know how to kill one," Melanie said grimly. "As does Sean. . . . I think maybe now they'll have to tell Blake Reynaldo what's going on."

She fell silent, thoughtful.

Scott had a million questions he wanted to ask, though he wasn't sure he really wanted all the answers. Can you fly? Can you turn into a bat . . . ? How about a wolf? Can you disappear in a cloud of dust?

When did you become a vampire?

He decided to let it rest for the moment, except for one critical question.

"In a fight, how does this work?" he asked. "Do you have any special powers I should know about?"

"We can be injured, but we heal quickly,"

Rainier answered. "Lop off our heads — and we die, just like anybody else. A stake through the heart will do it, too. That much is true. We do need blood to survive. Neither Melanie nor I have bitten anyone in . . . well, a very long time. We acquire our blood, if not always legally, at all times morally. And, yes, we can do something that's a lot like flying. It's something to do with the molecules in the body, but no one — not even the scientists and doctors among us — has actually figured it out."

"And you paid for a flight?" Scott asked Melanie. "First class, even."

"It's very hard to get this far," Melanie said, looking out the window. "It's draining. I needed my strength for when I got here."

"All right," Scott said. It certainly made sense, anyway.

Rainier leaned forward to talk more easily. "I was the defender of the church," he said. "I was knighted. I could best any man at a tournament. Then a noble of Ascencia attacked and tried to sack the church. We fought them off, but I was badly wounded. The priests tended to me in the church, but despite their efforts, I died. The thing is, I had been having an affair with the nobleman's daughter, and I hadn't realized just how thoroughly I had been seduced. She

328

was one of those wickedly passionate lovers. I'd never really realized that her ardent grazes and nips were *bites.* I woke that night in the church with a ravenous hunger, and so I went after my enemy and his cohorts. Not a man survived. It was a bloodbath, and when it was over, even I was horrified. I was a hero, yes, but everyone was terrified of me. I managed to stage a new death for myself, and I watched as I was buried with tremendous honor. I spent hundreds of years wandering, and for many of those years, I — and the others of my kind I encountered — stayed hidden, and we were selective in choosing our victims. Many of our number were destroyed, and many more should have been. For quite a while, I was a kind of vigilante. When someone was slipping through the loopholes in the legal system after committing a terrible crime, I decided they were fair game. But as the world and technology changed, blood banks and hospitals became far more available. I met Lucien, and I went back to my church. The priest you met today knows who and what I am, and has helped me, as his father helped me before him. I've traveled widely, but Roma is my home, and I cannot see it destroyed."

Scott knew that he was looking expectantly at Melanie, but she wasn't saying a thing. He'd claimed that it didn't matter. Maybe he needed to prove that to himself.

Once again, he parked as close to the church as he could get, and they walked the rest of the way, each of them carrying one of the canvas bags. Looking around as they approached, Scott couldn't see a single sign of the battle they had fought that morning.

"Do you think Sister Maria Elizabeta is still here? That she's all right?" Melanie asked, whispering suddenly. "Or do you think they've taken her back to the convent?"

"I think she's here," Scott said. "I'm sure some of the other nuns are with her, but I don't think she would have left."

He was right. The elderly nun was still there, as were Sister Ana and a few of the younger sisters. Sister Maria Elizabeta was still lying on one of the pews, her head on a small kneeler pillow, and they had brought water for her. Her fellow nuns surrounded her as if she were the queen penguin and they were her offspring.

Scott walked over and knelt down in front of her. "Is it time?"

She looked at him, and she seemed distraught. "This church has guarded the world from evil for many years. The catacombs themselves are not evil, nor are the dead. It is the demon who lurks below the earth, hating us for basking in the light of the sun and the love of God. The demon is seeking escape, and my fear is that he will find it because there are people who fear the wrath of the prophecy and so, whether they mean to or not, they will make it come true." She took a deep breath, her expression one of pain, and not only physical pain. "I wasn't strong enough. He has slipped through because of me."

"No, I don't believe that. We were down there. Perhaps we somehow freed him."

Melanie knelt down, too. "He may be raising an army of the damned, but we will find the way to stop him."

The sister lifted her hand and placed it on Melanie's. "Do you know how old I am, child? Did Lucien ever tell you?" There was suddenly a slight twinkle in her eye. "Not so old as Conte Rainier, but I am over a hundred, and as I measure time, that is a very long life indeed, so long that I am afraid I haven't the strength to play my part anymore."

Scott was stunned. It had never occurred to him that she had known all along that she was allying herself with vampires.

"We will be your strength, I promise," Melanie vowed to her. She patted the canvas bag she had slung over her shoulder. "We're ready for whatever comes."

The sister continued to look disturbed. "I can feel that he has found cracks and weaknesses across the world. We must work fast. He can animate the dead, he has collected hordes of the damned, and they all stand ready to do his bidding. Not even I know what you will face down there. He plays with the mind, and he can slip into your thoughts and dreams."

Yes, Scott realized, he'd had proof of that.

"If we're going to do this, we must start now, before the moon rises," Rainier said.

As if the church were a stage and they had received their cue, the sisters fanned out across the pews and fell to their knees.

It was a nice send-off. And a frightening one.

Scott rose, looked at Rainier and started for the trapdoor. He pulled it open and started down, aware of the darkness first, and then of something else.

A pulse. A feeling of hot, fetid breath. The presence of something vile and evil that seemed to throb throughout the underbelly of the church, the catacombs and beyond, into the depths of the earth.

Bael, Baal, Balor . . . By any name, whoever, whatever he was — he was waiting.

12

Scott paused on the steps, steps that had changed, even in the course of night. The ancient stone now seemed to be covered in something lichenous and sticky, like a strange quicksand.

He lit one of the flares they had acquired at Rainier's church, and he tossed it down to the ground below. In the light it gave off, he saw the altar with the panels written in three languages and the walls of the crypt. He hurried down the last few steps, letting the flare burn on the cold earthen floor. He waited until Rainier and Melanie came to stand beside him.

Rainier dug into his bag and lit another flare, which he tossed down the nearest tunnel that led away from the altar.

"Wait," Melanie said, and dug around in her bag until she found a cross.

As she handed it to him, Scott realized it wasn't just a cross; the bottom end had been honed to make a stake of it, as well. He wondered if he should expect to meet vampires down there. *More* vampires, he corrected himself, remembering the alley outside the church, not to mention his companions.

From above, he heard a sweet chanting, and he knew that the sisters were in prayer, raising their voices high. He smiled.

"What if he's called upon Jewish vampires? Or Buddhist ones?" Scott asked, his voice a whisper so as not to drown out the comforting sound of the sisters above.

"It's not their faith, it's your faith in yourself and your quest that matters," Rainier told him.

"And in Sister Maria Elizabeta," Melanie added quietly.

Scott knew they were all thinking the same thing. She was the Oracle, and they had been called to her side. What were they without her — except sitting ducks?

"Let's see what he has waiting for us, shall we?" Rainier said.

Rainier's flare lit the way. They were all tall and the ceiling was low, just inches above them. Scott moved slowly, knowing that he had now truly reached the nightmare place of his dreams. He looked to both sides. Some of the crypts were empty, some held ancient bones.

"God's waters," he heard Melanie say, and he saw that she had taken out a vial and was sprinkling water from it on the corpses. He assumed it was holy water, given to Rainier earlier.

She repeated the words, but if she'd been expecting the bones to respond, she was doomed to disappointment, because nothing happened.

Scott led the way farther down the tunnel, and when Rainier's flare went out and the darkness ahead took over, Scott lit another and tossed it ahead to light their way. He could see that they were coming to the place where the ancient pagan altar stood and where the eleven other tunnels met, and he blessed whatever lucky spirit had led Rainier to choose this tunnel instead of one of the others.

"God's waters," Melanie said again.

Rainier stopped for a moment. "Did that one just move?" he asked, pointing to one of the skeletons she had just sprinkled.

Neither Melanie nor Scott had an answer.

"No matter, why take a chance?" Rainier asked, and he used his cross to smash in the skull.

Scott continued in the lead, and he was nearing the tunnel's end when he heard the whisper in his head again.

Vampires. Good vampires. That's a laugh, a joke. They are vile creatures, tearing at human flesh and thriving on human blood. They are not human as you are, not anymore. They have lured you here. They will bring you to the altar and lay you upon it. They will rip out your throat and bathe in your blood, and then they will fornicate there, slick with the blood of your body as they writhe together in lust and hunger.

Scott stopped short and looked back. Rainier and Melanie just looked at him expectantly.

"He's whispering to me," he said, fighting the fear the whisper evoked in his heart. "He's entering my mind, and he'll try it with all of us."

Melanie let out a little sound. "He's already told me that I'm evil, vile and loathsome."

"He wants me to believe that I'm a coward. And that I should kill you, Scott, because you're not one of us."

Scott smiled. "He thinks we're weak," he announced loudly. "But we're not."

A roaring sound began to shake the very walls of the tunnel.

A fetid wind rose.

Scott kept walking, and when he turned

to look back, they were nowhere in sight.

Melanie and Rainier were gone.

He was alone, facing that ancient altar and the wind that blew, filled now with black mist and sharp grains of sand. He blinked against it, holding the cross in his hands.

Such a fool. They are coming. You know in your heart that they are the evil. See her now, see how she comes. She is naked and laughing at you. Her fangs are bared, and he is behind her, both of them ready to tear you apart. She'll sink her teeth into your throat, and she'll rip at your genitals, until the blood pours over her. She'll watch you die as he stands behind her, and then they'll touch one another and rut on the floor while you breathe your last and the blood drains from you. . . .

As the words played in his mind, he saw the exact images the whisper promised. He saw Melanie, and she was naked and laughing, her teeth bared, fangs that dripped in salacious anticipation. She was coming toward him, and Rainier, just as naked, was laughing with the satisfaction of a great cat that had finally treed its prey and was now awaiting the first taste of blood.

Melanie kept coming, but something in his heart denied that it was her. He raised the cross and began chanting a prayer remembered from childhood, and when she was close enough, he drove the pointed end of the cross into her chest.

He heard her scream rise shrill and furious into the air, and he finally saw her clearly then. It wasn't Melanie, but it was a vampire, and as he watched she decayed before his eyes, skin drying and cracking. Her flesh flaked away, leaving only bone, a skeleton with its jaw gaping in that final scream that still echoed through the crypt, and then she fell, dust to dust and nothing more.

The man behind her was real, but not Rainier. In a fury, he seemed to levitate and come flying at Scott, who lifted his weapon in both hands, caught the creature dead center in the chest and twisted, finding the heart.

The man, too, decayed and fell, then exploded into dust upon the hard ground by the altar.

The whisper in his mind came again.

They are watching, laughing at you, whispering, because you are just a man and a fool. Rainier will take what you want, and the witch is ready for him, crawling atop him, licking him, fornicating with him. . . .

Scott almost laughed that time. "Oh, go fuck yourself!" he snapped, and when he turned, he saw that Rainier was there and looking at him curiously.

"What is it?" Rainier asked.

"Nothing important," Scott assured him. "Where's Melanie?"

"Right behind me — just like I'm right behind you. I saw you take down those two vampires, and I took down a third."

"But where's Melanie?" Scott asked again, beginning to panic. "Turn around and look. She's not there."

She didn't know what had happened. One minute they were right in front of her, and then, suddenly, they were gone. She turned and looked frantically around, then came to a dead standstill.

Scott *was* there, staring at her — and he had his cross raised, ready to strike. "You're the evil here," he said, "and we both know it. You've made the others believe in a demon, but we both know that you're the real demon here. You're not a woman, you're a snake. You're every creeping thing in the night that is filthy and disgusting. When you are destroyed, evil will be destroyed."

He was coming toward her, and she needed to defend herself. "I am not evil." She meant to scream, to cry out, but she barely managed a whisper.

"Melanie!"

Scott! He was calling her name from somewhere ahead. The thing in front of her was not Scott. It was a skeleton, nothing more than bones, a skull with black eye sockets and a ridiculous grin clicking its jaws. She screamed in fury and tossed holy water it. It crumpled and turned entirely to dust.

And then Scott was there, the real Scott. He took her into his arms and lifted her chin, and she saw his dark eyes, fierce and protective. "Never believe his whispers — never. It's a mind game. You are everything that is good and fine. Remember that. I know what you are, and that's everything pure and decent. Believe it, Melanie. Even if you doubt yourself, believe *me*."

She smiled at him and straightened. "Rainier!" she cried suddenly. "We have to find Rainier. We can't let the demon separate us."

They rushed forward back to the altar room, where Rainier was just withdrawing the business end of his cross from a decaying corpse, one that smelled to high heaven and didn't decay into dust. Rainier looked at them as he wiped his weapon clean on the dead creature's coat.

"Apparently he didn't realize just how

damned old I am," he said, and kicked the corpse. "New vampires. Idiots."

The wind rushed at them again with a screeching and wailing that grew in fury and pitch. Suddenly bones began spinning about, and they heard feet running. From each of the twelve tunnels, the dead — and the undead — suddenly came running.

"They're here!" Melanie cried.

And they were. The three of them braced their backs against the altar as the onslaught rushed toward them. Melanie hurled her almost-empty vial at the slim virago hurtling down at her, flesh not bone, and then, as the vial shattered against her and splashed its contents over her, bone and not flesh. Melanie grabbed another vial as Scott realized in shock that there really was something to that belief thing. Apparently holy water could destroy an evil vampire, perhaps simply because the evil undead believed in its power, while Rainier could cross himself with it with impunity.

And speaking of Rainier, he lit an oil-soaked torch and thrust it into the chest of an attacking cadaver, which burst into flames and, whirling, took more of its fellows down with it. They came, soldiers of the bone army that had to be killed by crushing their skulls, accompanied by Ba-

342

el's other army of the undead — vampires, cruel in life, now cruel in death.

Scott felt hot breath at his back, so close. Melanie turned from her own battle to sprinkle the creature with the deadly water.

But they kept coming, more and more of them.

Scott had never felt his own strength so keenly. Like the others, he used fire, holy water, his cross, his fists and his feet, and the ground grew deep around him with the detritus of bone and flesh and decay. But still they came.

Scott began to chant, the words coming unbidden to his lips. He heard Melanie join him, then Rainier, and they followed when he switched to Latin, and then a language he didn't even recognize, but he knew the prayer was the same each time. *Yea, though I walk through the valley of the shadow of death, I will fear no evil. . . .*

So, so many of them.

And then, so suddenly that the silence seemed deafening, the crypt went silent. The three of them stood, waiting, startled by the sound of one another's movements.

"It's over — for now," Scott said.

"This was just the prelude," Rainier said.

"It's him. Bael. We have to find him and destroy him, or at least send him to some eternal damnation. It's the only way to win," Scott said wearily.

He looked at the others. "The most important thing is this — we can't let him into our minds. He preys upon our slightest fear. He's trying to turn us against each other. He hopes to destroy us from within, just as he hopes the havoc he creates with earthquakes and his minions will cause people to turn against each other, paying with their souls as well as their lives."

"He was getting to me," Melanie whispered. "I never knew I could be so weak."

"You're not weak," Scott protested. "None of us were prepared to have him slip into our minds."

"Let's go," Rainier said. "We're done for now. He's licking his wounds, and we're worn out. If he's preparing, we need to do the same."

They trudged back along the tunnel. Scott took the rear that time, and he splashed holy water on all the skeletons remaining in their niches. Most fell to dust as the water hit them. Good. That meant there would be fewer left to rise against them later at the demon's bidding. But Rome was ancient. There were millions of bodies hidden in catacombs and cemeteries all through the eternal city, empty shells just waiting for the demon to reanimate them. Millions of them.

As Scott followed Melanie back up the steps and into the church, he heard her sharp intake of breath.

He quickly followed her to the pew where the nuns were grouped around Sister Maria Elizabeta. Several were sobbing softly.

"No, no, she can't be . . . dead," Scott said. She was lying on the pew, just as she had been before, but her face was the color of death.

"She's still breathing," Sister Ana said. "But . . ." She sat back, stretching her spine and neck as if she had been bent over for too long. "He is coming," she said. "He is coming."

"Bael?" Scott asked.

"No," Sister Ana said. "The Oracle."

"But Sister Maria Elizabeta is the Oracle," Scott protested. She couldn't die. If she did, they were lost.

"Just as you were chosen to receive the power of another, so will there be another Oracle," Sister Ana said. "We must keep her alive until he comes, lest the weakness of her flesh let Bael in to corrupt her soul."

"Then let's get her to a hospital," Melanie said.

"A hospital will not change things," Sister Ana said.

Sister Maria Elizabeta opened her eyes then. She saw Melanie and reached out, groping for her. Melanie took her hand and sank down by her as the old nun squeezed her hand painfully. Then the aged nun began to speak.

"The fissures . . . they are opening all over. Everywhere. Faith comes from within, and it's what . . . I've seen them. Tell your friends that faith comes from within. . . . For centuries this church, and even the pagan temple below, have caged him, but he is escaping. The battle begins here, but it will not end here. I was weak, and he broke the seal. You've seen . . . you've seen the shadows. There is another place. I have seen it in my sleep, and you . . . you have felt it. Do not worry. You will find it. But the word must be spread. Tell them . . . to remember, faith is what frees us. We bear it within us, and it is different for us all."

Her grip on Melanie eased, and Melanie stared at Sister Ana in panic. Sister Ana smiled. "She is still with us. She will not leave until the new Oracle is with us."

"Should we take her back to the convent?" Rainier asked.

"She is comfortable here. I have her heart medicines, and so long as we are here, we can see what comes from the earth, can stand what vigil we are able to, and she can still touch you in her dreams. You must rest now, and prepare for the next assault."

"Perhaps we should take the offense, rather than waiting for the attack," Scott said.

Rainier disagreed. "There's so much we still don't know. If only we understood what it will take to win the *final* battle . . ."

"The Roman Empire did not collapse because of a single great cataclysm," Sister Ana reminded them. "It was eaten away from within and weakened. You must fight your battle and your battle alone. The answers will come if you hold true to your course. Go now and rest. We are watching, we are guarding."

There was nothing else to do. Scott nodded. Melanie planted a kiss on Sister Maria Elizabeta's forehead, and they filed out.

The sun was still high above the horizon. Birds chirped, and a soft breeze blew. It was a beautiful summer's day. The world seemed ridiculously normal as the three of them stood before the church, looking at one another in shock and exhaustion and fear.

"She *is* dying. And she's our link. If we don't finish this . . ." Melanie said. "And we *can't* finish it without her."

"You heard Sister Ana. Someone else is

coming," Scott said.

"Well, we're not getting anywhere standing here," Rainier said. "We need to reload and rearm, read more, keep going until we do have the answers."

"I know what we need to do," Scott said, suddenly certain. "Take a tour."

"What?" Melanie said, puzzled.

"A tour. The Coliseum, the Palatine Hill, the Forum."

"Scott, I'm not really sure this is the time for seeing the sights," Melanie said.

"I know what you mean," Rainier said, looking at Scott. "The shadows."

Scott nodded. "Maybe I'm crazy. But, hey, everything else is crazy, so why not me, too?"

"Let's do it," Rainier said. "We'll stop by the church for some more weapons, then head out like good little tourists and see what we can see."

"Why not? It's not like I'm going to be able to sleep, anyway," Melanie agreed.

"One day, hopefully, I'll get to sleep for a week," Scott said. He looked at Melanie, not caring that Rainier was there in his certainty that she needed to hear what he was going to say next. "With you beside me," he said softly.

She studied him gravely. "I guess we have

to keep the world spinning on its axis if we're going to sleep for a week."

"Shall we get on with it, then?" Rainier suggested. He was staring at Scott with an odd light in his eyes and a half smile curving his lips. The other man approved, Scott thought, and the knowledge made him happy.

As they headed to the church for supplies, Melanie, heedless of the time back in L.A., put through a call to Maggie and repeated everything that Sister Maria Elizabeta had said.

Especially the part about faith.

Maggie, Sean, Blake and Judy were all gathered in Melanie's apartment, along with both dogs. Blake, Maggie knew, was worrying about Judy's sanity, and Sean was silent, just looking out the window, watching.

"Blake, you didn't see them. I did," Judy insisted stubbornly.

"Sweetie, *vampires?*"

It was Bruno who warned them with a huge baying sound.

"They're here," Sean said, and stepped back from the window just as a massive black bat came crashing through the glass.

Sean was ready, but the creature was fast. It began to transform even before it landed.

The face became that of a wizened old man, whose expression mirrored the creature's snub-nosed visage. The fangs didn't change at all. They only enlarged. The vampire was bald and hideous.

Sean grabbed the broomstick he had broken and sharpened earlier; even as the thing rose, he slammed the point into its chest. It let out a furious shriek, and began flapping and jerking spasmodically, before bursting into ash and dust.

Blake Reynaldo, seasoned cop, was on his feet then, staring in disbelief. "Jesus, Mary and Joseph," he breathed and crossed himself.

"There will be more," Maggie warned.

There was a sudden flurry of wings and shrill, squeaking cries that filled the night, and then the creatures began coming and coming and coming.

Judy Bobalink didn't scream when one of the creatures headed for Miss Tiffany. "Bastard!" she declared, and she grabbed a lamp from the table, swinging it with all her might against the thing. It crashed against the wall, and Sean speared it.

Maggie went to work. Even before her conversation with Melanie, she'd made sure that she was sitting with the fire poker and a lighter in hand. She set several of them on fire, and when they faltered and fell, she speared them with the poker. Blake was one hell of a good cop; he caught on quickly. He drew a lighter from his pocket and mimicked Maggie, going after them with fire.

The dogs bayed.

The creatures screamed, burst into ash and fell.

And then it was over.

Blake was shaking, and staring at Judy.

"See?" she said.

Blake nodded, then looked questioningly at Maggie.

"They're coming out of at least one of the fissures left from the quake," she said.

"What the hell are we supposed to do? I can't arrest steam or smoke or — bats!" Blake complained.

"No, you can't arrest bats, and you can't force the world to believe," Sean said. He looked at his wife, and smiled that smile she loved so much. "What did Melanie say?"

Maggie looked over at Judy and Blake. Judy looked stronger — and angry. Blake was still in shock. Bruno and Miss Tiffany were staring up at her, too.

"All right," Maggie said at last. "We have to go to the fissures and . . . well, douse them with holy water and perform the ritual of exorcism."

"Vampires are living in the fissures?" Blake asked.

"No. The . . . the spirit possessing them and people like your physics professor is coming from the fissures," Sean explained.

Blake grimaced. "What if I'm recognized by some of the other cops on the street?"

"What if some of the other cops on the street start getting bitten — or worse, taken over themselves?" Sean asked.

Blake sat down heavily on the couch, then looked up at Maggie and Sean. "Ah, hell. Do I need to know Latin to help perform an exorcism?" he asked.

The Forum was like a time capsule. Century after century, rulers and rich men had changed it. Christian houses of worship had replaced temples to forgotten gods. To wander this ancient relic of the one-time empire was fascinating. Scott remembered his first visit, when he'd thought that the large stone containers he saw were some type of strange ancient urinal, only to find out that he was sadly mistaken — they were part of the world's first fast-food cafés, where a passerby could purchase a glass of wine dipped from one, along with food to eat as he hurried on his way.

" 'The area was drained at the beginning of the rule of the Etruscan kings,' " Melanie read aloud from the guidebook in her hand. " 'In the iron age, it was a necropolis. At other times in its history it was frequented by lawyers and politicians, strumpets and shopkeepers. Legal matters were dealt with at the basilicas.' "

Rainier had wandered off on his own, so Melanie and Scott strolled along together.

They passed by the Temple of Vespa, and he marveled that the architecture, even in ruins, could still provide incontrovertible proof of ancient talent.

Scott stopped, looking beyond massive pillars and arches, and blinked.

Black mist was swirling through the air just beyond his reach.

Melanie was still reading, but he didn't even hear her.

The mist — or maybe it was smoke? — kept eluding him, keeping just ahead of him as he tried to catch it.

"Scott?"

Melanie's voice seemed to come from far away. Suddenly he saw a girl in front of him. She had long blond hair, and wore a fashionable blouse and plaid school-uniform skirt. She looked very serious, even worried, as she stood there just staring at him.

"Help me," she whispered.

"What's wrong?" he asked her.

"Please, come help me," she repeated, her tone desperate.

He was tempted to do as she asked, but something held him back.

"You have to tell me what's wrong," he said.

He noticed that the sun was setting, the shadows beginning to lengthen.

He thought he heard a hint of the now-familiar sound of fluttering wings on the air.

The girl looked around, then took a step toward him. "I need . . . I need . . ."

She flew at him. Her fingers, like talons, hooked into his shoulders. He gripped her around the waist, trying to rip her away and felt the searing heat of liquid fire as she opened her mouth, still clinging tenaciously to him.

And then he felt the first scrape of her teeth.

13

"This is insane," Blake whispered.

It was the wee hours of the morning in Los Angeles, and the street was quiet. A car went by now and then, and the distant sound of music from a late-night bar down the long stretch of the road wafted by on the air.

"You know, I'm Roman Catholic," Blake said. "I could wind up excommunicated for this."

"Blake, dear, shut up," Judy told him.

"I'm ready," Sean said. He took the prayer book they'd acquired at Judy's church and he started to read.

Maggie began to sprinkle the holy water they'd acquired at the same place over the gaping break in the road.

"Insane," Blake said again.

Then he froze, as Sean skipped a beat.

The earth was moaning. A low howl was emanating from deep in the fissure, touched with fury and the coarse sound of nails on a blackboard. It was soft at first, but was increasing in volume.

"This is real, isn't it?" Blake whispered.

Sean's voice rose as he began to read again; Judy screamed as the ground began to tremble, and she lost her balance, but Blake caught her before she could fall.

Maggie joined in with her husband's chanting, followed by Judy and Blake, all of them reading as if their lives depended on it.

The moaning rose to a high pitch.

Black dirt suddenly blew into the sky with the force of water from a geyser, then thundered back to earth.

The moaning stopped.

They stood, covered in dirt, staring at one another.

"Is that it?" Judy whispered.

"I don't know," Maggie admitted.

"I know that there are a dozen more of these in the city," Sean said. "I know that we need to keep moving."

Maria Elizabeta was young and beautiful, trusting, and naive. She believed in goodness, and she was also at that age where the world was filled with adventure. She stood in that middle realm between reality and dreams, between the dark and the light, the truth sleeping somewhere in the back of her mind, and the wonder of her fantasies at the forefront.

He was an arrestingly handsome man. He sat down beside her, and she realized that they were at a café. A half-filled cup of cappuccino sat before her on the table, and her friends had wandered off. She thought she heard them laughing and tittering behind her; they had been raised by the sisters at the convent school where they lived, and boys — and certainly men — were objects of deep intrigue. They all dreamed and fantasized and talked about the opposite sex. Even those who were destined to go into service to the Church liked to talk and tease and dream. It was allowed, because they were still so young.

He had winked at her, and asked, if he might take the chair next to her. Then he asked her name, and told her that she was beautiful. His eyes were dancing and dark, and his voice was husky and masculine and seductive. In the end, he wanted to walk with her, and she didn't mind taking a walk. He was a perfect gentleman, never touching her, just making her laugh, because he was so charming.

But that night she was suddenly awakened from her deep sleep.

He was there, standing by her bed, and he brought a finger to his lips, warning her not to cry out. She tried to tell him that she was worried about him, that he had to get out, that someone else might awaken. "You will become a bride of illusion," he told her. "Thus you cannot betray your calling. After all, you must know what it is that you will miss."

She said no, but something within her was weak, because suddenly, she was no longer sleeping in her sparse little cot at the girls' school. She was with him in a room where the fire in the hearth burned hot and she, too, was warm. She felt as if there were a strange drumbeat in the air, something that whispered of passion and urgency. She could feel him; more, she could feel herself. She could feel the throb and the fire in her own body, and she wanted so desperately to feel more of his. He touched her flesh, and she longed to know everything that was carnal between a man and a woman, wanted to feel his kisses, and his hardness between her thighs.

He was so handsome, so strong. His dark eyes elicited her response as pleasurably as the sound of his voice. Whispers deep in her mind told her that this shouldn't be happening, that she had made up her mind long ago. She had felt her calling, and she believed it to be a true one. She would be needed one day; she had known it, just as she had known that she always had to be strong.

However beautiful he might be, she had to break away.

"I cannot," she told him simply. "I cannot. I am sworn to another."

And that was when he changed.

His voice became like the roar of thunder; his breath was a blast of rancid heat. And the face that had been so charming and handsome changed. She saw the flesh tightening into a horrible mask. His nose lengthened, and protrusions rose from his reddening forehead. He was not straight but hunched, and his backbone was studded with knobs, like the scales of a crocodile. His chin grew pointed, and his eyes glittered with the greatest malice and evil imaginable.

"I tried to give you beauty, but you would rather be an old hag. Well, old hag, you are weakening. You almost believed in youth and passion, and you almost surrendered to me. Your days are numbered. You will die without first succumbing to my fires, and you will know that you betrayed your life and yourself."

She cried out in horror. He had become a demon.

Scaly, red, with pustules breaking through his skin and a cruel fire burning in his eyes, a fire that reflected an inferno of lives and souls, the silent screams of those who had been seduced, then fallen from his grace to burn and smolder in agony forever and ever.

"Sister! Sister, wake up!"

She wasn't alone. Someone was coming. It was Lucien DeVeau, and though he was still far away, he was racing toward her, trying desperately to reach her. "Sister, please, he's only in your mind. He hasn't touched you. He can't hurt you if you don't let him. He's only in your dreams, trying to seduce you from your task."

She looked at her own hands then, as the demon howled with rage and thrust her away. She saw the wrinkles on her hands, the age spots. She had lived her life; she wasn't a young girl. She had grown strong with the years. She had known in her heart, since she was very young and had turned away from all the material pleasures of life, that hers was more than just a calling by any one religion. It was a calling to goodness.

She was old now, dying.

She was weak, and he was preying upon her. But Lucien, too, could enter her dreams, and he was coming to help her.

"Sister! Maria Elizabeta!"

The horrible face of the demon, was gone, and she heard Sister Ana's voice calling her from the torment of her dream.

She knew that she was dying, losing

strength. She was falling easily now into those fantasies of youth and beauty. She was letting him come closer and closer.

She couldn't forget her mission; she was the Oracle. Until she could pass on the burden and the knowledge in her soul, she had to find the strength to withstand his temptations.

Around her, many of the sisters were softly crying.

"Do not cry," she told them. "I will be strong," she vowed. "Foul creature cast from heaven!" she cried out, addressing the demon. "You can do nothing to hurt me."

The ground trembled.

Scott's grip on the young female vampire intensified, but she was like a snake, limbs wound everywhere about him. His shirt pulled open as he strained. She screamed suddenly, and he realized that the cross on the rosary Rainier had given him had touched her naked flesh.

He smelled the burning that rose from the spot.

He wrenched the girl away from him at last, throwing her hard against a tall pillar gleaming golden as the sun set and the moon began to rise. The great fluttering of wings began again, a cacophony that rose along with the sound of chattering and screeching. A bellow seemed to roar up from the earth.

The ground trembled beneath his feet.

"Scott!"

He heard Melanie calling to him, but he couldn't see her.

And suddenly, once again, he was facing a horde of bloodthirsty creatures, teeth bared and lips drawn back in furious snarls, hatred sizzling from their eyes.

His canvas bag was in the car; he had never expected the attack to begin in daylight. Bael must be growing stronger. Now Scott's rosary was his only weapon, and they were flying at him with a vengeance. All he had was his strength, and he sought desperately for a way to use it.

He pulled the remnant of a broken pillar from the ground and hurled it lengthwise at the crowd descending upon him. It bought him time. Small bushes and trees grew in the area, and he wrenched a small olive tree from the earth and used it to impale the large man who attacked him next. He backed away, taking stones from the ground and aiming for their heads with his most merciless pitches. Still, they kept coming.

He could still feel her teeth scraping his neck, so close to his jugular. Even as he fought, not daring to lose focus for a split second, he felt the burn of her touch, the blood drying along the thin scratch in his flesh.

He bent low, watching as they began to circle around him, and searched the ground blindly for another weapon. He ripped a bush from the ground and hurled it, then a massive rock and then another jagged pillar. The pillar struck home, smashing a head. And still he wasn't killing them quickly enough.

"Scott!" He turned at the sound of Rainier's voice. And then the other man was at his side, tossing him one of the stakes. Scott grinned. Melanie *had* seen him, then found Rainier, and they had gone to the car for their weapons.

He was no longer on the defensive. Melanie was uncorking vials of holy water, spraying the crowd that ringed them. Rainier was battling with sharpened crosses and a fierce resolve.

Scott moved forward, impaling one after another of the creatures. His power seemed to have multiplied with the presence of the other two. He was quick. They were dying, exploding, decaying and falling to bits around him.

There were screeches, cries and howls of

fury. Then he impaled his last. They had all died or were fast retreating in a cloud of smoke.

He heard another scream and turned. Melanie was holding the blond girl who had first accosted him. He moved forward, ready to strike.

"No!" Melanie cried. "No, we need her."

The girl let out a cry like a wounded banshee. Her teeth were gnashing. She began to change before them, a bat's face replacing the youth and innocence of her human form. She shook, and fur seemed to cover her flesh as her arms morphed into wings. She escaped Melanie's hold but flopped to the ground, and Melanie stepped hard on one wing, then reached down for the thing, shaking it until the girl began to morph back, furious but exhausted.

"We've got to get her back to the hotel," Melanie said.

"How?" Rainier demanded.

Scott stepped forward, sized her up and took aim. He planted a firm right hook on her jaw. Vampire or no, she went down flat.

"That'll do," Melanie said. "Until we can take better measures. Rainier, we can't let her get too close to Scott, we can't take the chance. Help me. We'll make it look as if she's drunk."

They each slipped an arm around her. She wasn't walking at all; they had to drag her, but she was slight and small, and it worked. Scott looked around for any of their paraphernalia they might have left, then headed after them, cross at the ready.

They got her to the car easy enough. At the hotel, Melanie explained to Signor Marchetto that her young niece had gotten in with the wrong crowd, and she was going to take care of her.

Scott had the feeling that Marchetto knew the girl wasn't Melanie's niece. He also had the feeling that Signor Marchetto knew exactly what Melanie and Rainier were.

They got her to the suite. Rainier set her in one of the upholstered chairs. She lolled back, still out cold.

Scott sat down across the room from her, staring at her and trying to rub away the tension in his neck. She looked like a kid, no more than eighteen or nineteen. Slumped down and unconscious, she could have been a sweet sorority girl, one who'd had a few too many at a fraternity bash.

"Watch out," Melanie warned.

"She's just a kid," Scott said.

"She had enough evil in her for *him* to be able to use her," Melanie warned.

"Do bad vamps ever go good?" he asked.

Melanie hesitated, looking at Rainier. He shrugged. "It's rare, but it's happened," he said. "But Mel is right — you have to watch out for her." He moved as he spoke, and Scott realized that he was ringing her chair with crosses. Melanie took a vial of holy water and splashed that around the chair in a circle, as well.

Scott found himself thinking of something Lucien had said that night in the bar in L.A. *The blood of the pure is toxic to the darkness of evil.* Strange. Well, he wasn't pure — and it was damned certain that her fangs scraping his neck hadn't been at all toxic to her. He had no better idea now of what those cryptic words meant than he had then.

He said them out loud.

"The blood of the pure is toxic to the darkness of evil."

"What?" Rainier asked him.

"Something Lucien said," Scott explained.

Rainier smiled grimly. "Well, don't be worried. You're hardly pure, and I promise you, we aren't planning on using you as a human sacrifice."

Just then the girl began to stir.

Her eyes flew open as she came to. She looked at them, and her face — so sweet and innocent in her stupor — instantly turned into a snarling mask of hatred and venom, teeth bared, fangs glistening and wet. She started to bolt from the chair, then fell back, a growl of fury escaping her.

Rainier said something to her in rapid Italian, and she curled up on the chair, looking coy. "My English is quite excellent," she told them imperiously, and smiled at Scott. *"Americano! Bello Americano."* She leaned forward slightly. "Help me, *signor.* Help me, *per favore.* They don't understand."

"Can it," Melanie told her. "We all understand perfectly."

Scott touched his neck without thinking; the scratch was still burning.

The mask of fury quickly returned to her face. She let out a hissing sound and stared at Melanie. "He will make you suffer. He will win, and you will burn and burn. He will take your soul, and your soul will burn in agony. You might have been one of *his,* but now you will suffer agony forever and ever, when he finally takes you down."

"Who exactly is he? Where exactly is he, and why doesn't he have the courage to come out and meet us himself? Why does he use sad lost souls — like you?" Melanie asked.

The girl had big hazel eyes and long blond hair, and she put on a look of great injury. "You hit me. You hurt me," she told Scott

367

plaintively.

"Sorry."

She clutched her stomach and bent over suddenly, moaning, then looked up again, a pained look that lacked cunning in her eyes. "I'm hungry. So hungry. The pain is unbearable. You must know," she said to Melanie.

Melanie looked uncomfortable; Rainier just shrugged. "*Si, ha fame.* We know the hunger. It *is* terrible. It burns, and it gets worse and worse."

"Then . . . help me," the girl whispered.

Scott leaned forward. "We intend to help you. But first you have to help us."

The girl sat back, her face pale and ashen. "He will destroy me."

"Hey, I was already about to destroy you. Melanie saved you," Scott said.

"Just help us and we'll take care of you," Rainier said. "The hunger will grow worse and worse. It begins slowly, in the pit of your stomach, and then it spreads. It's like poison ripping through your muscles and bones. Your head aches as if it will explode. It feels as if rats are eating away at your insides."

She stared at him, stricken at first; then she snarled again. "You don't know anything. Rats! That's what you'll be, all of you, rats in a cage, tearing one another up, cannibals. Not just the monsters like you, either, but all of those who think they're so good. One thing will happen, and then another. The earth will tremble, and all the dead and undead he has drawn to him will spew forth. He has created the doorways for us, and his essence will come out and possess those who think they are so good, so holy, and they will be like rats!"

Scott felt his blood run cold at the venom of her words. The hairs at the base of his neck began to rise. But he forced his voice to stay calm when he told her, "But first *you'll* writhe in agony. You'll want to die, but you won't be able to. You're starving now, aren't you?"

"Of course she's starving," Melanie said. "She thinks that her dark commander will gain control of us, but he's had control of her and the others like her for a long time." She turned to the girl. "He's used you as cruel men have used dogs throughout the years, starving them before a hunt."

The girl blinked, snarled. She was out of arguments.

A moment later, she let out a cry, gripping her stomach.

Melanie strode into her room, and Scott watched her go. She returned immediately with one of the bottles from her refrigerator — the ones that didn't contain cherry soda.

She sat down in front of the girl, slowly uncapped it and sipped, letting a little sigh of complete pleasure escape her.

The girl started to surge forward, then screamed, her flesh suddenly sizzling, as she tried to burst through the ring of crosses and holy water.

She began to spew every oath imaginable at Melanie, obscenity raining down upon obscenity. Melanie only smiled and watched her. She didn't move a muscle.

Scott glanced at Rainier, who gave him a barely perceptible nod, telling him to try whatever tack he thought might work.

Scott moved in closer, keeping his distance just outside the edge of the circle. "We know so much already — and, in case you haven't noticed yet, we took on your boss's army of bones and bloodsuckers, and won. We know that he has evil escaping from fissures across the world."

"There are a lot of us out here," Rainier said. "Your leader doesn't have that much strength, because he's just a demon. Just a demon, trying to prove his worth to Satan. He has to start this ball of destruction rolling, or he'll be an outcast before his own vile kind. He has used his base below the church for a long, long time, and he has worked hard to animate the bones of the long dead. As to your kind . . . I'm assuming he started beckoning you with promises of an eternal place where hunger and every vile expression of greed, lust and vanity were free to be reveled in forever."

"But we can kill your kind, and we will," Scott said.

She snarled suddenly and let out a laugh that was unearthly and unnerving. "He is killing your Oracle. The old hag! She will die. He enters her dreams, and he lets her know that she has failed. He makes her believe that she will betray you, and because she believes it, it will happen, and you will all die even before the end of days. I think that's too kind. I think you should be destroyed slowly. You should suffer. You should starve. Perhaps he will manage that. Or perhaps he'll send you swiftly into the fires of eternal damnation, just to rid himself of the annoyance you cause."

Melanie stood up, casting her head back languidly and draining the last drop from her bottle of blood. She licked her lips, staring at the girl. "One a day. Just a pint. And the world is wonderful. Food tastes good, and wine with it. And there's no pain. We cause no pain, and we don't feel any. It's a great way to live. We don't have to hunt anyone down, so we don't risk a stake, a lynch mob, and no one wants to lop off our heads. . . . But we do stop murderers of any kind, and we *will* kill you, if that's what's necessary." She smiled.

"Know what? A nice meal sounds pretty good to me right now. We should check out the dining room here."

"I could definitely eat something," Rainier said.

"Sounds good to me," Scott agreed.

They started out of the room.

"No, come back here. *Per piacere!*" the girl cried. "You can't leave me here like this. You can't let me starve." They kept heading for the door. "I'll scream. I'll bring the servants, and I'll eat them up when they come to help me. And then the foolish *polizia* will arrest you! So let me go. Let me go this instant!"

They stepped into the hall and closed the door.

"We're really just going to leave her?" Scott asked.

"No . . . give it a minute," Melanie said.

They heard the girl sobbing then. Terrible sobs that tore at Scott's heart. She still looked like a kid — when she wasn't baring her teeth.

"Come back! Please, I'll tell you . . . I'll tell you where to find him," she cried.

They opened the door to the suite and went back in. The girl was strained, her features contorted. There were tears streaming down her cheeks.

Scott stood in front of her again, making sure to stay outside the circle that kept her in her chair. "Look, I'm very sorry for you, despite the fact that you were determined to make a meal of me. I'd like to help you, but I know that you'll just lie, no matter what we ask you."

She began to rattle off a flurry of oaths in Italian then.

"She isn't going to help us," Melanie said. "I say we stake her right here, right now."

"No," the girl moaned softly. "No, no, no, no."

"Like I said, I'd really like to help you," Scott said. "But my friends . . . they seem to know your kind better than I do."

She stopped crying for a moment, looking at him with a sudden cunning in her eyes. "They're the evil ones. You can't see it, because they've blinded you. They will kill you and cut you to pieces, drink your blood and eat your flesh. They've seduced you, and now they're just waiting for their chance to strike. You think they're your friends, but they're not."

"They can stop the hunger, the pain," Scott said. "They can give you sustenance."

She leaned toward him. "So can you," she told him. A flash of coquettish mischief touched her eyes. Scott hadn't realized how close he had leaned in until she jerked forward and almost sank her teeth into his neck. He threw himself back behind the invisible walls of her prison.

"We really should stake her — now," Melanie warned.

"No!" The girl sat up and looked at Melanie with a hate-filled gaze, and yet she spoke with a real plea in her voice.

"Please," she moaned.

Rainier looked at Scott, shaking his head. "She isn't giving us anything. I think we do have to destroy her. It's going to be messy, though. She's a young vampire. She won't just disappear in a cloud of dust. She'll become a pretty nasty corpse, and we'll have to get her out of here."

"No, no, please, you can trust me," the girl said. Suddenly she was speaking in a rush. "My name is Celia. Celia Mero. I was at a club down off the Spanish Steps when . . . I don't know who made me, but I just wanted to get through my last year of school here and go to America for college. I learned my English well, yes? I am not . . . bad.

"Haven't you ever known the hunger?" the girl whispered.

"Yes, I have," Melanie said. "We all know it, we all feel it. And some of us make the choice to sate that hunger without killing. I don't think you were a killer before you became one of us. I think you were a flirt, a tease, but a normal girl. You went to a club, where you met someone who wasn't normal. He turned you, and he taught you to be cruel, taught you that the only way to ease the pain was to kill. He left you open to the demon's influence. You're still young — in life and in death. You might have had a chance to find a place among those of us who have learned the way and are always ready to welcome others. You might still. But you have to be strong. You weren't strong when it happened. But you didn't know — you couldn't know. *He* is not one of us. He calls to those who are hungry, those who are afraid, and those who are cruel now just as they were cruel in life, and he makes them seduce and kill for him. Those who are long dead no longer have souls to offer up, but he can make their remains dance to his tune, make them do battle for him. Many prophecies have warned that this time will come, but they have also said that we who have free will can fight — and win."

Celia stared at Melanie dully. "He doesn't have to force his minions to seduce and kill. We do it for fun, just like him. Don't you understand? He can kill you no matter what you do, because he can slip into your mind. He makes you see things, feel things, believe things."

"We know that," Scott told her. "But what you must believe is that he *can* be fought."

Celia glared at him. She looked worn out, beaten. "How? How can you fight him when he comes first as if he is gentle and charming, handsome to a fault? How can you fight what starts off as comfortable as a pillow? As a whisper? When he welcomes you in, and you find that you're where you belong, and there are others like you?" she whispered.

"We can help you," Melanie said. "You saw that — I have what you want, what you need. But you have to give us what *we* need first."

Celia looked at them and shook her head. "You two . . ." she said to Melanie and Rainier. "He will destroy you. You should be his already, but you've fought him. And you —" she broke off to stare at Scott "—

you're already as good as dead, and you just don't know it."

"Believe what you want. I know that I will fight him tooth and nail — and win," Scott told her.

Melanie let out a long sigh. "Should we give her more time? Or just get it over with now?"

Again, the girl started to sob.

Lucien had chosen to fly, in order to save his energy. But because he was traveling at the last minute, he hadn't been able to get a direct flight. Now he was flying against time, and the day was waning.

Perhaps flying had been a mistake.

Because he hadn't been able to close his eyes without seeing not his own dream, but the Oracle's. He had closed his eyes, and somewhere in her heart, Sister Maria Elizabeta had cried out to him, knowing that the demon was in her mind, in her dream. And the demon was growing stronger, making it hard for him to reach her in time.

He had barely made it, and now he was exhausted.

He glanced at his watch. Two more hours. Two more hours and he would be there.

Scott opened his eyes. Somewhere along the

way he'd fallen into a doze.

Celia had been crying. Tears streamed down her cheeks as she sat inside her prison of crosses, holy water and belief.

"Scott, you must get away quickly. She's going to kill you. Don't you see? She's a vampire, an old vampire. She's been using you. Don't you know? Haven't you seen? She's playing with you. Defend yourself!"

He turned swiftly. Beside his chair, Melanie was on her knees. Beautiful, sleek, as graceful and sinuous as a cat. She was reaching for him, her lips parting, and he could see her fangs as they glistened in the stray beam of moonlight that fought its way through the shadows.

Fear shot through him like a bolt of electricity. He started to jump up; there was a sharpened cross by his side, and his fingers curled around it.

But . . .

Distantly, so distantly, he heard the demon's laughter.

He turned away from the image of Melanie, wondering if he'd killed her in his dream, would she have died in reality.

"Bull," he told Celia flatly. Except that she wasn't real, either, he realized. She was just something that Bael had somehow made him see in his mind.

She faded away. In her place he saw red glowing eyes that seemed to hover in front of him, staring, before fading away. Bael. Scott smelled something disgusting, like burning flesh, and then . . .

14

The plane landed. Lucien couldn't afford the time to go through customs or to deal with his baggage, so he didn't.

He closed his eyes for a moment, imagining himself as wind and air, moving swiftly through time and space.

Shape shifting. Not all vampires could do it. But he was old. He had learned a lot through the years, and he knew that he was strong.

He hoped he was strong enough.

He opened his eyes and saw the church hidden in the woods along the Appia Antica. He heard the chants of the nuns as they let their prayers rise toward the heavens.

He saw Sister Maria Elizabeta lying on the pew, barely breathing — and barely blinking. She did not want to fall asleep again.

He burst through the doorway of the church, and everything was as he had seen it in his dreams, as he had known it before, so many years ago. Sister Ana leapt up as he entered, like a true soldier, though she knew she might face certain death.

"He's come!" Sister Maria Elizabeta gasped out. "Don't be afraid. The Oracle has come."

Lucien hurried to her side and took her hand. "My dear Sister, I know you feel you must be here, but it's time for you to get to a hospital. You have done your duty, and now you must let yourself rest and heal."

She smiled at him. It was the beautiful smile of the young girl he had seen in the dream, the sister herself, but so many years ago. "This is the beginning. If the earth signs don't stop the demon, there is no hope. The Oracle must be there when it is time for water, fire and air to go into battle."

"Sister," he said gently. "You cannot stay here as you are. You are old, and very ill. You won't be able to fight again if you don't get some rest, not to mention medical care. And you must get better. We need you — the world needs you."

She closed her eyes, and her smile deepened, some of the wrinkles that betrayed her great age beginning to fade.

"I know," she whispered. "I knew . . . all those years ago, when I first saw you. You thought you were damned, and you played the part well. But I knew — as you knew, in your heart — that you were not meant to kill and destroy, but to go on. You thought your role now was just to show the others the way, but . . . our connection is strong. You entered the dreams I sent to Scott, and you saw what was happening. Already, you were the one. You have acted as the Oracle."

He looked up a little helplessly at Sister Ana.

She shook her head. A dull thud of fear struck him. He was not ready for this responsibility. Sister Elizabeta could not die.

Her eyes opened, and she looked at him. "Lucien, don't you see? You are the Oracle now."

"No. I haven't your faith, your strength."

"I am old, and so weak that he is slipping into my mind. My heart is pure, but my body is weak. *You* are strong. And you will find the resources you need within your soul."

Lucien wasn't even sure that he had a soul.

"My son," she said softly.

Her grip was suddenly strong. He felt something, as if he had been struck by lightning. He almost cried out, almost wrenched away. But even as the power of the Oracle burned through her touch into him, he suddenly understood.

And he was very afraid.

"Sister," he whispered.

"Bless you, child."

"Sister, please, no."

"Let me die, let me die in the light in which I have lived, for it is time, and I will not risk my soul to such as he you must now fight."

She touched his cheek. He felt her love, and the strength that would never leave her, not even in death.

Then she closed her eyes again. This time, they would not reopen.

"Scott, please, wake up. What's wrong?"

Melanie was terrified. Scott had suddenly begun tossing about wildly, his muscles straining, his features taut, as if he were in extreme pain.

But worse than that . . .

The air had an odd smell about it. Like flesh charred by fire.

"Scott!"

At last his eyes opened. He looked around anxiously, saw her, and his eyes filled with relief. He reached out, drawing her to him. His heart was pounding. "My God," he whispered. "You're all right, you're here with me. Unscathed." He smiled at her, and she was startled by the wealth of emotion in his eyes, the force in his arms as he held her. His smiled faded suddenly. "Where's Celia?"

"In the sitting room, where we left her. Rainier is standing guard."

He eased back, and his grin returned slowly as he reached up and touched her hair. "He — Bael — tries hard, but, you know what saves me every time?"

"What?" she asked.

"You."

"Me?" she asked, both puzzled and afraid.

He nodded gravely, studying her with a passion and warmth in his dark eyes that both thrilled and frightened her.

"Whatever you are, I know there's not an ounce of cruelty in your body," he said. "I couldn't love you if you were cruel. And I even believe that you feel something for me — dare I suggest you love me in return?"

Love? No, it couldn't be — could it?

It could.

And suddenly she was afraid. Afraid of the force of her own emotions — and his. She was afraid of his complete and utter faith in her.

She eased down, laying her head upon his chest. "You believe that I'm a vampire, don't you?"

"I do, yes," he told her, stroking her hair.

"Don't you want to know more?" she asked him.

"Whenever you're ready, yes," he said without hesitation.

She didn't believe that he would judge her harshly. Still, the fear remained.

She was quiet for a long time, and he didn't push her. At last she sighed. "Do you know how old I am?" she whispered.

"No, but it doesn't matter."

She rose up on an elbow, looking down at him. She wasn't sure what she was going to say, but she knew she didn't want to look at him while she was talking. She eased back down on her back and stared at the ceiling as she began to speak. "It happened during the potato famine," she said quietly.

"What? What potato famine?" he asked.

She winced. "The Irish potato famine, eighteen-forty-nine. They were truly desperate times. We were raiding an English estate near Dublin. My father, mother . . . brothers, sisters, all told me it was time to go, but I was determined to get more food. I pretended that I was right behind them, but I wasn't. We knew that Lord Miller's stockroom was full, but for some reason no one wanted to go near it. Miller had acquired a reputation for being not just cruel, but evil.

Maids had gone into his manor to work and never come back out. Still, that night . . . you can't imagine how hungry I was. How hungry we all were. So many people starving to death."

"Miller was a vampire?" he asked.

She nodded, still not looking at him. "The worst kind. He loved being a lord, being able to rule his property, to drink — lots of wine and alcohol, as well as blood — and to take whomever he wanted to torture and abuse. No one stopped him. He was a member of the ruling class. No one dared."

Scott rolled over to look at her. His eyes were deep and gentle, but he was such a strong man, in his own quiet way. He smoothed hair away from her face. "He caught you that night."

She nodded. "I was always a fighter, I suppose. I had to be. So when he caught me, he had a great time torturing me. He'd let me think I had gotten away, then catch me again. And then I would fight him some more. Actually, I'm pretty sure I did hurt him several times. I was willing to die rather than let him have me. I just didn't realize that I *would* die . . . only to awaken and find myself still in his home. With him. Then it got worse. He wanted me to feed upon my own people. I do know what Celia is going through now, because I went through it then."

Scott pulled her against him as she spoke, and she didn't stop him. Instead she looked him straight in the eye. "I killed one of his friends instead. Another English lord."

She was surprised that he still managed a gentle smile. "You didn't kill your own."

"But I *did* kill. Don't you understand? Maybe the bastard even deserved it — he'd certainly been cruel enough to his tenants. But . . . I never wanted the power of life and death over others. And . . . you have to understand. He was just the first. I made my horrible misfortune into a war of vengeance." She rose to a sitting position, trying to make certain he was really paying attention. "A serious enough bite . . . enough blood taken, and you do die, then become one of us. But there's an ancient law — one all of us, good and bad, are afraid to break — that a vampire can only make one of his or her own kind three times in a century. Survival of the fittest, you see. So I didn't just *turn* these people, I killed them. I staked them or beheaded them after I had drained them."

She wondered if she was trying to force him to turn away. Better now than later, when her heart was even more vulnerable.

But he didn't turn away.

"Who finally helped you? Was it Lucien?"

She shook her head. "It was Rainier, though Rainier eventually introduced me to Lucien. In the days when we had to fight to stay alive, Lucien was what you would call the king of the vampires. He's still the head, though there are rebel factions across the globe, those who want to stick with the old ways and kill indiscriminately for survival. They usually die," she whispered.

"But not always?" Scott asked.

"No, not always. It appears that Bael has a way of gathering the disgruntled and the cruel around him. He's managed to exert a mental power to keep them under control — the same power he uses to slip into our minds and our dreams."

Scott nodded slowly. "I think I understand. It's like a world within our world, and most of us don't even suspect, because so many of you are careful to stay under the radar."

She nodded.

"How did you wind up in California — and how did Rainier help you?"

"Lord Miller came to despise me. We carried the war into our private domain. He knew that I was killing anyone who helped him stay in power — and practice his cruelty. He managed to trap me in the dungeon of an ancient ruin for weeks with nothing to . . . eat — and then sent my baby sister in to search for me." She stopped. All these years later, even with all her immediate family long gone, she could still remember how she had grabbed the little girl who had loved her so much and barely managed to shove her away. "I didn't," she said, her voice barely finding breath. "I didn't kill her. But she went home and told my parents what she had found. Rainier had come to Dublin — to find an old . . . acquaintance. My parents ran to the priest and told him what I had become, and when Rainier heard the story he came to find me. He took me away before the entire town could come after me. My parents loved me, and my sister loved me, but they would have destroyed me to save my soul. Rainier got us berths on a ship to America. We settled in . . . New York first. Rainier taught me how to survive, far below the notice of those who might find me out." She drew a deep breath and let it out, still determined to meet his eyes. "We can subsidize our diet with other blood, of course, but when we're sick, injured . . . or need our strength, it must be human."

"I see."

"Over the years, I lost my accent," she told him. "Actually, over the years, I've learned several languages and can affect many accents. But I love my country. I am very much an American now."

"So . . . ?" He let the word trail off inquiringly.

"So now you understand what a totally loathsome creature I am," she said, trying to speak lightly.

"I don't think you're loathsome at all," he assured her. "I can't help but be curious, though, in all those years . . ."

"How many vampires have I created?" she asked, wincing. Her voice sounded cold.

And bitter.

But he shook his head. "You said that Rainier helped you all that time. Did you really never —"

She looked at his face; his tense features. She heard the slight twinge of jealousy in his voice — something he was trying hard to hide.

"He's my brother. My friend and my brother. But we haven't been close geographically in years. I moved on. I always move on."

He took both her hands and kissed them briefly but tenderly. "Please don't move on. Not away from me," he whispered.

She didn't have a chance to reply, because there was suddenly a long, low cry from the living room.

Scott leaped from the bed and nearly ripped the door off its hinges in his anxiety to discover what had happened.

As he raced to the living room, a million thoughts seemed to flash through Scott's mind: Rainier had fallen prey to Bael's mind games. He had fallen prey to the girl. Someone else had come in and fallen prey to the girl.

But when he reached the room he saw that nothing had changed. Rainier was sitting calmly in a chair, one long leg crossed over the other as he read. Celia was still sitting in the midst of her circular prison. The wail he had heard was hers, an agonized cry of hunger.

Scott understood; he hadn't eaten, and his stomach was rumbling. Then he thought guiltily about what Melanie must have suffered during the potato famine, about what this girl was suffering now, and imagined his plight a thousand times over.

He could wait a bit longer.

"Where's Mel?" Rainier asked, yawning calmly, as if he hadn't even heard the girl's howl.

"She's coming," Scott said.

To prove his point, Melanie emerged from the bedroom right then.

"Everything all right?" she asked.

"Celia is apparently very hungry," Rainier said. "But not talkative. So . . ."

"I don't know what else I can say," Celia moaned.

"You know where he is," Scott told her, folding his arms across his chest.

"You know where he is, too," she said, pouting, then wincing and doubling over in pain.

"We've tried finding him below the church," Rainier said, turning a page in his book, then looking up at her. "And he does have power there. But there's somewhere else where he's actually hiding. Somewhere that gives him a better opportunity to send his evil seeping out into the world. That's where we need to go to find him." He turned to Scott and Melanie. "And I believe our friend here knows how to find him. If we just give her a little more time, maybe she'll talk to us."

"Sure." Scott yawned. "Well, I think I'll go out and find a sandwich or something," he said. "Can I get you anything?" he asked the others.

"No! Don't leave me here alone with . . .

them," Celia pleaded.

For a moment, Scott was convinced that she was going to remain stubborn. Then she whispered, "*He'll know.* He'll know if I tell you, and he'll kill me."

Scott moved as close as he safely could. "He won't kill you, because you'll be with us. And we're here to stop him."

She winced. Scott heard a twisting sound behind him. Melanie had gone for another "cherry soda."

"We *will* protect you," Scott promised.

"It's by the north end of the Forum," Celia whispered, giving up the fight all at once. "There's a huge rift . . . it's covered by an old Roman archway. There are tunnels beneath, older catacombs still. He's waiting for the full moon. The full moon gives him some kind of power. He'll send out the rest of his armies to clear the way, and then he'll appear and cause the earth to crack open everywhere. People will die, some in the cataclysm and others at the hands of their fellow men. It will be like a plague. A plague of desperation and cruelty, because mankind is only decent when things are going well."

That's not true, Scott thought. Trauma and tragedy could bring out the worst in people, yes. But they could bring out the best, as well.

Melanie passed Celia what was left of the bottle.

Celia drank it down greedily. Some of the blood dripped to her chin. She lapped it up with her tongue, not losing a bit.

Scott turned away.

Celia finished drinking, then started sobbing softly.

"The full moon," Rainier murmured. "That would be . . ."

"Tonight," Scott told him. "We don't have much time."

"What do we do with her?" Melanie asked.

Celia's sobs ceased; she'd heard the question and now stared at them in horror. "No! I gave you what you wanted. Please don't kill me. Please. I never meant to . . . I didn't *want* to kill people. . . . I don't want to go to hell, to burn for eternity. . . . All I ever wanted was to have fun and go to America."

"Listen," Scott said, "we have to start moving fast. Rainier, we can take Celia with us to your church to get every symbol of faith we can lay our hands on. Then the nuns can arrange some kind of prison for her and keep an eye on her. Then —"

He broke off, frowning. Melanie looked as if she had gone into a fog; she wasn't paying any attention to him, just staring straight ahead.

"Melanie!" he said sharply. "What is it?"

She didn't answer him right away; it looked almost as if she were communicating with someone who wasn't there — or hearing voices in her head.

"Melanie?" he asked more gently.

She looked at him. "Lucien is here."

"Here? Where?" he asked, frowning.

"At Sister Maria Elizabeta's church," Melanie said.

"You can . . . feel that?" he asked her.

She nodded. "Lucien can . . . communicate. I don't know how. He's always had a certain telepathy with . . . with our kind. That's how he entered your dream. The thing is —"

She broke off suddenly.

"The thing is what?" Scott pursued with exasperation.

"Sister Maria Elizabeta is dead," Melanie said.

"What?" Suddenly Scott felt blank, as if they were now an army fighting without a commander. No new Oracle could possibly take her place.

"She's dead," Rainier said, as if he were in on the same telepathy, "but —"

"But — what?" Scott felt his anger rising, mingling with his pain over the loss of the wise old nun. "Will the two of you please stop this? What the hell is going on?"

Melanie looked at him, her forehead puckering in thought. "Lucien is now the Oracle," she said.

Scott stood still for a moment. He thought about the sister, who had reached out to him in his sleep and brought him here. He thought about her beauty as a human being, the light within her that had been so special and unique, a strength that defied the years. And now she was gone.

"So Lucien is the Oracle now. What does that mean?" he asked.

"I don't know. I'm not sure he even knows," Melanie said.

"Let's go," Rainier said.

Scott looked at him, about to complain, then realized the other man was right. They didn't have time to mourn their loss. They didn't have time to do anything but try to survive.

"How do we get her out of here?" he asked.

"She stays between Mel and me," Rainier said. "We can't take any chances. You drive, and we'll keep her in back with us. Lucien will be waiting for us when we get there."

As they moved out through the lobby, Scott found himself pausing. The television set was on in the bar area. The announcer was speaking in Italian, but he didn't need to understand the language to grasp the import of the footage being shown.

The scene might have been taking place in Greece or one of the eastern European countries. There was mayhem in the streets, people screaming, some breaking windows, looting, some running in despair. The camera caught a large break in the earth, jagged asphalt reaching up to the sky and a huge cloud of black dust billowing from it. As he watched, a small group of men and women approached it, including a priest, a rabbi and a Moslem imam. The group stopped beside the hole, and the religious men began chanting, one swinging a brass incense brazier over it. The group around them protected them as the maddened crowd tried to attack.

"The Alliance is out," Melanie said, then turned to Scott, her eyes filled with love and pain. She touched his face, a caress like a whisper. "We have to hurry. We need more supplies . . . lots of holy water. The main battle is ours."

Scott studied the scene on the television screen. "We need more than holy water," he said quietly.

"I know where to go," Rainier told him.

■ ■ ■ ■

Lucien stood before the altar in the church, and, despite himself, he found his entire existence flashing through his mind.

Hundreds of years.

Years of life.

And afterlife.

The bad and the good.

He didn't understand how he could be the one to take the place of a *nun.* A holy woman like Sister Maria Elizabeta. Someone who knew humanity and, despite her strong religious faith, was able to sense and accept how much more the world held, and that the world wasn't black and white. Decency could be found in the shadows, just as terror could be found in the brightest light of the sun.

Sister Ana came up behind him. She didn't touch him, only cleared her throat to alert him to her presence.

"We must . . . do something," she told him. "I am not . . . I am not of the chosen, but I can sense that our time is slipping away."

He turned to her. Her eyes were warm and steady — and filled with trust. He nodded. "Leave me for a few minutes, please, and then we'll begin. I have to finish getting my message out, and those in the Alliance must hear and take steps."

She nodded, stepping away.

It was difficult, but he cleared his mind. He waited until he felt as if he were standing in a world that was nothing but white mist. He lifted his arms, and it looked as if rays of light extended from them. He knew when he touched the minds of those near him; he felt Melanie's presence, Rainier's, and even Scott's. But he had to go far beyond that. He reached out to Maggie and Sean, but they already knew, so he reached further, including to those who were in New Orleans.

His wife. His beloved Jade. He should have been with her.

He did his best to touch all the members around the world, concentrating heavily on places where the occult was accepted, where folklore had long been accepted as truth, and far more than fantasy or insanity.

The full moon would be rising here soon; to the east, it was already climbing higher in the night sky.

He reached out, as if his fingers could touch all those he needed to tell, and sent his message, then waited until the mist began to fade, until he felt his own strength waning.

He fell to his knees, drained.

Sister Ana came to his side, and he smiled as he allowed her to help him up.

"We have an army around the world," he told her.

"I never doubted it," she assured him.

The sisters had brought Sister Maria Elizabeta to the altar. "We have to lift the marble altar top and use it to lock the trapdoor," he told the sisters. "It's very heavy."

It *was* heavy. He had the strength of Atlas, but even with the help of the sisters, he could barely budge it.

They were still struggling with it when the other three arrived.

Scott, the first to be called.

Melanie and Rainier.

The three earth signs.

Capricorn, Virgo and Taurus.

"Hurry!" Maggie urged.

Sean was driving, she was at his side, and Judy and Blake were in the backseat, along with Miss Tiffany and Bruno.

They were headed north, nine hours behind Rome, so they still had plenty of daylight left to reach the huge fissure that had opened up after a quake just south of San Francisco, exactly the kind of thing Lucien had told them to watch out for.

"We're only about ten miles away now," Blake said. "Sean, take the next exit and run along the auxiliary road."

Sean did, and when they arrived, there were barricades and crime tape around the giant slash in the earth, so he eased off the road to park on the embankment, next to a California Highway Patrol vehicle. They left the car and hurried over to see that the fissure was now about twelve feet long and at least ten feet deep. It looked much deeper at the northern end, though, like the proverbial bottomless pit. A middle-aged and paunchy man who looked to be a geologist was studying the fissure, consulting charts and taking notes.

"Hey, hey!"

They turned as one to find themselves being approached by a highway patrol officer. "No sightseeing — this thing is dangerous," he told them. He was about thirty, fit, and he wore his authority well. As he spoke, a young man climbed out of the hole.

"What the hell are you doing, you fucking idiot?" the middle-aged man yelled at the newcomer. "Where did you get your degree, dickhead? Toys 'R' Us?"

The younger man sprang out of the hole faster than a whiplash and socked the older man in the jaw, sending him staggering back, falling. Recovering, he picked up a trowel and went for his attacker.

"Hey!" The patrolman shouted, racing over to the two men. "Hey!"

The older man slammed the cop in the head with the trowel; the cop cried out in shock and pain, and when the younger man let out an unearthly howl and threw himself into the fray, the cop began to scramble for his gun.

He didn't have a chance to draw it. Blake

fired into the air, and the sound was deafening, causing everyone to pause for a minute.

Sean moved forward without being told, wresting the gun from the patrol officer's hand and reaching for the trowel.

Suddenly Bruno let forth a basset bay that staggered them all.

Filthy steam and smoke came gushing from the hole. "Get the holy water — quickly," Sean ordered.

Even Maggie had gone still in shock, but now Sean's words catapulted her into motion. She was afraid, but she approached the hole, reciting by rote words she had learned as a child as she doused the area with the holy water. As she did, it was as if the miasma took on a life of its own and shifted direction to wash her. She felt it like something black and rotting, covering her flesh, slipping into her veins. She felt it take hold of her, and she was tempted to turn and fly at her husband. She wanted to gouge his eyes out.

But then Judy and Blake were at her side, reciting the ancient words of deliverance with her, and the feeling of being invaded by something disgusting and evil faded.

The black, billowing cloud of smoke and steam disintegrated, leaving behind the scent of brimstone.

The cop, still on the ground, had propped himself up on an elbow. The geologists were in the dirt, trying to scramble up, dazed.

The older man was rubbing his chin.

"What the hell just happened?" he whispered in a tone of shock.

"Here, let me help," Scott said, striding across the church.

He paused when he realized that Sister Maria Elizabeta was lying on the slab of marble — even in death, somehow beautiful and seeming to glow with serenity and warmth. He paused, touching her cold face and feeling the sense of loss again. He thought he heard Melanie let out a jagged little sob, and then they were all silent.

Rainier took over from the sisters, and together the three men lifted the marble and laid it over the trapdoor. Again, they all paused. Sister Maria Elizabeta looked as if she were simply sleeping peacefully. The nuns had placed her rosary in her hands, which were folded, prayer fashion, just below her breasts.

"She's still with us," Melanie whispered. "She will guard us from any evil that lies beneath this ground."

She was absolutely convinced, Scott thought. She turned and smiled at him, albeit a bit sadly.

They were all startled when Celia, who'd been dragged in between Melanie and Rainier, then given over to the nuns, let out a cry, shook and wrapped her arms around herself. "He's angry, and he's close, so close. I can feel him. He's furious that you've blocked his army. And he knows I'm here. Oh, God, he knows I'm here! He's going to rip me to pieces, bit by bit. Disembowel me and burn the pieces before my eyes!"

Scott walked over to her, forgetting for a moment how dangerous she was, and took her by the shoulders. "Forget him. Don't let him into your mind, do you hear me? You can fight him. He'll make you see things, but they won't be real. You're with us now. Do you understand?"

She blinked and stared at him.

Then she wrenched free and backed away. "You! You will be my death! You are Capricorn, and you are sworn not to protect the earth but to destroy it. And you'll kill me if you can. He's telling me so, and he knows. He knows!"

Suddenly her features twisted into that mask of fury, hatred and evil. She prepared to leap at him, and none of the others were near enough to prevent her. Perhaps instinct saved him; he reached for the rosary around his neck.

She stopped, as if frozen. Her expression was stricken, and she closed her mouth, covering the glistening fangs she'd extended in anticipation of a strike. She looked around and saw where she was, then let out a shriek and fell to the ground, shaking.

"Bambina, bambina!" Sister Ana said, hurrying to the girl. She placed her hands on the girl's shoulders, then stroked her cheeks, heedless of any danger. She crooned gently to her in Italian. Tears began to slide down Celia's cheeks. In a moment, she had curled into Sister Ana's arms.

The sister looked up at Scott and smiled. "We look like skinny old women," she told him. "But we are strong."

Scott looked at Lucien, who had appeared at his side as Celia began to change.

"So now," he said, "you're the Oracle?"

Lucien nodded grimly. He was staring at Celia. "She was one of *his,* and you three captured her." It wasn't a question. He was staring at the girl, reading her mind, Scott thought. "And she told you where to find him."

"Yes," Scott said.

"It's tonight," Lucien said.

"The full moon." Scott shook his head in

puzzlement. "Okay," he said. "So tell me —
how are three of us supposed to stop an evil
that's escaping from the earth all around
the world?"

"You're not," Lucien said. "There are others out there, taking on that fight."

"All right, so . . . ?"

"You three have to take on Bael *himself*.
Darkness is coming, and it is the night of
the full moon. The fight begins now."

Sean Canady wasn't even in the right state
to use his police credentials, and not even
Blake Reynaldo was in a city where his
badge counted. But there they were, at
police headquarters in San Francisco, trying to explain the need for a public alert,
and not just in California but around the
nation.

Chief Brady Donahue stared at them as if
they had completely lost their minds.
"You're trying to tell me that something is
coming out of the ground and possessing
cops?" he asked politely. "Oh — and geologists, too."

"Yes," Maggie said flatly. "Look, I know
how ridiculous this sounds, but ask the
highway patrol officer. He was there."

"It's the truth, the absolute truth," Judy
said, holding tightly to Miss Tiffany. "They

would have killed each other if we hadn't been there to stop them."

Chief Donahue, a pleasant-looking man with a dignified demeanor and iron-gray hair, leaned back in his chair and smiled slowly, and then pointed at Judy. "I got it! You're an actress — I recognize you. What is this? A new reality show? Try to see if you can get a police chief to do something really stupid, like go get a priest to exorcise a piece of highway?"

"Chief Donahue," Sean said, leaning on the desk and looking squarely at the man. "I'm not asking you to do any such thing. I'm asking you to put out a public health alert. There's some kind of toxin escaping from the fissures around the state and probably beyond — that apparently affects the centers of the brain that control logic and violent impulses."

"Hey, Chief!"

They all swung around at the sound of the voice calling from the doorway. A young officer was standing there. "Switch on CNN. You gotta see this. It's spreading like a plague!"

The chief frowned and turned on a small flatscreen TV. A tense female reporter was describing a rash of violence in Japan in an area recently struck by serious quakes and tremors. Scenes of a riot in the streets of Tokyo were next shown, and then a second reporter came on, live, to report that a region in Estonia, recently struck by minor quakes, was facing something like mass hysteria, with people lashing out at one another everywhere. Even as the live report aired, the on-scene reporter let out a sudden gasp and keeled over, struck in the head by his cameraman.

"Holy mother of God," the chief said quietly. He stared at Sean and Blake and said, "I'm calling the governor. He can get it on the television stations."

As he reached for the phone, Sean said, "Look, you just saw Tokyo — and Estonia. The governor has to call the president, and the president has to warn the country and the other world leaders. People have to stay the hell away from those fissures."

"Great," Donahue moaned. "The world will think I'm an idiot."

"Toxic fumes that affect the brain," Blake said firmly.

The cameras had switched again. A fault-line along the Mississippi had suffered a series of tremors. There was a scene of looting in Biloxi.

Sean swore. "Call fast, talk fast and talk well!" He was already on his own cell phone, calling his chief back in New Orleans.

Maggie sat back, staring at Judy. They had done everything they could for now. She just hoped they wouldn't be stopped as they moved through the area as quickly as they could, praying over holes in the ground and dousing them with holy water.

Celia was sleeping and seemed, to Melanie's eyes, to be at peace.

She looked like a strangely contemporary Sleeping Beauty, in an odd way. The nuns had made her a bed on a pew, with prayer books and a sweater on which to rest her head. She was surrounded by a circle of holy water and votive candles, with a kneeling sister at every compass point. She was going to be all right.

Lucien, Rainier and Scott were huddled together by the altar. It looked almost as if they were holding a vigil for Sister Maria Elizabeta.

The sisters who weren't watching over Celia were busy filling more vials with holy water and adorning the church with every cross, crucifix and scripture verse they could find — along with a few ancient symbols from even older religions. Melanie was vaguely aware of their soft chanting in the background.

She had found herself a seat on the ground near the rear of the church. She could vaguely hear the men discussing strategy, and she didn't know why she wasn't dragging herself over to join them, front and center.

She felt the need to be alone — even in the crowd — and she wasn't sure why. She felt vaguely — detached. She wasn't at all sure that she was going to survive the night, and she was worried about the future. She had never known anyone like Scott, a man who could stay strong and steady no matter what. He didn't lose his temper, or if he did, he quickly controlled it. Whatever had occurred to him that night in the alley had made him able to accept the bizarre and terrifying with little argument or emotion.

He seemed to accept her for what she was.

After all these years, why couldn't she do the same?

She wondered if it was a more subtle voice of the demon in her head, continually telling her that she was vile, no matter what course she had taken in the years since her change. Or was it simply her own guilty conscience? She wanted so badly to believe that she had a future. That she could build something approaching a normal life.

Lucien had a wife and a very happy life. Other vampires married mortals, but . . .

What happened at the end?

"What is that?"

She looked up, startled. Scott had come over to her and, amazingly calm and composed, hunkered down by her side. Somehow he seemed more appealing than ever, and at first she didn't even see what he was pointing at, because she was thinking about how much she loved his hands, his long, artistic fingers and the warmth with which they held her. She flushed suddenly, feeling an urge to throw herself against him and just be with him as the world came tumbling down around them.

"Mel?" he said.

She shook her head, forcing a smile to her lips. "Are we ready to face the demon?" she asked him.

He nodded. "But what did you draw?" he asked her.

She looked at the floor beside her. She had been using her finger as a pen, drawing in the dust.

She had somehow sketched a perfect rendition of Sister Maria Elizabeta, standing with a sword in her hand. All around her, there were raindrops, and beyond the raindrops, an array of demons was falling back.

"It's Sister Maria Elizabeta," Scott said.

"As she cannot be anymore," Melanie replied, then stood, dusting off her hands. Rainier and Lucien had followed Scott, and now Lucien touched Melanie's face with the affection of a brother.

"We all miss her, and I know how much we needed her," he said. "But it's really always been about you three. She was the Oracle, and the Oracle's mission was to bring you together, and then . . . well, there isn't really a 'then' if you don't succeed."

"How will we know if the demon is dead?" Melanie asked. "Is it even possible to kill a demon? I mean, I'm supposedly dead, and —"

"And you can be destroyed. As can a demon," Lucien assured her.

"We need to head out," Rainier said.

But Scott wasn't ready. He was still staring at Melanie's drawing. "What if we were to analyze the picture?" he wondered aloud.

"What do you mean, 'analyze' it?" Lucien asked.

Scott flashed him a smile and pointed to the picture. "Melanie's drawings have always meant something. In the body, Sister Maria Elizabeta has left us, so this picture of her fighting demons indicates her spirit. Somehow she's still here with us."

"Why the rain?" Rainier asked.

"I don't think it's rain. See how she's holding her arms and her hands? I can't actually cut up the ground and move it around, but imagine moving her a bit to the left, and . . . then it's as if those drops are coming from her wrists," Scott said.

"As if she'd cut them?" Melanie said in horror. "She certainly wasn't a suicide," she protested.

"No . . . ," Scott agreed. "I think it's to show the power of her spirit to drive the demons away. And I'm not sure that what she's holding is a sword. I think it's more of a dagger. I'm not sure what the drawing means, really, other than that she's with us."

"We can only hope," Lucien said.

Melanie looked at him. She realized that he was still disturbed by his new responsibilities.

She looked over at Celia, still asleep, eyes closed, caged within the boundary of nuns and symbols. The girl looked so young, sweet and peaceful. But she had been under the demon's influence and perhaps still was.

She turned back to Lucien as Scott hunkered down by her drawing, studying it further. "Are you coming with us?"

He shook his head. "This is a battle the earth signs must fight. I can only rally what help I can across the globe. It's growing late. It's time now for you, Rainier and Scott to head out to Bael's lair beneath the earth."

"I know what they mean!" Scott proclaimed, looking up excitedly.

"What?"

"The words you told me," he said to Lucien. "That night when we went to the bar. 'The blood of the pure is toxic to the darkness of evil.' You said you'd heard those words but you didn't know what they meant. Maybe Sister Maria Elizabeta knew she wouldn't survive until the end, so she sent these words to me after establishing a connection in the dream. She needed you to hear those words, to know . . ."

"What are you talking about?" Melanie demanded.

"There was probably never a human being who had so pure a heart," Scott said.

"You want us to cut her open and take her blood?" Melanie demanded.

"We don't have to cut her open," Rainier said.

"Look at your picture, Melanie," Scott said. "We . . . uh, only have to slit her wrists. The blood of the innocent, the blood of the pure. Maybe it's even a test, in a way." He cleared his throat. "I mean . . . you two need blood. But this isn't blood for sustenance. This is the blood of someone totally pure. She's offering it to us. It's her final act against Bael, and the part she was given to play in this battle to prevent Armageddon and let the world live on."

Melanie turned away. "I can't do it," she whispered.

Scott looked at Lucien, then at Rainier. He groaned softly. "I suppose this has to be my task."

Rainier shrugged. "It's not that we won't, it's just best if you deal with this situation."

Scott left the picture drawn in the dust, then walked away to kneel beside the aged nun's body. Melanie couldn't watch. She walked to the other side of the church, wondering how she, of all creatures, could be so squeamish. She just prayed that Scott was right in his interpretation of her drawing.

Sister Ana, ever competent and prepared, walked over to Scott and gave him a small scalpel from her medical bag. She also offered him several empty vials, the kind often filled with holy water for supplicants to wear around their necks. The most amazing thing, Melanie thought, was that Sister Ana didn't question anything.

She worked with them based on faith alone.

Faith — including faith in me, Melanie thought.

She knew that Scott was careful and tender, but to her distress, the scent of fresh blood seemed to hang on the air, and she winced as the scent aroused the hunger she always prayed she had learned to quench.

"We're ready," Scott said.

I'm not good enough for this. I'm not pure, Melanie thought.

No, she wasn't pure, not in any way, shape or form.

As night began to fall, the hectic pace of the business heart of Rome started to slow. Tourists no longer thronged the Coliseum and the Forum. Actors dressed as Roman soldiers and gladiators disappeared from the nearby sidewalks, along with their photo-selling assistants.

The Forum was now given over to the cats that came out to slink through the darkness. And the nearby streets grew quiet.

Deadly quiet. Melanie was certain that the news about the worldwide epidemic of violence was probably keeping people in. That was a very good thing tonight.

They had left the car in a nearby parking lot and walked from there. Along the way they saw a number of police cars cruising the streets. They tried to stick to the shadows, because they looked like a strange group to be walking the city streets at that hour. Choosing what they might need had not been easy; they couldn't be too encumbered to move, so their pockets held vials of holy water — and one vial apiece of Sister Maria Elizabeta's precious blood. Scott had opted for the flame thrower they'd found at the church in the city, while Rainier had acquired a semiautomatic pistol — just in case, he'd decided.

"I wonder what we're looking for," Melanie said, walking at Scott's side.

"I don't think we need to worry. Whatever it is, it will find us," he said.

They were nearing the arch Celia had described. Scott suddenly slowed his pace as Rainier, who had been walking just ahead of them, stopped.

"We should do this without Melanie," Scott said, staring down at her. "Seriously, I think maybe you should be back at the church with Lucien. Helping the nuns keep Celia under control."

Melanie smiled slowly, touched. He was trying to protect her. Her cavalier, hoping to fight the battle for her.

"I think those nuns will do just fine. And

I believe that Sister Maria Elizabeta's body will be an effective deterrent to whatever part of Bael tries to escape through the catacombs," Melanie said softly. "I'm needed here. With you."

Rainier had been looking away, trying to give them a private moment. Now he shook his head impatiently. "She's right. It has to be the three of us," he said to Scott. "Capricorn, Virgo and Taurus. That's the prophecy." He started walking again.

Scott was still staring at Melanie. "I just wish you —"

She reached up and touched his face. "Scott . . . you've led a decent life. I wasn't always so upstanding. Maybe this is my way of earning . . . earning a right to go on existing. It doesn't matter. We have to do this together. But it *is* strange. For so many years I've been content just to exist, but now . . . now I want to *live*."

His grin was crooked. "With me?" he asked.

She nodded, meeting his eyes. He had beautiful eyes. Deep, dark, expressive, intelligent. She felt an inner pang. Where had he been all these years? Why hadn't she met him, gotten to know him, until . . . now?

They were startled by a hoarse cry from ahead. Scott sprinted forward, Melanie following on his heels.

"Rainier!" she cried out.

He was standing in the center of the sidewalk, huge black shadows swooping all around him. He wore both his rosary and a large silver crucifix on his chest. The shadows weren't touching him — yet — but they were swooping low enough to keep him busy. Scott raced and positioned himself back-to-back with Rainier, so that neither of them could be taken from the rear. Melanie went on the offensive, tossing holy water at the creatures every time they drew near. She measured her success in hisses and cries of fury, and then the black shadow-bats began to fall.

One of them fell at Melanie's feet, and she looked down. The creature had been caught in midmetamorphosis, half in human form, half still shadow-bat, burning, hissing and steaming. But it had a grip on her leg and was drawing itself to her, fangs gnashing.

She stooped low, a sharpened cross in her hand, and slammed the point down into the creature's head. The jaws snapped, and the thing went up in a puff of smoke.

She saw Scott using a large cross like a scythe, swinging it back and forth, batting the creatures away. She moved forward, tossing more holy water as she went.

Slowly they began to even the odds against them. As the battlefield narrowed, Melanie tried desperately to stay at his side. She was afraid for him; the gnashing fangs and teeth could not do to her or Rainier what they could to Scott.

Scott was still swinging when the last of the shadow-bats went down.

Rainier set a hand on his shoulder. "They're gone," he said.

Scott went still, but he only said, "We've just begun." He pointed ahead of them. They had reached the place where Bael waited.

They crossed beneath the remains of the ancient arch and saw, to the far right of the roadside, a ledge of stone, perhaps a fallen roof. Beneath it, the world was entirely black.

"Do we go down?" Melanie asked.

"I think we have to," Scott said, but before they could go farther, a shriek of pure terror sounded from around the corner ahead.

Even as they sprinted toward the sound, someone threw a rock at the nearest light, pitching the street into darkness as another flurry of pitch black shadows began to take form.

A young woman was being tossed back

and forth between two groups of hoods. Some had spiked hair; a few sported tattoos. The young woman was clearly terrified.

"Polizia! Polizia!" she screamed.

One of the thugs grabbed her and turned her toward him, showing his fangs as his face twisted into a monster's mask.

She let out another horrified scream.

At that moment a police car came screeching around the corner. *"Polizia! Polizia!"* she shrieked again.

The police car jerked to a halt. Two officers jumped out, shouting for the thugs to let the girl go, but the vampires only laughed derisively.

And then several of them flew at the officers.

"Hell," Scott whispered, then sprang forward, Rainier and Melanie following close behind. Melanie was ready with the holy water, and Rainier lifted off the ground himself, flying toward the creatures and catching two of them, then heaving them aside with a force that sent them crashing into the nearest building.

Scott drew out the flame thrower, catching the cocky bastard who had nearly bitten the young woman.

The first officer fell back against the car,

fingers trembling as he drew a crucifix from beneath his shirt and held it out before him. The second swore and started shooting into the melee.

But bullets didn't stop the things. And though their triumvirate had saved the young woman, they weren't close enough to reach the gun-firing officer before one of the thugs took hold of him, lifted him close and ripped his throat out.

The sound was horrible. The ripping, tearing wetness of it seemed to drown out everything else.

The vampire finished with his victim, twisted the neck and ripped the head from the shoulders, then tossed the pieces to the ground.

Scott let out a horrific wail of pure fury and raced in. Melanie cried out: he hadn't taken out a weapon, he had merely thrown himself at the vampire. He was moving at an amazing speed, but she flew after him, terrified. She knew the power of her kind, knew the ferocity of well-honed fangs.

Rainier was engaged with the others, bringing most of them down quickly with his expertise in wielding the sharpened crosses. But Scott . . .

She was stunned to see that he had already engaged the vampire, which had made a run for Scott, like a bull, and Scott hadn't even tried to dodge him. He'd met him head on and caught him by the shoulders, slammed him against the police car, and then taken hold of his head between his hands.

And twisted.

The creature fell to the ground.

"He's not dead!" Melanie shrieked. "Stop him!"

The vampire had been playing possum, trying to gather his strength and his fury. As Melanie cried out, he reached for Scott's leg. But Scott was ready; he slammed the spiked end of a cross straight through the creature's head.

She heard a babbling sound and realized it was the remaining police officer.

"Get into the car! Now!" she shouted at him.

The officer, shaking, let her maneuver him into the car. As she did so, Scott reached for the man's gun, then turned and shot another of the creatures in the head.

Screaming and still babbling, the officer drove the car straight into the wall of the ruins.

Melanie was about to turn to run after him, but Rainier let out a hiss, and then she heard it.

Marching.

An army of bones was rising from the depths now. Some had only one arm, others were missing ribs. Mouths dropped open and snapped closed; hands carried old knives and swords.

Melanie began swinging one of her crosses, knocking the first rank to pieces, but Scott stepped quickly past her.

"They'll just put themselves back together," he warned, then he used the flame thrower again, charring the bones to ash. When one slipped through, he used the snub-nosed revolver he had taken from the cop to explode its skull. Rainier became a whirl of motion, kicking and shooting, bringing them down in piles of dust, stamping on limbs that continued to move blindly across the ground.

Someone screamed from a block away; Melanie decided she was the least important in the current fight, and turned and ran in the direction of the scream. "I'm on it!" she shouted back over her shoulder.

The night seemed unnaturally dark. Even with the full moon rising in the sky, the ruins cast impenetrable shadows, and the surrounding trees blocked out the glow. She heard the hair-raising scream again, a cry of pure terror, but she saw nothing.

Finally she saw a dark form in front of

her, low on the ground, curled up like a large ball. She slowed her pace, staring all around, looking for danger.

A breeze rose from nowhere, lifting her hair.

The next sound she heard wasn't a scream but a low moan, which quickly turned into the wrenching sound of a child's sobbing.

"It's all right," Melanie said soothingly, moving more quickly toward the huddled shadow. "It's all right. Who are you? *Sono gentile. Che . . . ?*"

She reached the huddled child and hunkered down, lifting the child's face by the chin. And then she gasped, stunned. She was staring into the face of her little sister, the child she had been so tempted to rip into and drain so many years before.

"No," she moaned, trembling.

And then her sister laughed and grew to a massive height, a giant shadow that covered the face of the moon. She backed away as it suddenly exploded into a massive rain of fetid decay, and charred flesh and bone, all of which began to swirl, like a nightmare eddy, all around her.

16

Scott swung around, certain that he'd heard something behind him. When he turned, he saw that Rainier, too, was reconnoitering, anxious to be prepared for whatever form of the living — or the dead — might be coming after them next. But for the moment they were alone in a field of bone dust and scraps of rotting shrouds. The air was alive with the remnants of gunpowder and bone dust, and the smell of charring was strong. The fissure to the black gaping underworld was quiet, as if waiting for them to enter.

"I think we have to go in," Rainier said regretfully.

"I agree. But . . . where's Melanie?" Scott asked.

"She ran after that last scream. We . . . have to prevent all the violence we can, but . . ."

"He's trying to split us up," Scott said.

Together, they turned, racing as one in the direction Melanie had taken. As soon as they rounded the corner, they saw her.

She was caught in the center of a strange back whirlwind. Her eyes were dazed, and she was making no attempt to move.

Scott rushed forward but was thrown back by the violence of the storm. Rainier helped him scramble to his feet.

"Together!" Rainier roared over the wailing of the whirlwind. "The holy water!"

Scott made it to his feet and braced himself. They approached the maelstrom together, tossing holy water as they went. Scott started chanting Latin prayers he remembered from school as they made headway, a fraction of an inch at a time. When they got closer, both men yelled Melanie's name, but she showed no sign of having heard them. They penetrated the whirling black storm at last, and Scott's fingers touched Melanie's arm.

But they couldn't pull her free. All three of them became caught up in the black eddy, trapped where they stood. There was one weapon they hadn't used yet; none of them had wanted to use it — it was their last measure. But now Scott reached into his pocket, straining against the force of the dark whirlwind, to slip his fingers around the vial of Sister Maria Elizabeta's blood.

And he released it into the stream.

A terrifying shrieking rose around them, as if a thousand banshees were wailing all at once in fury.

You will die in the end. You will die in the mire of the earth, in the fires of hell. You will suffer eternal agony. . . .

But despite the words that insinuated themselves into Scott's mind, the storm began to slow. Scott strained with all his might and dragged the others with him. They crashed down onto the ground a few feet beyond the borders of the dying storm, and as they lay there the fetid muck hailed down over them.

"It worked," Melanie said in awe. "Maria Elizabeta is still with us. But Bael . . . I saw . . . my sister, Scott." The pain in her eyes was agonizing to see.

Scott pushed himself up, offered Melanie a hand.

Rainier was already back on his feet.

"It's time to go in," he said quietly.

They could hear the sound of chaos in the city around them, but they would have to count on the Alliance and the police to take care of that. The creature in the catacombs had to be bested or not only the city but the world would be lost.

"Are you all right?" Scott asked Melanie.

She smiled as confidently as she could and glanced over at Rainier.

"Let's do it," she said.

"Yeah," Scott said hoarsely. "Looks like this is it."

There was only a small opening for them to actually slip through — apparently one reason so many of the skeletons had been broken was from their efforts in escaping — and that was barely visible. They dug away at the rocks and dirt and brush that blocked the opening. When they had enough cleared away, Rainier shined a flashlight into the crevice. Old stone steps, built right into the earth, were visible in the flashlight's glow.

The darkness — and Bael — waited beyond.

With Rainier's light leading the way, Scott made it down to the bottom step.

It was like stepping into a nightmare.

The catacombs here were truly ancient, and they held a scent of brimstone as well as mold and decay. The earth beneath his feet was hard packed, the walls stacked with narrow, tightly packed shelves holding the dead, and he was dismayed at the number remaining. He'd hoped they had already fought off most of this army. He looked warily, right and left, as he passed along the corridor. Melanie was directly behind him, with Rainier bringing up the rear.

They all stopped at the same time.

The head of a skeleton to Scott's left suddenly began to turn of its own accord, as if driven by the ghosts of muscles and tendons long gone. Scott was tense, waiting, and he knew that behind him, Melanie and Rainier waited, too, wondering if the thing would knit itself back together and come after them.

A terrible, rasping whisper began to hiss through the broken and toothless jaws. It became a laugh, a low, evil chuckle. Then it uttered dry words. "Bael is calling you," it said. "Now, begins the end of days."

Broken bits of finger bone began to form together, and the skeletal hand was suddenly whole and pointing toward the darkness beyond. "Go," the voice commanded with military authority. Then the terrible laughing began again.

Enough.

Scott swung his bare fist into the bony head, splintering it into a hundred pieces.

Wind, coming from nowhere, suddenly began to rush around them. The skeleton whose skull Scott had just crashed clattered, but couldn't seem to pull what was left of itself together.

But the other skeletons didn't seem to be having the same problem. As if a switch had been turned on, they began to rebuild themselves in monstrous numbers.

And the wind that seemed to be giving them life was not coming from the hole in the earth that had allowed them entry.

It was coming from the darkness ahead.

Melanie stared at Scott, shouting above the clicking and clacking of the bones. "Go on! Stop Bael! We'll follow."

Scott didn't want to leave her alone with Rainier to face the growing skeletal army, but she was right. Someone had to go after Bael *now*.

And then there was a voice in his head. Lucien's voice, this time.

There are three of you: Capricorn, Taurus and Virgo. Virgo will be reason. Taurus will hold the line. Capricorn must go on ahead alone.

The skeletons were rising en masse. Scott demolished those he could on the way to find Bael, anxious to rid his companions of as many as possible while he made his way to the source of the evil power.

Ahead was only darkness that swallowed all light.

He had no choice but to move forward. The dead were awakening everywhere, but as Scott made his way deeper under the earth, it seemed that their purpose was changing. Heads lifted, arms pointed, and there was the eerie sound of malicious laughter. The clattering of bony jaws as they tried to work grew louder, as well, but the sound no longer seemed to be coming from the skeletons he passed, it was issuing from the far depths of the tunnel.

I am waiting, foolish man. I am waiting, and I am ready to end this interference now. Come now and it will be you and me alone, and you will finally see the face of Bael.

Through the darkness ahead, he saw light at last. It wasn't the natural light of the full moon outside, nor was it the artificial light of a flashlight. It was a flickering red glow.

The smell of brimstone on the air was so thick he could barely breathe.

He stopped, pausing to get his bearings as he realized that he was approaching a central room, just like the one in his dream. The tunnel widened slightly where he stood, and the unearthly glow that had guided him was located just ahead.

He moved forward slowly. There were burning sconces all around the room, and what looked like a massive sarcophagus in the center.

The tomb was cracked and ajar. There was

ancient lettering etched into the top of it. And standing there, shrouded in a black hood and cloak, was a presence.

The laughter began again.

And then the thing's voice reached him loud and clear.

"Time to play this farce out to the end, foolish man. In your dreams, you saw the nun. I am certainly no nun, my friend. So . . . let's finish the game. All that has happened thus far has been a game, don't you know? It's been fun to jerk the strings of the puppets, fun to watch men rip and tear into one another, and bleed and die. And the vampires and other creatures of the night? They are damned already, of course, but I enjoyed it as they followed me, worshipping me, believing I would give them eternal pleasure. As if I could be bothered. I eat flesh for breakfast, my friend, and finish out the day with souls for a nightcap."

The scent in the air, the sound of the demon's voice, the weird red light and the scent of brimstone mixed with death, all worked on Scott's fear, on his natural instinct to survive.

But Scott stood his ground.

"Fuck you," he said, praying that there was no tremor in his voice. "A game? Then it might interest you to know we're two steps ahead. All across the world, the forces of light have prevented the mayhem you thought you would cause. This is a game, all right, and you're nothing but a two-year-old crying on the playground."

The roar that rose from the creature's mouth was like the rush of a blast furnace, hot air searing Scott and filling his nostrils with the scent of foul black earth. Scott fought to remain standing against the onslaught.

Then the earth began to tremble.

Suddenly the thing by the altar started to grow, it's evil laughter deepening as it grew in size. It rose higher and higher, and grew tentacles as it stretched, powerful cords of muscle and sinew and death that began winding around him, choking him, stealing his breath.

"Silly man, you will die so easily," it said.

"Rainier!"

Melanie cried out. A skeleton was poised at his back, holding the skull of another in its hands, ready to smash it down on his head. Behind it, an army massed in numbers too great to count.

Rainier spun around. He pulled out his vial of pure blood, and tossed it at the skeleton and the hordes standing behind it. The thing paused, and suddenly the skeletons were attacking each other, bones fighting the bones.

"The blood!" Rainier cried. "The blood has turned the tide. Any skeleton touched by it is fighting for us now. We can finish off the rest and get to Scott. Where's your vial? You need to use it."

"I can't. We might need it when we get to Scott," Melanie said.

He stared at her and nodded. His flashlight had fallen in the battle, and he quickly retrieved it. He played the beam down the length of the tunnel, and they started forward.

The earth suddenly exploded before them, sending bits of rock, mud and bone showering down on them.

The demon's tentacles were around him now, choking him slowly. Very slowly.

"I can't have you die too quickly. Mortals are so fragile, but I like to take my time. I will make talons for myself, rip your flesh inch by inch, watch you bleed until you are nearly dead, and then see the light go out of your eyes as you suffocate. That you thought that you could go against me . . ."

The demon's tentacles began to grow and

change; they became like the talons of a huge bird, stubby and gnarled, razor sharp at the tips. And there were so many of them. So many. Scott couldn't breathe. He'd been so foolish. He thought, his pride in his own strength too great. . . .

But he'd never fully tested himself. He concentrated on building strength within his mind. He flexed his shoulders and caught hold of the closest talon, the one threatening his eyes. He twisted it with all his strength. He forced himself to think of the kindness and the knowledge of Sister Maria Elizabeta, and he thought that he heard her voice in his head.

You are Capricorn. The strength of the earth. A man, but also the earth, itself. You have the power. You have the strength.

The demon howled as Scott snapped the talon in two, to hang uselessly in the air. He ripped at another and another, tearing at the rubbery arms with the razors at the end. The more he fought, the more adrenaline seemed to rush through him, and the greater his fury grew. The thing began to loosen its hold on him bit by bit. It was losing strength.

The earth trembled again, accompanied by a deafening roar, and then Scott fell; he was free. But he knew from the scent of brimstone and death that he hadn't beaten his enemy, only staved him off temporarily. The darkness deepened, and from somewhere within it he heard a sudden scream.

Melanie.

"Melanie! Where are you?" he cried.

A sobbing sound followed. He inched his way through the dark, trying to discover the source of the sound. *Where was she?*

He touched something that seemed like flesh and blood, but his eyes were tearing from the sulfur in the air, and in the darkness he could barely see. "Melanie?"

She reached out. He felt her hand; he saw her eyes, filled with horror and pain. "He has me, Scott, he has me. He says that I belong in hell, and that I have to burn there forever, left to feel my flesh scorching and charring, smell the odor of it, forever and ever. Hold me, Scott. Stop him."

"I have you, Melanie. I have you."

"Oh, God, Scott, he has to have one of us. Save me, for the love of God, save me. Give yourself to him so I can save my immortal soul."

Scott paused, still holding her hand, but an alarm began ringing deep in his brain.

This wasn't Melanie. He was suddenly sure of it. Bael had tried to use Scott's emotions against him before. But he knew Melanie. She would never ask another to sacrifice themselves in her place. He didn't let go, only eased back on his hold.

"This is the worst charade I've ever seen," he told the demon. "You're nothing like Melanie, nothing at all."

Again that roar that shook the earth.

And the face he was staring at began to change.

It was Melanie, but a Melanie grown so old that her skin began to crack, turn a nauseating yellow-brown and drip down her face like melted candle wax. Finally her beautiful face was nothing but bone, a paper-white skull staring at him from empty eye sockets, roaches spewing from the mouth, while snakes began to slither from the nostrils and eye sockets.

Scott pulled back in horror, so stunned that he released the creature.

The roar of fury became peals of laughter. And then the face changed again.

At last he was seeing the true face of the demon.

The eyes were becoming red glowing pits, and scaly flesh began to cover the naked bone. Bael bore a passing resemblance to a man, but a man with stubby horns growing from his forehead, a pointed chin, giant black wings and skin that was far more like that of a reptile than a human being. Again he began to grow, until he barely fit into the confines of the tunnel. His arms were long, and talons grew at the ends of his gnarled fingers. A tail grew from the base of his spine, a sharp barb growing at the end.

He heard Lucien's voice in his head again.

Beware of the shapeshifter's tricks. Run when you must, fight when you can.

Bael reached out, seeking Scott's throat.

Scott dived low and raced back to the room with the sarcophagus. When he rose, he saw that the demon wasn't even looking at him.

It was staring down the tunnel from which he had come. Scott could just make out Rainier rushing forward, a pointed cross ready in his hand. He didn't stop; he plowed into the demon, piercing it in the gut.

Bael let out a roar of pain and fury, then set his crocodilian hands on the cross and ripped it from his flesh, sending Rainier crashing against the wall of the room with one casual swipe.

"No!" Melanie cried, rushing in, a stake of her own in hand.

This time the creature was ready; he caught the stake and hurled it powerfully across the room, knocking Melanie against the sarcophagus.

Scott let out a cry of fury, leaping up and throwing himself onto the creature's back.

It burned, and he could hardly keep his position.

Rainier, though dazed, was up again. He found his broken cross and ran for the demon again.

"The eyes!" Scott shouted. "Go for his eyes."

With Scott struggling to hold the mammoth scaly head still, Rainier struck home. The bellow that escaped from Bael then was horrible, shaking the entire catacomb, bringing chunks of earth and stone raining down on them.

The creature whirled and bucked, using its tail to send Rainier flying with bone-cracking violence against the wall again, and this time he didn't get up.

Scott found himself sliding down the length of the scaly back, felt the creature trying to impale him with the spike on its tail.

Melanie was still down, trying to rise, trying to clear her head.

"Melanie, the tail! Help!" Scott called.

But Bael could still hear them clearly, even though a viscous fluid was oozing down his face from his destroyed eye.

Suddenly the demon was changing again, growing smaller and tucking his tail beneath him, forcing Scott to slip to the ground.

"No!" Scott roared himself.

Smaller, smaller . . .

He got his hands around the creature's throat and began to squeeze.

It began to grow again, the neck bulging until Scott's hands could no longer surround it and he was forced to climb onto its back again, his arms encircling that muscle-bound neck.

Melanie was ready, circling the demon to reach its slashing tail. She finally found her aim and caught the tail with the pointy end of her cross, pinning it to the ground.

The demon began to thrash and roar, and Scott had to keep fighting to maintain his hold.

Rainier was up again at last, searching his pockets desperately. He found a vial of holy water and started sprinkling it over Bael, whose movements became more frenzied, making Scott's position ever more precarious.

This time Bael put on a human face. Scott's face.

"Melanie, you bitch," Bael seethed. "Look what you've done. You've twisted everything good in me because you want to hurt me, you want me to be a monster just like you are."

Melanie was stunned for a moment, staring, just long enough for the monster to snake out one taloned arm and bring her down.

"No!" Scott raged, his stranglehold tightening in fury.

"Melanie — the blood. Do you still have it?" Scott demanded. His hold was weakening. There was nothing left to do but pray.

She had the blood.

She came to life in a flash, drawing the vial from her pocket, daring to stand mere inches from the demon, which was still moving beneath Scott like an enraged bull. She uncorked the vial and she splashed the blood dead center into Bael's face, catching him first in his remaining eye.

The demon screamed and strained, growing to impossible size, and sent a whirlwind of earth, dust and bone swirling around them. Scott was blinded, but still he held on.

Then . . .

Still roaring, Bael began to shrink again. Scott's hold tightened. And tightened. He twisted with all his might, and to his amazement, he heard a snap, and the head lolled bonelessly to the side.

The earth shuddered again and the demon fell, with Scott on top of it, and then a wall collapsed right on top of them.

"Scott!" Melanie's voice was frantic.

He reached out blindly in the rubble and found her fingers.

In seconds they were clasping hands.

A moment later Rainier was on his feet and helping them free of the pile of rock.

They looked down at the demon Bael. He was only the size of a man now, and he was hideous: his skin was pocked and diseased, his limbs a mix of a goat's and a bird's. The horns still protruded from his head, and the end of his tail oozed some kind of loathsome fluid.

But he was down, and the earth was still.

Rainier hunkered down, then drew out a knife and sliced through the creature's neck. He decapitated the great demon Bael, who, in the end, had proven that his true self was small.

"We need to burn the body," Melanie said.

Scott didn't question her. He and Rainier started to gather what flammable material they could find and built a pyre.

They set Bael's body on it and lit the fire, and the corpse cracked and smoked as it began to burn. They watched it, making certain that both the body and the head caught fire.

"So small . . ." Scott said.

Rainier looked at him. "That's the thing . . . it's the least of men, and the demons within them, that can cause the greatest tragedy."

"Let's get out of here," Melanie pleaded. "The fire is growing . . . the heat . . . Oh, Scott, your hands!"

He looked down at them. They were red and blistered and cracking. And all three of them were absolutely filthy, as if they had been working in a coal mine.

He laughed suddenly. He didn't feel the pain in his hands. He cupped her face with them and kissed her lips.

"Men may be monsters, and monsters may be angels," he said. "Yes, it's time to leave the dead behind and revel in everything that's beautiful here on earth — here in heaven on earth."

Rainier rolled his eyes but clapped him on the back. "Yeah, let's get out of here, so I can get away from the two of you before this mushy stuff kills me."

Melanie just smiled and, still holding Scott's hand, started down the tunnel that led back to the world of freedom and goodness.

And when they left the catacomb behind

at last, Rome was quiet, with a beautiful
moon glowing in the sky above.

EPILOGUE

I Am

The headlines across the globe following that summer night of the full moon were fairly uniform. In various languages, they declared in bold print: **TOXIC FUMES CREATE HAVOC ACROSS THE WORLD; GEOLOGISTS SCRAMBLE TO PREVENT A SECOND OCCURRENCE.**

It was absolutely fine; it was the best possible scenario since the world, divided in so many ways, would never accept the truth: that a minor earth demon had done exactly what many a dictator had done before him. He had tried to rule the world through fear and, in doing so, bring about its destruction.

As we talked about events after that night, we realized just how much Bael had preyed upon the minds of so many. He knew the secrets of controlling not only the dead and the undead, but even the weakest among the living. As we continued to research the many prophecies about doomsday, we found references that described him as a wily demon, but certainly not one as powerful as the devil himself, under whatever name.

One of the biggest lessons was that fear can be far more potent than any weapon.

And then there's the importance of free will.

We could, I believe, have chosen to run. What that would have meant over the ensuing years — because, of course, the struggle to prevent the apocalypse is far from over — we'll never know. Lucien believes that our immediate role in this has been fulfilled. There are others who must take on the next threat to the world, and whether that will come in the form of air, water or fire, we don't yet know. He is ready, however, and waiting. He has accepted that he is now the Oracle, and he will be on guard. And the rest of us will all still be around, too, of course.

Bael played upon our personal fears so well. He seeped into Melanie's mind and tried to convince her that she was a monster, that no one could love her. I still don't entirely understand the world of the vampires, but Bael did. He knew where to attack, where she was vulnerable, and since we haven't really figured out how to get along as human beings, it's easy to see how Melanie could have been afraid that I might loathe her.

I've decided to dedicate my life to proving to her that quite the opposite is true.

Anyway, here's the aftermath. Sister Maria Elizabeta was given a quiet Catholic funeral, just as she would have wanted. Her sarcophagus now rests over the trapdoor to the catacombs below, guarding that gateway forever. Sister Ana has taken her place within the convent. She doesn't have a special title; she simply seems to have a special wisdom, and the others often turn to her.

Rainier is planning a trip soon; he wants to visit the ruins at Chitzen Itza.

Sean and Maggie returned to New Orleans and their family. And Celia, who seemed to become more peaceful after Bael's demise, will eventually be returning to New Orleans with Lucien and Jade.

As for me . . .

I still don't have the answers as to why I, of all people, was chosen to receive such extraordinary powers. I don't think I'm meant to live forever. The time may come when I know it's my turn to clutch some-one's hand and pass on the power. Sister Maria Elizabeta knew that she was weak and dying, and she passed her power to Lucien. In the meantime, though I know it sounds a little strange to say that I was chosen to help save the world, I believe that to be true. There will be another group of three to face the next challenge, but they may need us, as well, so we'll all have to be alert and on guard until then. Whatever comes, I'll be ready.

Which brings me back to L.A.

Judy Bobalink and Blake Reynaldo have joined the fight. Anything to do with the Alliance — which I was finally invited to join, by the way — is of course under the radar. But they both earned their entrée into the world most people don't know. Anyway, it never hurts to have a seasoned cop around. And Judy's place is a new kind of safe house for anyone from our side who might need it.

As for me . . .

I know I can never go back to the life I used to have, and these days I don't want to.

I want to go forward.

I'll never forget the day I asked Melanie to marry me. She turned those beautiful blue eyes on me and tried to tell me that I shouldn't love her, but I just told her that there are powers on the earth over which we don't have any control — and love is the biggest of those. I told her the only thing that would prevent me from haunting her to my dying day — whenever that might be — would be her telling me that she hadn't fallen in love with me. Pretty cocky and presumptuous on my part, maybe, but luckily it worked.

So, on a beautiful late summer morning, we were married. We had the ceremony in L.A. My family and friends came from New Orleans, Melanie had people in from everywhere, and all our new friends from California came, as well. Maggie was Melanie's matron of honor. Since I didn't want to hurt either Zach's or Emory's feelings, I asked Lucien to be my best man. That way, the Unlucky Three could play for both the ceremony and the party we threw afterwards.

The Unlucky Three have never played more harmoniously.

In fact, it was all so perfect I felt as if we'd walked into a dream.

But it was real when she said her vows to me, and very real when I returned them. And when I kissed her, when we were man and wife at last, nothing had ever been more real, more life affirming and more beautiful.

Our friends surrounded us — the living and the undead — and as they applauded, Bruno bayed and Miss Tiffany yapped. It was perfect.

We took off that night for the South Seas.

We had a bungalow right on the beach, and that night, when she smiled, and drew me to her, it was indeed heaven on earth.

ABOUT THE AUTHOR

Heather Graham is a *New York Times* bestselling author of over 70 titles, including anthologies and short stories. She has been published in more than 15 languages and has over 20 million copies of her books in print.